PARALLEL LINES

ALSO BY STEVEN SAVILE AND AVAILABLE FROM TITAN BOOKS

Sherlock Holmes: Murder at Sorrow's Crown

Primeval: Shadow of the Jaguar

PARALLEL LINES

A NOVEL

STEVEN SAVILE

TITAN BOOKS

Parallel Lines
Print edition ISBN: 9781783297917
E-book edition ISBN: 9781783297924

Published by Titan Books
A division of Titan Publishing Group Ltd
144 Southwark Street, London SE1 0UP

First edition: March 2017
10 9 8 7 6 5 4 3 2 1

Names, places and incidents are either products of the author's imagination or used fictitiously. Any resemblance to actual persons, living or dead (except for satirical purposes), is entirely coincidental.

A CIP catalogue record for this title is available from the British Library.

Printed in the USA.

Jane
For then, for now.

But mostly for the park bench in Covent Garden where you put up with me trying to work out what happened next, animatedly acting out the story and the aha! moment when I realized it wasn't about that at all, it was about this.

So here it is, twenty-five years in the making, your book. Believe me, it couldn't have happened without you and Beryl Reid's bench. That's my way of absolving myself of blame. It's all your fault.

PARALLEL LINES

1

KEEP AWAY FROM BABIES AND SMALL CHILDREN.

The words were printed on the bottom of the plastic carrier bag like some irrefutable law of the universe. *The wisdom of the supermarket checkout*, Adam Shaw thought, trying not to focus on what was inside the bag. His hands trembled. That happened a lot these days. Dyskinesia. That was the fancy word for it. He'd got other *dys*es to look forward to over the coming months, too: dysphagia, dysarthria, and dyspnea. Dys. In his head he always called them the "dies"; after all that's what was going on, slowly, increasingly painfully, one treacherous muscle at a time.

Live fast, die young, and leave a good-looking corpse. One out of three wasn't a great showing on the old scoreboard of life. 33.3% recurring. A big fat fail in mathematical terms. It certainly wasn't the deal he'd wanted to make with the universe back when the universe was up for making deals. It wasn't as if he was going to rage against the dying of the light, he was just going to take it, because when it's your own body killing you, really, there's fuck all you can do to stop it. Fuck dignity, fuck being brave, fuck taking it like a man, and most of all just fuck. Fuck fuckity fuck-fuck-*fuck*.

All he wanted to do was scream, but the dysarthria made it difficult to vocalize his anger. *Now there's some first-class irony for you*, Adam thought, stuffing the bag into the deep pocket of his coat. It was heavy and pulled at the shoulder.

That was a giveaway.

It would be recognized for what it was by someone who knew what they were looking for. *A passing cop on a donut run, say*, he thought, watching a cruiser roll slowly down the blacktop away from him. The air around its tailpipe shimmered in the rising July heat. There was a food truck on the corner, a small line of customers waiting. *Do they even do donuts these days?* he wondered, *Or is it all fro-yo runs and healthy-living shit now?* He couldn't remember the last time he'd seen a fat beat-cop anywhere apart from on TV.

Adam's mind was all over the place. Stress, obviously. Understandably. He was struggling to keep it all together.

This wasn't him.

He wasn't a bank robber.

Or at least he wouldn't be for about another thirty seconds.

When he opened the door, it'd be different. Then it would be him. And it would be him for the rest of his life. Right now he was still a good man. A good father. He needed to focus on that.

It didn't matter how many times he'd gone over it in his head, how meticulously he'd planned it to be sure no one would get hurt, there were always variables. Things you couldn't plan for.

When he stepped through the door of Chicago Liberty Bank he wouldn't be Adam Shaw, probability specialist for Humanity Capital, one of Chicago's biggest private insurance concerns; he'd be walking into a brand new life. Then it would be all about keeping his shit together. Not easy with the shakes. Even with the meds, he couldn't control them, though he'd timed his Zanaflex so it ought to be at its most potent. He could already feel the tingling sensation in his fingertips. That was one of the side effects of the drug. It was better than the spastic twitch that would replace it in a couple of hours. His mouth was dry, too. That was another side effect, but given the fact he was about to rob a bank, a mouthful of saliva would have been a miracle on the bread and fishes scale.

In and out.

That was the magic.

He figured he'd have a two-minute grace period. It wasn't a lot, but that didn't mean a lot couldn't happen in that time. Life-changing things happened in less. He was living, breathing proof of that. His entire world had changed in two almost identical fragments of time. Two-minute blocks. Both of them had been in doctors' offices.

The first one was back in 2005, holding hands with Lily, listening to the results of her prenatal screen. It had taken two minutes for two words to sink in: chromosome abnormality.

What the doctor meant was Down's syndrome, but he was working towards naming the disease slowly. Yes, there was the possibility of a false positive. Yes, more tests would be needed. But for now they needed to be prepared to make a tough choice. In their place most people opted for termination. Neither of them wanted that.

The second time, seven months ago, he'd been on his own. It had been a different doctor in a different office in the same building. The specialist had delivered his diagnosis and explained how he could expect the disease to progress. It was his problem and only he was going to be broken by it. That made it easier. Right up until the realization that it wasn't only his problem. It was Jake's problem, because he was all the boy had in the world. That had almost broken him.

Both times the words had been delivered in disinterested tones, the message utterly matter-of-fact even though the doctors were taking a sledgehammer to his existence. He understood in a very real way why ancient kings wanted to kill the messenger when presented with bad news. He could have wrung the specialist's neck if it meant he could go back just a few minutes in time, to a point before the sledgehammer hit and the first cracks started to appear.

Some nights Adam lay awake envying those lucky bastards who went out with an aneurysm on the toilet. There was something glorious about the idea of straining so hard something in your brain ruptured. It was so radically different from the fate that awaited him.

His death had begun with the shakes. Few people could point to the actual moment in time they began to die. It wasn't a gift he would have bestowed on anyone. Actually, it was nothing as glamorous as a fully-fledged tremor. He'd woken up one morning eight months ago with a twitch in his little finger that wouldn't stop for more than an hour, while he stared at it, fascinated by the errant digit doing its own thing, he'd assumed it was a trapped nerve or something equally mundane. The disease would progress into difficulty swallowing, forming words, and ultimately, breathing. In other words Adam Shaw was dying one muscle-dependent bodily function at a time.

He'd been living with the diagnosis for seven months: amyotrophic lateral sclerosis. The disease had a Major League Baseball All-Star as its poster boy. Lou Gehrig's disease. It sounded like it should have been a stat printed on Adam Shaw's rookie card. To stretch the baseball analogy way beyond breaking, the last seven months had taught Adam one single excruciating truth: life delights in throwing one beanball after another and doesn't give a shit about the rules. It's all about hitting you until you go down. If he'd been in the batting cages, they'd have turned the pitching machine off to put him out of his misery long before now.

He couldn't afford to be sick. It was as simple as that. It wasn't just about phrases like "Medicaid," "pre-existing condition," "insurance premiums" or any of the vast array of other magic words that made up the vocabulary of the high cost of a slow death in the United States of America. It was about Jake. It was always about Jake.

His son was eleven now. It had been his birthday last week. They'd worn paper hats and had cake Adam had dropped on the floor because of his fucking treacherous hands. They'd giggled about it, but Adam could have cried as he struggled to scoop up the mess. He hated what was happening to him. Jake didn't understand. He just blew out the candles and made a wish. Even with that duplicate chromosome and a host of other problems that had come to light over the last eleven years, Jake had a conservative life expectancy of thirty-three, meaning he was going to outlive his father by a good twenty years.

Adam was good with numbers. He had to be, with his job. He spent every day calculating the different ways people would die given their age, education and other environmental factors. He knew better than anyone that the numbers never lied. Lily had always joked that he was on the autistic spectrum, the way he could rattle off statistics and draw correlations between seemingly unlinked numbers. It was just what he did. Slightly obsessive, just a little bit odd, and one hundred percent Adam. In every good joke there's a grain of truth. He knew his nature made him difficult to live with. His obsessions ruled his world, but they were what made him indispensable to his employers, saving them millions as they withheld hope from other desperate people who had no idea how badly the game of life was weighted against them.

Latest estimates had the cost of raising a child—a healthy

one—from birth to adulthood up near four hundred thousand bucks. Working with the theory that Jake would essentially never leave childhood, that was basically two childhoods, or in terms of cold hard cash, eight hundred thousand dollars. Just thinking about it was dizzying. They were the kind of numbers that made you go blind if you stared at them for too long, and the absolute worst of it was that they weren't even close to the truth. Jake's special needs multiplied those costs, conservatively, threefold, meaning Adam needed to lay his hands on two and a half million before he died.

Sometimes he felt like Rain Man with stuff swirling round and around in his head day and night, mocking him. They weren't just numbers now. They had dollar signs attached. One hundred and thirteen thousand six hundred and thirty-six dollars and thirty-six cents a year. Nine thousand four hundred and sixty-nine dollars and seventy cents a month. Say it quickly enough and it didn't sound too bad, now. Two thousand one hundred and eighty-five bucks, thirty-one a week. Round and around they swirled. Three hundred and twelve dollars and nineteen cents a day. Doable, surely? Thirteen dollars flat an hour. That was four bucks seventy-five more than minimum wage in this town, but in reality it only equated to a measly twenty-two cents a minute. Not even half a cent a second. But he couldn't find it. That was the ultimate kick in the nuts. Not even half a cent a second.

His entire savings would be eaten up in ninety-six days.

Three hundred and fifty-two days carved up into four

seasons of eighty-eight days a piece. In other words, he'd got enough money banked to see his boy looked after properly for one spring, summer, autumn, or winter, no more, no less. That was the reality of Adam's bequest. Ninety-six days of living.

The burden of care shouldn't have rested solely on Adam's shoulders.

There should have been safety nets and safeguards and fallbacks and all sorts of checks and balances to stop a kid like Jake falling through the cracks, but with the infinite wisdom of pencil pushers with quotas to meet, the Disability Determination Services had put an end to Jake's Supplemental Security Income, declaring that his disabilities didn't result in "marked and severe functional limitations." It was a joke. They'd had reports from his teachers, from his doctors, even from his physical and speech therapists. It didn't matter. It had taken them five months to decide that Jake's symptoms weren't severe enough. Maybe they used astrology or called in psychics to gaze into a future where Jake Shaw was able to fend for himself without constant care and supervision? Or maybe the DDS just didn't give a crap about Jake one way or the other?

There was CHIP, of course. The Children's Health Insurance Program, but Adam's salary was a couple of thousand over the threshold, making it another dead end.

Everything was about keeping Jake out of care, keeping him self-sufficient not only after Adam was gone, but during the months or maybe even years of disintegration where he wouldn't be able to care for him.

Sure, there were appeals, but appeals took time, and time was just another thing he didn't have.

He was never meant to go through this alone. That had never been the plan. It had always been him and Lily in it to the end. Only it hadn't worked out that way.

And that was why he stood outside the door of Chicago Liberty, about to radically change what little remained of his life.

Did that make him a good father?

Was it even a good excuse?

In both instances, he needed to believe the answer was yes.

The best way to rob a bank is to get a degree in finance, get into a business fraternity, network your ass off and land a plum job pulling down a hundred thousand per annum plus bonuses. Better still, have a frat brother in the Treasury willing to look the other way when you dabble in a little usury, plying the unemployed and students with high-interest credit cards they can't possibly meet the repayments on, or invest customer funds poorly and wait for the government bailout, giving yourself a nice incentive bonus for keeping the bank open. Then you're just making money.

Then there was that line from *The Godfather*: "A lawyer with a briefcase can steal more than a hundred men with guns." Wasn't that the truth? It had evolved of course. Now it was: "Give a man a gun and he can rob a bank; give a man a bank and he can rob the world." But the principle held.

Bank robbery was a fool's game. Much better to lie, cheat, and steal your way onto Wall Street; less work for a better payout. Adam Shaw didn't have a degree in finance or law, and lacked a bank to call his own; his options were limited and he was desperate. He'd been forced to come up with another strategy. His gift was for numbers.

He'd done his homework.

He'd started by watching a lot of movies that offered a crash course in heists—some bank, others more elaborate in their nature. Unfortunately, if Hollywood had taught him anything, it was that there were as many different ways to rob a bank as there were movies on the subject. Over the last month he'd watched them all: *Inside Man*, *The Italian Job*, *The Silent Partner*, *Run Lola Run*, *Ocean's Eleven*, *Twelve and Thirteen*, *Point Break*, *Butch Cassidy and the Sundance Kid*, *Dog Day Afternoon*, *Heat*, *The Bank Job*, *Reservoir Dogs* and *The Usual Suspects*. His Netflix history was a veritable how-to guide that could and would be used in court against him.

He'd done his reading, too. The FBI had published a wealth of information on the subject. And dispiriting stuff it was, given what he had in mind.

The average bank robbery netted the thieves a princely 7,500 dollars, but went up to sixteen grand if a gun was involved, hence the contents of the plastic bag with its life-affirming message: KEEP AWAY FROM BABIES AND SMALL CHILDREN. Of course, the presence of a firearm turned it from robbery into aggravated robbery, and meant a fifteen-year sentence in

Cook County if the shit hit the fan. If the gun went off, he was looking at thirty. Not that he'd be alive to serve either term out.

He'd even posed the question on Reddit, crowdsourcing a solution to the problem. "How Would You Rob A Bank?" had garnered a good fifteen hundred helpful comments from devious minds. Most involved hurting someone or were straight rips-offs of movies like *Die Hard 3*, loudly proclaiming they'd detonate a bomb in a public place to divert police attention, or hit the Federal Reserve dressed up like a clown. One guy came closer, suggesting he'd hack the bank's mainframe and upload a virus to do the dirty work.

Getting his hands on the Beretta had been simple: a kid called Chris whose brother mowed the lawns in his neighborhood was a gun guy. Chris had bought the piece legally, using his own permit, scratched off the serial number and sold it on for twice the shop rate; if Adam was caught he'd just claim it had been stolen. The cops called people like Chris's brother "straw men." The city was full of them. Drug guys and gangs used them to tool up for drilling. That's what they called it, "drilling," like the blood that sprayed out of the back of their heads was oil and they'd hit the mother lode.

Another person on the job pretty much doubled the take, with an additional fourteen thousand per head. It was smart to specialize, divide and conquer. Have a getaway driver, have someone in place watching the lobby, someone to accompany the teller to the vault, but then you were looking at a lower cut, with more people to keep quiet.

It was hardly surprising that a quarter of all money stolen ended up back in the vaults eventually. And of course, every penny was federally insured. The tellers were trained to comply, hand over the cash and get you out of there as quickly as possible without hurting anyone, but they'd never hand over two and a half million in cash.

Branch size didn't matter, neither did location—apart from the obvious demands of the getaway—what did make a difference were those fast-rising security screens that shielded the teller from the would-be robber; but at upwards of seven thousand dollars to install, they just weren't worth the investment for a lot of the smaller branches, like the branch of Chicago Liberty he stood outside right now.

The truth was armed security vans and the river casinos offered more attractive targets, and easier ones, too, but neither would work for what Adam had in mind.

He opened the door.

How could such an inconsequential action change everything?

It wasn't just Newton's third law; that could be distilled down to an essence of "for every action there's an equal and opposite reaction." There was nothing equal about the relationship between the door and his future.

The cold blast from the air conditioner hit him full in the face, a frigid counterpoint to the stifling summer heat out on the sidewalk. It was only going to get worse as the day progressed. The music of the waking city played on around him, a landscape of sound that stopped as soon as he entered the ATM vestibule with its piped music. He didn't recognize the song. Some nineties tune stripped of vocals and made bland in the process. He didn't bother with a disguise, or a mask. He'd been in a few times over the last month. It was a small provincial branch, but not so small they knew who he was. There was a remote possibility someone might remember the guy with the uncontrollable twitch. He looked up at the camera eye. They didn't bother hiding them these days. Everyone knew there was heavy surveillance in place. Right now he was being recorded from seven different angles.

At five eleven, Adam Shaw was an unremarkable man. He was thinner than he had been in the last decade thanks to the wasting disease eating away at his muscles; the hair at his temples and the stubble on his cheeks was graying. The only thing that made him stand out that day was the long raincoat he wore in spite of the heat. He was always cold these days. That was one of the side effects of his lack of body fat.

Aside from the staff behind the counter and the guard on his chair by the door, there were three other customers in the lobby: a big black man in one of the green loungers; a white woman beside him half hidden by the leaves of an overgrown potted plant, one side of her face badly bruised; and a middle-aged white man in a tweed jacket with worn-out elbow patches, who Adam stepped aside to allow to leave. Then there were two.

Adam walked up to one of the two women behind the counter.

Her name badge said SASHA.

She looked up and smiled at him. She had no idea that he was about to ruin her day.

2

Introspection was supposed to be good for the soul, wasn't it? Surely Buddha had some great wisdom to share on the subject. If not Buddha, maybe Laozi or Confucius? Not that she knew much about any of them.

Sasha Sumner was seriously beginning to doubt the wisdom of looking anywhere but forwards. Looking back only brought home all of the fears and inadequacies of childhood she'd fought so long and hard to get over.

Looking at the here and now left her riddled not with doubt so much as performance anxiety. What was she doing working as a teller in a bank? Why, when all was said and done, did she have the shit version of the Midas touch, where every man she became interested in turned to crap?

The answer to these and so many other insightful questions, when she turned the magnifying glass inwards, was a wholly unsatisfying series of "don't know"s.

It was funny in a pathetic kind of way.

Sasha's last relationship consisted of meeting a guy called Barry with bad hair in a wine bar downtown (Barry with the bad hair—that really should have been a bright neon flashing warning sign) on a Tuesday night. A bit like Barry, the wine bar had been trying too hard to be sophisticated and came off as cheap.

First kiss, Tuesday night. First proper grope (his) also Tuesday night. First proper date, Thursday night, drinks at the Telegraph, a fancy wine bar with a killer view of the water.

First and last fuck, technically Friday morning, 2 a.m.; slightly drunken, very wearisome, not very thrilling, even less fulfilling, hence the emotional and physical epitaph on their fledgling relationship: Sometimes you just knew it wasn't meant to be.

In that short space of time Barry had, however, managed to come up with a not-so-cute nickname for her: Goldilocks. It had sounded okay when he had first said it, but then he'd gone through his thought process: she had been standing, naked, looking at herself in the full-length mirror when Barry had said, "Goldilocks' ass," and grinned like he had just said the funniest thing in the world.

"What?"

"Your ass. You know, not too big, not too small. Just right."

He had obviously been saving that one for a while. It didn't have that spontaneous feel. Things got so much worse a couple of minutes later, when she came back from the bathroom to see Barry spread out on the bed, licking his lips.

"Who's been sitting on my face?" he said, doing an impression of Daddy Bear's throaty grumble.

That was it.

That was the exact moment Sasha knew that he and she would never make us.

The men in her life had been a string of Barrys, some well-intentioned, some unlucky, some just downright mean.

Now, thirty-three years old, habitually single, with a half-century of notches on the bedpost, she'd reached the lightbulb moment where she'd finally realized she didn't need someone else to make her life complete.

The fact that her number had crept over fifty this year was depressing. She had slept with fifty-one people in her life. Even when she rationalized it by saying that she was thirty-three and had been sexually active since she was sixteen—seventeen years with an average of three sexual partners a year, or one every four months—it just felt like an outrageous number. Yesterday it had left her feeling like a complete slut. The question had come up over an after-work drink. "What's your number?"

Eight women ranging from eighteen to fifty-six years old, and she'd fucked more men than the rest of them combined. She'd lied about her number and still got looks that spoke volumes.

You can take the girl out of the 'hood, but you can't take the ho out of the girl, she thought bitterly.

She looked at herself in the mirror again, alone in the room this time, and wasn't depressed by what she saw. She *was* Goldilocks, not too big, not too small, and not just her ass. She had good proportions all over and a flat stomach, capable of stopping a man dead in his tracks. Her breasts were big enough to give cleavage without being pendulous, and she liked the way her nipples still pointed upwards. All in all, she liked what she saw. A lot.

Fifty-one.

Worst of all, she seriously doubted she could remember all of their names, and definitely not their faces.

She could remember some of the sweeter more intimate gestures, including Charlie Fletcher, who touched her face so tenderly during their lovemaking that he burned himself forever on her memory. It had been so unexpected, so gentle, so unlike those pioneers who came before him. Sasha smiled, enjoying the memory. It was one of the few that regularly conspired to convince her that love might just exist after all.

She turned on the radio to catch the news and traffic reports. The day was full of the usual violent crimes and threatened teachers' strikes, political unrest in unfamiliar countries, and the traffic was already congesting into tailbacks, bottlenecks and contraflows.

She dressed conservatively in a trouser-suit and white cotton blouse, and at 7.29 a.m., made the short walk to 63rd and the red line station that'd take her from her place in Englewood through changes in the city to the Metra at Glenview. There were no whistles. Appreciation was much cruder in Englewood these days. They barracked her with promises of just what they'd love to do to her. It was a poverty-stricken, predominantly black neighborhood, but she'd grown up here and the place had a pull on her. Plus her rent was affordable, and thanks to the color of her skin, she fit in just fine. She might work in a bank and own her own four walls, but under her skin she still felt like Sash, the same old girl from the block even if that kid would have ripped the shit out of her for the trouser-suit and blouse.

She walked quickly, head down, focused on where she was going. Only tourists and gangbangers walked with their heads up.

Other girls she'd run with growing up didn't have their own places, at least not nice ones, not without the kind of debt they'd called indentured servitude back in the Dark Ages. It wasn't the banks that owned them; it was either the gangs or the welfare people and both were as bad as each other.

The walk took her around the corner of Wallace, where H.H. Holmes's murder castle had once stood. Now it was a couple of trees and a post office, hardly the eerie domain of the country's first serial killer; still, people flocked to the spot eager for a taste of the city's macabre past. There was no sating the thirst for blood. Give them a month living in Englewood instead of passing through and see how they liked it then.

The early summer sun felt good on her skin, the breeze just slight enough to be refreshing, not cold. Give it an hour, though, and it would be uncomfortably hot.

There were seven people at the train station: the usual suspects. Sasha regularly amused herself by imagining names and stories about her fellow commuters, their lives littered with dirty secrets. There was Clive, a secondhand car salesman who'd hidden the body of his ex-wife in an old Caddy at the back of the lot that wasn't for sale. Next to him was Richard. Tricky Dicky, the stock-exchange wizard. He wasn't just in *this* line. He was in the pre-op line for his sex change. Tricky had such fine cheekbones. Next was Sister Grace, a pharmacy assistant who was selling prescription tranquilizers and anti-depressants to her boyfriend who sold them on… (Only her name was Emily, not Grace, and she worked in a bakery, Sasha now knew. Sometimes a little knowledge took all the fun out of life.) Betsy, mother of two, cheating on her perfect husband with his best friend's wife. Riley, distinguished second son of a Texan oil baron, slumming it in Englewood because he had a habit. Gorgeous Graham with his greasy ponytail and thin neck, perpetually tired from his late nights holding forth as the comrades rehashed Better Dead than Red plots and subplots in the basement of his squat. And last, but by no means least, Maya, a beautiful Cherokee princess forced to take refuge so far from her homeland because the big chief wanted to sell her to the white man.

It was all bullshit, but bullshit made life fun. Their real lives had no hope of being as exotic as the ones she dreamed up for them. Dealers, lawyers, tinkers, tailors, soldiers, sailors, priests, cops and bank tellers, utterly banal lives for ultimately banal people. At this time of the morning, she preferred her version of reality.

By the time the train rolled into the platform another dozen commuters had joined them. The carriages were already full, but as people disembarked, a seat opened up. It was twenty-two miles to the bank, through streets haunted by the ghosts of her life and loves; where she'd met, kissed and left people because they were frogs not princes. Cafés where she had taken a leisurely coffee, gulped down a burning macchiato, spilled chocolate sprinkles, and snorted espresso out through her nose when laughter had ambushed her. Lingerie stores where she'd carefully selected ammunition, the warfare of her love life. They had one thing in common. They were all places that had been full of hope at one time or another. But hope washed away like footsteps in the sand.

She followed the crush as workers left through the various exits at Glenview, treading a familiar path to Chicago Liberty.

On the corner beside a brightly colored food truck a youngish man stood counting the cars. He was there every morning, and everybody who worked in the neighborhood knew him: Brian, the compulsive counter. Brian appeared to be adding up the number of cars crossing the intersection without turning left, marking them off methodically in his notebook. Not all cars, she realized, as he didn't mark off two in a row. Cars of a certain color.

"Hi, Brian," she called.

"Hey, Sasha." His smile was childishly wide. "You look pretty today."

"You don't look too bad yourself, Brian." She blew him a kiss and breezed on down the street to the bank.

As usual, the lights were out and the blackened façade offered no glimpses of life beyond the glass. She rang the staff bell and smiled up at the security camera. A few seconds later the door buzzed and she pushed it open. She was surprised to find that she was the last to arrive. The entire staff had gathered on the main floor and there was a soft but insistent buzz of conversation, with Richard Rhodes, the manager, at the center of it. She didn't like the guy: he was needy and always tried too hard to be liked. She thought for one terrible minute she'd got her days wrong and was late for the staff meeting. She hadn't and she wasn't. The reason everyone had gathered around Richard Rhodes was obvious the moment she saw him properly. He looked like shit. The entire left side of his face was covered with purple-black bruising, his forehead was cut up with a mesh of small grazes, and his lips were swollen. The swelling made his voice slur.

"...followed me out of the bank last night. I didn't notice him at first, then I heard his footsteps right behind me and looked back..." Rhodes looked up uncertainly, as though seeking understanding. His staff hung on his every word. He could have told them how he bumped into Mike Tyson and volunteered to spar a few rounds and they would have nodded and smiled encouragingly. "He was big." Rhodes rubbed at his chin. "He was an animal, snarling and swinging his fists... I thought he was going to kill me." Rhodes paused just long enough for that one to sink in. It was the one nightmare they all shared: a bank robbery with violence. "When I fell down he started kicking me, yelling about keys to the bank. I tried to explain that we have a time-lock on the night safe, that even I can't open it, but he just wouldn't believe me."

Sasha looked at her co-workers as they absorbed his bullshit. And it *was* bullshit. It wasn't even good bullshit. She'd grown up around liars, both good and bad. Rhodes was at best economical with the truth. She couldn't understand why they couldn't see straight through him; he was twitching and shifting, clearly going through a well-rehearsed speech. Worse, he kept looking for affirmation in their eyes. But why was he lying?

"Did you call the police?" she said, looking Rhodes straight in the eye, challenging him to try to brush her words away. "He could be out there now. And if not here, another bank in the city. You were lucky, Richard. Next time he might kill somebody."

Rhodes looked at her. She smiled as he swallowed and rubbed hard at his right eye as though trying to make the bruise disappear.

"God... yes. Yes... I should. I didn't even think..." he said sickly. He shook his head, his body language saying *no, no, no*. "I'll do that now while you girls open up. Everyone be safe today." He touched his cheek again, then shuffled away to his office across the lobby. That was another thing, he insisted on calling them "girls." She really hated that.

They had the routines down, so when the little hand ticked over onto the hour they were ready to open the doors to the world.

The morning dragged on. She wasn't a clock watcher. That would drive you mad in a place like this. She saw a guy with the twitch shuffling towards her counter.

She didn't know what was wrong with him, Parkinson's, maybe. She couldn't help it; she pitied the guy. She knew she wasn't supposed to pity people, that demeaned them and their fight, but how could you be human and not? She flashed him her most welcoming smile as he wrapped his left hand around his right elbow. His arm twitched almost like he was battling an uncontrollable urge to do the birdie dance.

Sasha kept on pitying him right up until he pulled out the Beretta 9mm.

3

ADAM HAD REHEARSED THE speech a hundred times in front of the mirror, and at least half a dozen of them had ended up with him channeling Travis Bickle and asking his reflection: "You talking to me?" Confronted with Sasha's smile he couldn't remember what he wanted to say.

He reached into his left pocket, the one that didn't have the Beretta in it, and closed his hand around the thumbdrive. That was his real weapon; the Beretta was just something to open lines of communication.

He was shaking.

He breathed deeply, closed his eyes, trying to master his limb, counted to five in his head, and opened his eyes. He managed a smile to match hers.

Focus on the plan. Don't think about anything else.

Don't think about the teller. Don't think about the big black guy in the chair over there, don't think about the woman with the bruises or the bank manager—who, Adam noticed, also had a black eye. Just focus on the plan. The plan is good. The plan is sound.

"How can I help you?"

Adam read her name badge. "Hi, Sasha," he said. He couldn't look her in the eye. "I need you to do something for me."

"Of course."

Adam put the thumbdrive on the counter between them. "I need you to put this into the terminal." He nodded towards the computer beside her.

Chicago Liberty had close to six million customer accounts across one hundred and forty-six branches across the State. He'd had to make allowances for dead-end welfare neighborhoods that would be dominated, statistically at least, by deadbeat accounts and low-yield deposits where his theft would be noticeable. A corporate branch in a reasonably sized catchment area would service somewhere in the region of forty thousand accounts. It was the Goldilocks principle: not too big, because the security would be too tough; not too small, because the reward vs. risk wouldn't pay out.

The branch where Sasha worked was just right. Goldilocks. Adam couldn't possibly have known that he was the second person to think of her that way in the last week, but armed with her age, the fact she'd never been in a long-term relationship and her background, he could have predicted her number. It was all just mathematics.

Forty thousand accounts meant he only needed sixty

bucks per account. A negligible amount, really. It could be hidden in charges or interest payments, larger than he would have liked, but with corporate accounts, small enough that the odds of the theft being discovered were slim to none. He wasn't out to hurt anyone, so he'd set a lower limit on balances held, meaning he was realistically looking at robbing seventy-five dollars from each viable account to secure his son's future.

Seventy-five bucks. Or, in other words, he was asking each person to pay for 341 minutes of Jake's care. Five hours, forty-one minutes. It was nothing in the grand scheme of things.

"I can't do that, sir," Sasha said, as he'd known she would.

One message on Reddit had caught his eye. It was unlike the others.

It was simply a clickable string of alphanumerics: 18681872I^2P.

At first glance it looked like gibberish, the kind of spam a bot left behind that, if followed, led to an advert for cheap pharmaceuticals. He would have ignored it if it wasn't for the final part of the message. The numerical string was a pseudo-mathematical notation, an invisible Internet protocol for web surfing, chatting, blogging and file transfers anonymously and securely. I2P had another name: a dark net. It wasn't a particularly sophisticated cypher, and once he'd worked that out, decoding the rest of the message was relatively simple.

18681872, eight digits that could easily be broken down into any number of sequences and combinations, but the most obvious was a simple four-four split, which offered up two years. 1868–1872, the dates that Ferdinand von Richthofen made seven expeditions to China and first coined the term "the Silk Road."

The modern-day Silk Road, despite being closed down multiple times by the FBI and Europol, was one of the dark web's most resilient marketplaces, offering drugs, fake driver's licenses and just about everything in between. He was after the in between. He could buy what he needed to pull off the robbery; all he had to do was look in the right place.

The where was a little more difficult, but the poster's identity offered the final clue. It was another number sequence: 12541324. The dates equated to the birth and death of the road's most famous traveler, Marco Polo.

186.81.87.2—one of only two viable IP addresses from the original message—gave Adam a direct peer-to-peer connection with a computer in Colombia. He felt like he was playing out some patsy role in a cheesy eighties movie. The alternative IP address was US-based and linked to a machine in one of MIT's computer halls, which could have meant a Treasury sting. Of course, that didn't mean either was the true site of operations; it was easy to mask an IP address if you knew what you were doing, shifting it across a dozen anonymizers. He couldn't worry about that. Running an anonymizer to mask his own path, he entered the numbers into the url bar. The second string confirmed Adam was in the right place, but not in the way he'd expected. He was offered an array of choices as an ASCI-style map of China scrolled up the black screen. Various cities were marked along the way. Three stood out, Xinjiang, Gansu, and Shaanxi, because they were listed as key destinations on the trade route Polo would have followed. The others weren't.

Adam selected them one after the other, and was rewarded with a simple welcome message: GREETINGS, WEARY TRAVELER.

He hit Enter and was rewarded with a second message: WHAT IS YOUR POISON?

Over the course of a week he traded messages with the mysterious Marco Polo, outlining exactly what he needed the computer worm to do. The seller promised his people had been developing something very similar, similar enough to cover Adam's needs. But he refused Adam's offer of a straight transaction, money for the worm. Instead he offered a mutually beneficial agreement. Adam would get the two and a half million dollars he needed as a payment for a small task, rather than direct from the bank. All Adam would have to do was insert a thumbdrive into a USB port with access to the bank's main system—not a sandboxed computer—and the worm would do the rest.

Adam needed Marco, whoever he was. If the guy had a way of getting the money out of the country, laundering it and filtering it back into the States it was the answer to his prayers. It didn't matter if he was mixing it up in the laundry with drug money or gun money or sex money. That was none of his business. He was simply being paid to put a thumbdrive into a computer.

He wouldn't have to live with the consequences of his action. His mysterious benefactor knew that. Adam knew that. He had nothing to lose and two and a half million to gain. The money would be moved to a place where the Treasury Department couldn't touch it and the bank couldn't claw it back. It didn't matter if the cops tracked his route out of the bank by CCTV, or even if some trigger-happy guard put him down. That eventuality would only rob him of a couple of months, and he'd willingly trade them for the money Jake needed. Those few minutes when the worm processed millions of calculations per second to move the money out of Chicago Liberty were all that mattered. And that, Marco Polo assured him, was covered by the wonders of the program he'd bartered for.

They'd given him a number to finalize negotiations; he could tell from the pauses in the conversation that it was a satellite phone. "I'm offering a marriage of convenience," the voice on the other end told him. Marco Polo spoke through a distorter, his voice coming out comically mechanical and stripped of any inflection of vocal pattern. "We'll offer you a return of twenty-five cents on the dollar recovered."

"That's not what I came to you for."

"But that's what you found. In a week you'll receive a visit from a benefactor working on our behalf. He will deliver two items: a thumbdrive and a key. On the drive will be an encrypted program that will do everything you need and more. It will be designed to work on a mainframe so you won't be able to test it on your home computer; don't waste your time trying. All you need to do is insert that drive into a computer on the network of the bank of your choice and it will do the rest. The key is for a left luggage locker in Union Station. Twenty-one days after you complete the transfer go to the locker. You'll find a hard drive with an encrypted private key that will unlock two and a half million dollars in clean Bitcoins. I trust you find this agreeable?" Even through the vocal distortion, Adam was struck by the man's command of English. He was a native speaker. His use of contractions was comfortable, and he used complex sentence structure and phraseology. That should have triggered a louder alarm bell than it did. That and the fact that putting a thumbdrive in a machine just wasn't a two-and-a-half-million-dollar risk. Any idiot could have done it; it didn't require any talent.

Adam knew he was getting into bed with dangerous people. It had even crossed his mind to go to the Treasury Department and turn himself in, but that wouldn't help Jake. So he clung to one simple maxim: desperate men do desperate things.

He had an idea how it would work from their side; the program would move the money offshore, to a country without a tax treaty or disclosure agreement with the US, then on to accounts in Columbia—assuming they really were Columbian—where they'd trade the currency to brokers on the Black Market Peso Exchange, filtering it back into the US as part of illegal currency exchanges of narcotics dollars, laundering it through purchases of household appliances, consumer electronics, liquor, cigarettes, auto parts, precious metals and even footwear. The vast majority of laundering went through banks, but the second most common non-bank exchange involved casinos. Even for legitimate South American businesses it was a way of avoiding paying import and exchange tariffs.

"You promise me that you will put the threshold in? I don't want to rob people who are barely getting by."

"You shouldn't concern yourself with anything you don't need to. Worry about finding the right bank, leave the rest to us."

"Twenty-five cents on the dollar means three hundred coming out of each account, not seventy-five. It's the kind of money that gets noticed and could really hurt an ordinary family."

"You do realize I could lie to you, don't you?" the voice said, sounding utterly reasonable. "But content yourself with this: we don't intend this to be a one-shot deal. This is a test run of our software. There are desperate people like you in every city in every state, and burning the operation before we've even begun isn't in our interests, that you *can* trust. We have invested a lot of energy in this, which is lucky for you as for the time being we have a coincidence of wants." Again with a complex concept, not the kind of language he'd expect from a non-native speaker. "We can help each other. Remember, you came to us, not the other way around. The hard drive will be clean. This way you walk away with two and a half million dollars. Any other way, you don't walk anywhere. Do you think you can just transfer money out of the country and the government will just let you transfer it back in as though nothing has happened? They monitor unusual activity and high currency exchanges. They would shut you down in minutes and you'd live out your days in Joliet. This way you have a chance. Assuming you can disappear, you get what you want. We get what we want."

"What's that?"

"A lot of money."

"How will you know when it's done?"

"We'll know. Don't disappoint us, Mr. Shaw." The line went dead.

Yesterday Adam had made a second set of arrangements, going to a small law firm to arrange for two trustees to administer Jake's inheritance: Lily's parents. He'd lodged the key along with advice on how to trade the Bitcoins for real money with the lawyer, leaving strict instructions that the letter was only to be opened by the named trustees in the event of his death or physical and mental incapacitation. It had taken an hour and cost him six hundred dollars of Jake's fund, but it bought him peace of mind. Even if he never walked out of Chicago Liberty, as long as he carried out his half of this devil's bargain the hard drive would be there at Union Station waiting to be picked up, and he could die knowing Jake was looked after.

It might have been a Pyrrhic victory, but even that was a win.

Adam didn't feel like a winner.

He swallowed hard, and with his trembling right hand reached into his other pocket for the plastic bag, fumbling with it as he lifted the gun out. "I really don't want to hurt anyone, Sasha. I promise. Just put the thumbdrive in and click 'run' when the dialogue box pops up. Please. I know you're frightened, but you don't need to be. I'm not going to hurt you."

"I couldn't even if I wanted to," said Sasha. "This is a dumb terminal, not a computer. There's nowhere to plug anything in. I don't know what's wrong, but this won't help." He hadn't even considered the possibility that the machines the tellers used would be anything less than normal—intelligent—computers. He was looking at a screen and keyboard, but there was no CPU, no processing power, and worst of all for his needs, no ports. Computations, data storage and retrieval depended on the mainframe.

"I'll tell you what's wrong," a third voice cut in from behind him. It was the black man. He was up out of his chair and walking towards Adam. "Twitchy here is missing his fix. Big man with a gun, huh? You wanna put that gun away before you get yourself killed."

"This isn't any of your business," Adam said.

"Oh I beg to fucking differ," the man said, less than ten feet away from him now. "I'm making it my business."

Random variables.

"Please, just go back to your seat, don't make this worse."

"What are you gonna do? Shoot me? I don't think so. You're fucked. Look at you. Junkie shakes. You might look all respectable, but you're just another fucking junkie looking for a score. Path-fucking-etic."

"It's not like that," Adam said. The tremor in his right hand was worse. The muzzle of the Beretta veered wildly as he tried to keep it steady.

"Of course it's like that. Look at you, man."

"No." He tried to focus on Sasha. He realized she had a block of money on the counter, ready to hand over to him. There was maybe eight thousand in the bundle. He shook his head. "No. I don't want it."

That seemed to confuse her. All of her training would have been geared to handing over the cash without argument so the threat would move on. He was the threat. She was just doing her job trying to get him out of there. What to do when a gunman refused a big stack of cash wasn't part of the training.

"Aren't you robbing the bank?"

"Yes," he said. "But not like that. That's not enough. I need more." She looked towards the other teller, a middle-aged white woman with a too-tight top button on her starched blouse and skin the color of a ghost. The woman reached down, presumably to press a button and trigger the cash drawer or the silent alarm. One or the other. Fifty-fifty chance. Adam shook his head again. "No. Please. Just do what I asked. I need you to put the thumbdrive into a computer on your network."

"Don't do it," the big man said, close enough to grab Adam now. Adam pointed the gun at him. He was too close, right up in Adam's personal space. "Look honey, just get the cops here to take care of Mr. Looney Tunes."

"Don't fucking move!" Adam barked, his hand jabbing towards the man. "Just… just…"

"You're not going to pull the trigger," the guy mocked. "My advice: grab the money and run. It'll keep you high for months."

Adam shook his head. "No."

There was more movement now. The bank manager with the battered face had emerged from his office. Adam didn't understand the look he gave the big man beside him. It was almost as though, for just a second, he'd mistaken the source of the threat and assumed the other guy was the one with the gun. Racial stereotyping at its finest.

"Is there a problem?"

"This tweaker's trying to rob your fucking bank, Rickie," the big man said. Adam was surprised that they were on first-name terms. "You gonna let that happen?"

4

THE SECRET WAS EATING Richard Rhodes alive.

He just wasn't built for a life of crime—which was a bit of a problem, because as of 4 p.m. yesterday he'd gone to third base with the whole Robin Hood myth, which, given he was the manager of the Glenview branch of Chicago Liberty Bank, was bad for business.

He crossed Sherwood Park every day on the way to work. He'd taken the name as a sign.

Day in, day out, he'd watched people lining up at his door to renegotiate their loans, desperate to sign up to repayment schemes for debts they couldn't hope to cover because their existing loans had been bought out, their interest hiked up and up over a bunch of transactions meant purely to put them out of house and home. It was heartbreaking. You had to be made of stone not to care. These were good people. People he'd grown up with and called friends; people who'd trusted him and taken bad advice from financial sharks swimming in the seas of the almighty dollar.

It wasn't fair. Idiots rode out the dot-com wave just long enough to avoid the wreckage, hipsters rolling their joints, content to leach a few more zeroes out of the next good idea that came their way. He kept trying to tell himself it wasn't personal when the bank foreclosed on someone's mortgage or repossessed a handicapped man's car, the only thing that allowed him to connect with the outside world. It was just business.

He knew all of their stories. He'd entertained thoughts of giving plane tickets to an old woman so she could fly back to Costa Rica and sit by her daughter's side as she went through chemo. He'd thought about Disney World passes for the young mother of two who'd lost her husband in a drive-by. He'd imagined the look on the face of single moms being presented with the start of a college fund, and the sheer joy of a lifelong Cubs fan given tickets for opening day. Little acts of kindness made the world go around.

Some days the inequality of life just pissed him off.

That was when he realized the extent of the resources he had at hand, and just how much he could help the people who needed helping.

When the last of the tellers left yesterday, he'd put his plan into action, though using the word "plan" to describe it was rather generous. All he did was a little digital shuffling, redirecting the interest payments from the accounts of the stockbrokers and other leeches to those of the genuinely in need, just enough to clear off overdrafts and loans he knew couldn't be met, and mortgage repayments where foreclosure was looking like a genuine possibility. Robbing the rich to give to the poor: the morally perfect crime. No one suffered. It wasn't even real money. It was interest.

Richard had even indulged in a daydream or two, imagining the press if he was ever caught. Chicago would adore him. It was an audacious crime, but more than that, it was a crime of the heart. In a city built on the foundations of organized crime the selfless nature of his would make him something special.

The Robin Hood bank manager.

How would the fame change his life?

Apart from winding up in a nine feet square cell with a new best friend called Bubba?

Perhaps one of those gorgeous women who habitually dated criminals would start to write to him, sharing promises of all that they would do when he got out? He could live with it if the universe wanted to pay him back that way. Or maybe he'd be headhunted by Saul Bonavechio or one of the other heads of the old crime families that ran the city? Who wouldn't want him on their payroll? He'd be the most celebrated criminal in Chicago since Capone.

The only sure thing was that Chicago Liberty wouldn't want him within five hundred feet of the place. He was a thief now. He could think of himself as Robin Hood all he wanted; it didn't matter that he'd given all of his ill-gotten gains away.

That was just a technicality, something the lawyers could argue over in court. A smart man would have tried to keep things as close to normal as possible, but the morning after, all of the evidence suggested Richard Rhodes was going to make a spectacularly dumb criminal.

His first real thought as he closed up was that it could be his last night of freedom. Once that notion took root he couldn't shake it. Everything he did from that moment on was predicated on the idea that it couldn't last so he'd better savor it.

Where did people like this new him go to relax?

As clichéd as it was, he knew straight away: they went to the riverboat casinos to blow a stack of money on blackjack and roulette.

For one night and one night only Richard Rhodes was determined to live the life. For that one night the world was filled with infinite possibilities. He could do anything.

So he dressed up, slicked his hair back with gel, put on a plain white shirt and a flamboyant tie and a black single-breasted jacket. The tie looked as though someone had thrown up on it. Richard flattered himself that he looked like Clooney or Garcia in his gangster get-up. In truth he bore an uncanny resemblance to Joe Pesci circa *My Cousin Vinny*.

Feeling like every one of the one hundred and fifty-three thousand dollars he'd diverted, Richard Rhodes put on his new life in much the same way that he shrugged into the single-breasted jacket and went down to the street to hail a cab. People like the new him didn't walk anywhere. People like the new him didn't have to. They were driven.

Contrails filled the sky above his head, parallel lines of white from each jet engine arcing across the curved earth, flying north from O'Hare across Canada to Europe. Never crossing. No doubt some conspiracy nut somewhere else in the city was looking up at them too, sure that the president was poisoning the populace to keep them docile and compliant.

As the first yellow cab he tried to hail accelerated past him, Richard felt a twinge of doubt. He might have given it all up right there and then if a second cab sixty feet behind it hadn't slowed to a stop beside him whilst he was still waving at the one that got away.

"Where to?" the driver asked as Richard closed the door behind him. It had all the finality of a cell door slamming.

"One of those riverboat casinos."

"Any particular area? West? Southwest?"

"Whatever's closest," he said, leaning in close to the Perspex partition. The driver nodded. A cab is a cab is a cab in the city: pine forest scent, no smoking roundels, charge sheets, Visa, MasterCard and Amex stickers and the impossible-to-expunge aftertaste of the nightlife.

"All the same to me, boss. Elgin, Joliet, Aurora, forty miles either way."

"You been to any of them?"

"Sure, we drop off fares out there a fair bit."

Richard nodded. "This is going to sound dumb, but what

kind of women go to those places? Are we talking grannies hitting the slots or…" His voice trailed off.

"Depends on the river. Elgin's mainly slots and video poker. Aurora and Joliet are good for table games. We're talking class women, you know. Real lookers. America's next top models on the hunt for high rollers with money they need taken off their hands."

"Nice," Richard said, nodding. "Take me to one of them."

The cab driver gave him a salute in the rearview mirror, and headed for the cloverleaf that'd follow the Des Plaines River out of town. No doubt the reality would prove much less glamorous, with bored housewives and call girls leaning against brightly flashing machines, but he liked the fantasy the cab driver had painted in his head.

He ran his fingers through his hair. The gel made it feel different, strange, hard. What would a classy woman think if she ran her fingers through it? Was gel erotic or uncomfortable, like touching something dead instead of something sensuous and alive? That made him worry. So much of life and attraction was tactile—the frisson of the first touch, the electricity of the first kiss, the sensory overload of penetration, every nerve-ending alive for the first and last time together. The gel had been a mistake.

The new Richard Rhodes wasn't a gel man. He made a mental note of that. He was learning himself as he went along, like Peter Parker after the radioactive spider had bitten him.

"Had me a classy woman once," the driver said, eyes fixed

on the road. "More than I could handle, if you know what I mean? Never thought I'd ever admit that there could be such a thing, but after three weeks she was killing me. Then, get this, I found out I wasn't the only one."

Richard wasn't in the least bit interested. That was new.

"I was her daytime guy. She was fucking the brains out of a nighttime guy as well, while I was driving fares to get the cash to take her to all the fancy places she liked to go. Give me a big girl any day of the week. They work hard to keep their men happy, know what I mean? They can't take it for granted that you'll come back the next night, so they work hard to make you happy."

Richard nodded in silent agreement. It wasn't so far from what his first girlfriend used to say, lovely Emma of the rose tattoo. In every relationship one partner is more in love than the other, and thus gives the power to the other. It wasn't a philosophy he wanted to believe, but the evidence certainly stacked up. Even back then he'd known instinctively that she was right—he was more in love with her than she was with him. Less than a year later Emma had moved on to pastures new. He made a point of never letting himself be the one to fall the furthest in any of his subsequent relationships, and always, always, made sure that he was the one who said things had run their course. It just made life easier.

They drove on, the driver sharing his various philosophies on the world. At night everyone was a philosopher, it seemed, especially when they had a captive audience.

The expressway took them through various neighborhoods of gradually declining wealth and increasing decay. Under the amber of streetlights Richard was sure he saw walls pitted with bullet holes. He had no way of knowing for sure, or if his imagination was running away with itself, but it felt like a fitting demarcation between his old life and this new one. Which, thinking about it, made the taxi driver the Ferryman.

"Here we go," the driver said, thirty minutes later as the yellow cab pulled up in front of what looked like an old steamboat river cruiser straight out of *Huckleberry Finn*.

Richard paid the man and emerged from the taxi like the king of Chicago.

It was all in the attitude.

The bouncers on the doors moved aside, nodding to him as though he was someone. He liked the feeling. These guys respected him. Right now, he really was the king. Richard tipped them both a nod, acknowledging their deference, and walked between them, up the gangplank and into the sumptuous foyer of the riverboat.

Inside, he was surrounded by lush reds and golds and thick heavy velvets and beautiful people at play. *Welcome to the jungle*, he thought. Part of Richard knew he was seeing everything through rose-tinted glasses, wanting it to be special, but that did very little to diminish his sense of awe.

A female concierge drifted towards him. Her smile was painted on with cherry red lipstick. "First time, sir?" she asked. The smile didn't so much as twitch; the war paint illusion was so well done.

Is it that obvious? Richard wondered how many other rubes had walked up the gangplank feeling like kings right up until meeting this woman, who took the wind right out of their sails.

"Yeah," he said, barely recognizing his own voice. "I'm in town with the circus for a few days. Thought I'd check out the competition." Only when he said it, "circus" sounded like something far more dangerous than clowns. He had no idea why he'd come out with a line like that: "checking out the competition" was bound to come back and bite him on the ass before the night was through.

The look she gave him said as much. People like her didn't use phrases like "free market economy" and "the competition," especially when they came in that order.

Still, her painted-on smile remained fixed firmly in place as she guided Richard into the casino proper with all the respect due to a visiting dignitary.

"Well, Mr....?"

"Rockwell," he said, surprising himself with the outright lie. He really was a new man. He smiled at that. "Like the artist. Milo Rockwell."

"Milo. That's a good name. I like it." The smile curled a little.

"Took a while to grow into it, but I like it now."

"Any relation?" she asked.

"Alas, no. I wouldn't have minded the bank balance to go along with the famous name."

Her smile never wavered. "Pity. Maybe we can make it up to you tonight. Whatever your pleasure, I'm sure you'll find it here. We pride ourselves on catering for every vice."

"Good to know."

"Perhaps you'd care for a drink?"

Somewhere ahead of him the slots paid out, lights and sound accompanying the jackpot.

"Someone's lucky day," he said. "I'll take a scotch, single malt, not the blended crap. Twenty-one years old or better, assuming you have it?"

"Of course. I'll have it sent to your table."

The croupier at the blackjack table caught his eye. There was something about her. Piece by piece she was nothing special, a yard sale of features, but as a whole they made magic.

He knew he was staring, but there was nothing he could do, even when the woman looked up from dealing a fresh hand of cards and saw his stare. Richard found himself smiling, but it wasn't *his* smile. It was, he realized, Milo Rockwell's smile.

He took one of the spare stools at her table.

It took him a moment more to realize what it was about her that was so compelling: she was *interesting* to look at, and interesting was so much more important than beautiful. Interesting people drew the eye. They demanded attention whereas beauty craved it. There was something desperate about beauty that worked to counteract its most basic and predatory lure.

He sat down beside an older man who might have been

a schoolteacher. He had that look about him. He dressed sensibly and without any real personality. The elbow patches on his tweed jacket were almost worn through. Richard liked to believe he was a good judge of character. It went with the job—the old one, not the new one—sizing people up, working out if they had money or needed it; and if they didn't appear to need it they had a better chance of getting it. He was good when it came to first impressions. And his first impression of this man was that he had a thing for the croupier. Richard read the woman's golden nametag: ALICE.

She obviously wasn't interested in him. She barely even looked at the old boy as he did a nerdy little trick with his cards, making them dance on their edges. It was quite impressive, but "Milo" wasn't the kind of man who'd be impressed by card tricks.

Something the hostess had said niggled at him. He worried away at it for a full two minutes, playing two hands of blackjack. He played the first too conservatively, staying early and letting the house win. He played the second too recklessly, taking a new card on seventeen and going bust on an eight. He knew people like him were supposed to be players, taking risks as and when, so he fought against his natural instinct to play it safe. His neighbor played the game the way he dressed: boringly.

Whatever your pleasure, every vice…

As the next hand played out—Richard claiming the spoils with a five-card trick—his single malt materialized by his right hand. He didn't notice who put it there or how long it had been waiting for him to take a slug.

He tasted it. It was good. And they hadn't ruined it by diluting it with huge rocks of ice. They didn't leave a bill, which suggested he was being watched. Instead of being intimidated, he felt strangely proud, like Milo Rockwell might actually *be* somebody.

They were probably up there now, trying to work out who sent him and just what kind of trouble he spelled for them.

He should have told them he was in from "the West Coast." Vague, but with the right kind of sinister connotations—another firm from Vegas looking to expand into their patch. That would rattle a few cages. Ah, well, something to think about next time. The way it just popped into his head that there would be a next time was both shocking and curiously comforting. He needed to think that there would be a next time. After all, Milo Rockwell had made his choice, talked the talk, and now he was going to walk the walk.

The schoolteacher went home after an hour of Richard spoiling his small talk with Alice, leaving them alone. To the victor the spoils.

There were surprisingly few people on this floor of the riverboat. Most of the punters gravitated towards the games they saw in the movies, the craps tables, the roulette wheels and the perennial favorites, the slots.

Richard turned over his third consecutive winning hand. He had to fight hard not to say something stupid like: "It must be my lucky day." That wouldn't be something Milo Rockwell would come out with. That was pure Richard. He wanted Alice to believe in Milo, the easy-come-easy-go, slightly dangerous man who'd turned up at her table positively radiating excitement and mystery. He didn't want her knowing about the nine-to-five bank manager in his soul.

"So," he offered, like the thought had just occurred to him. "What time do they let you out of here?"

"Two. But we're not allowed to fraternize with the customers. Golden rule."

"That's okay," he said, trying out a new smile. "I'm not a customer. I'm new in town, over from the West Coast. Just checking out the competition." He tried to read the look she gave him.

A giant of a black man, built like a linebacker, all brute strength and raw power barely harnessed by the expensive suit he wore, took one of the stools beside him.

"Well, then," Alice said. "You'd better talk to Archer." She nodded towards the new arrival. "He'll make sure you are taken care of."

5

ARCHER WAS KING OF all he surveyed.

He worked the muscles in his back.

Who would have thought it? A child of Cabrini–Green ending up king of this little bit of floating Chicago. Not exactly a rags-to-riches fairy tale, but certainly an underdog narrative, and wasn't that the promise the entire country was founded on?

He smiled. Samuel Archer, the embodiment of the American Dream.

The gaming floor was his domain. Everything between the slots at both ends of the floor: the video poker machines, the tables, roulette, blackjack, craps, even the girls running them. His. All his.

He walked down the red-carpeted stairs with their gold runners, pausing halfway down to drink it all in. It didn't matter how many times he saw it, he never grew tired of the view. Some kings might lord it over mountain ranges and skyscrapers, but he was quite happy with his own little paradise.

Archer nodded to one of the girls, Mimi—two kids, working three jobs and playing the ends off against the middle to keep her head above water—as she flashed him a smile, working her way through the players. He inclined his head slightly, a couple of inches to the left; just enough to say "I see you." That was important. They needed to know he saw them.

There was a romanticism to it all: the riverboat, the gaming tables, the rolls of the dice that promised that tonight, for one night only, those tumbling dice might just fall in the punters' favor. The whisper they made as they rolled across the green baize: anything is possible tonight.

Absolutely, Archer thought, *but nothing's left to chance.*

There was a science to the layout of the gaming floor; none of it was as haphazard as it looked. It was essentially a giant maze arranged to ensure visitors were kept disorientated, its sea of machines and tables creating obstacles and barriers that kept the players playing. The arrangement was absolutely logical once you grasped its purpose: a bank of slot machines to one side, another identical bank two hundred feet away. The player might remember that the exit was by the video poker machines, but what they didn't realize was that there were three banks of indistinguishable machines set up to create a labyrinth. The tall slots stopped people seeing over them, and, combined with the low ceiling, stopped them from spotting any obvious landmarks. After a few drinks, the gaming floor was one of those impossible-to-escape-from circles of Hell, which was why, of course, the cocktail girls were constantly circling. Alcohol dims the senses. Even shrewd players got sloppy when they'd had enough to drink. Plus, and this was the secret no one really talked about, the reality for a lot of the unloved and the unlovely that wound up in his kingdom was that chugging down drinks and playing cards was about as good as life got.

There weren't any clocks on the gaming floor, and there were no windows either. You didn't want Mother Nature marking the passage of time with something as pesky as dawn or dusk. You wanted people chasing their dreams—especially when those dreams were coming at fifty bucks per roll of the dice—and no one ever chased their dreams with one eye on the time. It was all pretty basic psychology. The lack of anchors helped the player slip slowly into that fugue state where money flowed steadily from their wallets to the croupier's till.

The rest was all ambiance: flashing lights, change slots clanging, the rush of the payout spilling into the metal trays, *ker-ching*, slot wheels whirring, the constant non-verbal stimuli crying "Win! Win! Win!" like the dupes really had a chance. It was all illusion. So many of those audible wins were nothing more than painful near misses meant to lure another handful of coins into the slots, because surely this time it was going to be different, wasn't it?

There was science behind everything here. Slot machines

constantly rewarded the gambler with small payouts, forever one cherry or star away from the real jackpot. At the card tables, players were always winning hands at blackjack, and each hand they won helped foster the misconception that the game was actually winnable. The entire business was predicated on that lie. For the house it was all about the long game. It just chipped away at the player's bankroll and slowly but surely the relentless turn of the cards left everyone losers.

And if all of that wasn't enough, there was Archer with his pocket full of comps. He never walked the floor without coupons for free meals and tickets for shows. He read the crowd and he knew who he needed to move on, who he needed to be sure came back, and whatever came out of Archer's pocket in comps the tables made back hundreds-fold from the same people sooner or later.

Yep, he really was the king.

He wanted a drink or a smoke; either would have given him something to do with his hands. The boss frowned on that kind of thing from his people, though. And if Archer was king, then Mr. Bonavechio—Saul to his aging mother, Mister B to everyone else in the city—was the Great Invisible Bastard in the Sky. God, to the Catholics in the audience, Allah to the Muslims, Mister B to the gamblers on the river.

Bonavechio wasn't big on personal vices, which was ironic given they were responsible for a healthy portion of his not-so-small fortune. He was what they used to call a self-made man, emphasis heavy on the last two words: made man.

He was *uomo d'onore* in the mother tongue. Not that Mister B had ever set foot in the old country.

He'd made his bones back in the early eighties with a high-profile hit in the wake of the Donnie Brasco trials, and after that people knew better than to fuck with him. Archer had been in short trousers back then, but even he'd heard the legends that surrounded Mister B.

So, if he couldn't drink or smoke he might as well do his job.

It was all about maintaining a presence. He liked to think of it as riffing on the "little boys should be seen and not heard" idea. At six four, packing just north of two hundred and forty pounds, Archer was hardly a wallflower.

He scanned the faces at the tables.

Who was feeling lucky tonight?

He made his way across the floor, throwing a comforting arm around a loser as he slipped two free tickets to go see Beyoncé into his hand. The man had lost fifteen thou in the last month and was fast on his way to losing his job, his house, and ultimately the wife who would be accompanying him to see Beyoncé in a couple of days. Archer took no joy in the knowledge that the man's life was slowly unraveling, but neither was he the guy's conscience. It wasn't his job to put the brakes on and say, "Hey, don't you think you've lost enough?" Instead, offering a rueful smile, Archer said, "Treat the wife, on me, my friend. She'll love you for it." And it was only partly a lie.

At the slots Archer saw a dowdy woman dressed in vintage

store chic clothes that hung on her like sackcloth. She was packing up to go. He thought about letting her leave, but money didn't discriminate. It all got spent just the same. Up close, he realized her dress wasn't vintage, it was just old, and the chicken wings of skin that hung slackly from her bones meant she was maybe fifteen years older than she'd first appeared when he'd seen her from across the floor. He changed his approach mid-smile and instead of silver-tongued flattery slipped a buffet voucher into her empty beaker. "Everyone's gotta eat, am I right?"

"You're too kind, Mr. Archer," she said.

He wasn't. He knew she'd eat, then hit the ATM beside the doors in the banqueting hall, change that for coins at the window and return with another beaker overflowing with life savings waiting to be fed one coin at a time into the hungry slots.

Ker-ching. Another winner.

Archer arrived at Alice's table in time to hear her say, "You better talk to Archer. He'll make sure you are taken care of."

"I will indeed," he said, leaning in. "Whatever your pleasure, I'm you man. Is this your first time with us?" The words were delivered with a salesman's forked tongue. It didn't matter whether the guy said yes or no, Archer would make the same offer.

"Mr. Rockwell here is just in from the West Coast," Alice said, "checking out the competition. I thought you might like to give him the grand tour?"

Archer inclined his head slightly. Otherwise he was absolutely still. He'd learned a long time ago that economy of movement was more intimidating than aggressive gestures. He would have to talk to Rockwell, obviously. He enjoyed talking. It was all about the delivery. People were more frightened by a calm sea than they were of a storm, because with the storm it was all on the surface. When he talked, Archer was dead calm.

"I would like nothing more, Mr. Rockwell."

"Milo, please."

"Milo Rockwell," Archer said it slowly, deliberately, sounding out every exaggerated syllable. "I feel like I should have heard that name before," he said, taking the man by the elbow and leading him away from the blackjack table. As he steered Rockwell around the bank of video poker machines towards the STAFF ONLY door and the fire exit that would take them top side, he asked, "You're not with the Milanos or Gambini, are you?" He deliberately made a mess of Gambino's surname. Anyone remotely connected to the Riverside or Los Angeles families would pull him up on the mistake without missing a beat. The family went all the way back to the Black Hand and the first days of organized crime on the West Coast. You didn't get the names wrong. You just didn't.

"I really can't say, you understand?" Rockwell said.

"Oh, I understand completely," Archer assured him, making the man for the liar he was. "Walk with me. We need to have a conversation."

If he'd been a smarter man, Milo Rockwell would have realized he was in trouble.

Nietzsche believed that people should exercise caution when examining the darker side of the soul: "He who fights monsters must beware lest he becomes a monster himself." There was a darkness inside Archer that *needed* the pain he inflicted, so to counterbalance that darkness he sought to understand it. He read Kierkegaard and Freud, Diderot, Kant, Plato and Descartes, and for all their wisdom, none of them could tell him why he had sunk so low as to feed off the pain of his fellow men, and why, more than anything else, he enjoyed hurting people. None of them understood the need in him to dispense hurt, but Archer was beginning to.

Archer's heartbeat didn't accelerate.

There was no adrenalin kick.

He opened the door, walking out into the fresh night air. It swung closed behind them on a hydraulic arm, shutting out the chaos of the gaming floor. The chill was bracing. It was good. It made him feel alive. It was quiet up here, giving the illusion of privacy despite the fact that several hundred people were gambling their life savings away less than thirty feet from where they stood.

Archer crossed the deck to the side of the boat. He didn't know if it was the starboard or portside. He could never remember which was which. He braced himself on the railing, looking out toward the bright lights of the big city in the distance.

"Hell of a view," he said, conversationally.

"Isn't it just," Rockwell said, joining him at the rail.

"Must be quite different to what you're used to," Archer said. "Living out in the desert."

"Yeah."

"What do you see?"

"Lights."

"Shall I tell you what I see? I see lives, hundreds of thousands of them, lit up like fireflies. And for every light I see an opportunity. You can be anyone you want to be out there, can't you?"

"I suppose."

"All you have to do is pick a light, you can try its life on like a new outfit, maybe a comfortable pair of jeans or some crisp Italian threads. Is that what you've done, Milo? Do you mind if I call you Milo?" He didn't wait for permission. "I think you're a liar. I don't think you're who you say you are. I think you're wearing someone else's life, trying to impress."

He leaned forward slightly, craning his neck to look the man beside him up and down with clinical calmness. Rockwell was nearly a foot shorter than Archer. Lean, but obviously out of shape. He had a desk jockey's physique. Maybe he went running a couple of times a week, maybe he played racquetball, but if he had any actual muscles beneath his cheap Italian suit the shiny fabric did well to conceal them.

"Is it Alice? She's a good-looking woman. I can understand you trying to impress her. Like that sad fucker

Maurice who sits at her table every night hoping she'll notice him. Thing is, like everything else in this place, she's mine. And when it comes to stuff I own I can get pretty protective, you understand?"

"I didn't mean any harm by it," Rockwell said. It was quite the most pitiful thing Archer had heard all night.

He took his time removing his suit jacket.

"I'm going to tell you something important, Milo, and I want you to take it to heart. Then I am going to hurt you to make sure you forget all about this place and any ideas you might have about pretending to be the big man again." He didn't take his eyes off the guy in front of him through the entire ritual of smoothing out the creases in his jacket as he draped it over the railing.

"You don't have to do this."

"I know. But that doesn't change anything. I don't *have* to throw you overboard, doesn't mean I *won't* throw you overboard. I'm not going to get hung up on worrying whether you can swim or not. Either you doggie-paddle to the shore, or you sink. It's all the same to me."

"Please."

"Don't beg."

"What do you want me to do?"

"Hurt," Archer said. The other man didn't have a good answer for that. "Do you know what I see when I look at you? I see a kid playing dress-up who really doesn't have a fucking clue what he's got himself into. I should take pity on you. Who on earth thinks coming out with some line about being fresh in from the West Coast to check out the competition is a good thing to say? That kind of dumb shit gets you noticed in all the wrong ways. Like I said, I get very proprietorial. So, what are you? I've got you pegged as a Bible salesman. Am I right?"

Rockwell shook his head.

"Insurance, then? Some other desk job you're bored of, something that's got you out looking for a bit of excitement?"

This time the guy just nodded. He looked sick.

"Figures. Okay, Milo, pop quiz: you ever heard of the Sufis?"

The man shook his head, eager to prove his ignorance. It really was pitiful.

"Then consider tonight's lesson on the house. You know the story about the scorpion and the frog crossing the river? Scorpion stings the frog halfway across and they both drown. I've got no intention of drowning, but I *am* going to hit you now because it's in my nature. It is what I do. I hurt people and I enjoy it. I'm one of life's scorpions and you, my friend, are a frog."

Before Milo Rockwell could move, Archer's fist slammed into his face. The bones of his knuckles exploded the gristle of his nose with a satisfyingly wet smack. The second punch to his gut doubled Rockwell up before a third hammered home the lesson. It was all over in three blows. Rockwell sagged against the railing and slumped forward, his legs gone.

Archer wasn't satisfied.

He grabbed a handful of the guy's hair and hauled him back upright so that he was forced to look at him as Archer's clubbing fist went to work with brutal efficiency. All told, it took less than sixty seconds to ruin the man's face.

He relinquished his hold, allowing Rockwell to slump to the deck, then crouched down beside him, reaching into the inside pocket of the man's cheap Italian suit for his wallet. "All right then, let's see who you really are, Milo Rockwell," Archer said, pulling out a driver's license. "Richard Rhodes," he read. "As I thought. You don't look like a Milo. Doesn't suit you." He wasn't even breathing hard from the brief flurry of exertion. He teased a business card out from behind what he assumed was a photo of Rhodes' girlfriend. It was good quality card stock. Very corporate. "Well now, isn't this interesting? You're the manager of the Glenview branch of the Chicago Liberty Bank? Someone up there must like you, Rickie, because this little piece of cardboard may have just saved your life."

"Richard," Rhodes said between bloody lips.

"Nah, I think you're more of a Rickie."

"Okay. Sure. You can call me whatever you want, just please—"

"Did I tell you I was psychic? I am. I know exactly what you're about to say. You're going to beg me not to hurt you anymore. I'll go easy on you, but only because Mister B is going to want to have a chat with you, Rickie, and without a Ouija board it can be pretty fucking tough having a decent conversation with a dead man. I'll be paying you a visit tomorrow. You're going to do me a service. I'm going to need you to move some money for me, no questions asked. You owe me that much for your life, understand?"

"There are rules," Rhodes protested weakly. "I can't just—"

"Rules are made to be broken. You want to walk away from here tonight, that's the price. I take it we have an understanding?"

6

ALICE FISHER WAS ONE of Archer's girls.

She loathed that label. She wasn't a girl. She was a woman. It was condescending. She wasn't the prettiest, but she had never cared about that. She wasn't blessed with a doll's face or any of those other impossibly perfect Photoshop features the world delighted in telling women they needed if they wanted to find love. What she had was a dancer's definition. Even now, eight months since she'd last danced, her abdominals, lats, quads, biceps and triceps, glutes and hamstrings carved out an impressive terrain beneath her skin. Some of Archer's clients would pay good money for muscle. A lot of what the big man did was trade in fetishes. It wasn't about being beautiful, it was about ticking certain boxes.

Alice hated herself, but she hated Samuel Archer more. That didn't alter the fact that when he whistled she came running.

She saw Archer crossing the gaming floor like a shark

in shallow waters, predatory, powerful and fully aware of both. He moved with an arrogance born of his brawler's physique. The pearl buttons of his crisp white shirt strained across his barrel chest, offering the occasional glimpse of the black skin beneath as he moved. He'd rolled his sleeves up and carried his jacket folded over his left arm. He flexed the fingers of his right hand, making a fist then relaxing it only to make it again. A vein pulsed in his temple to the same rhythm.

"Come see me when your shift's over," Archer said as she dealt a fresh hand for the only person at the table. "I've got a little extra gig for you tonight."

"Will do, Samuel," she said, the implications of those few simple words leaving her feeling sick.

"Hit me," the player said, tapping the edge of his cards on the green baize. Alice flipped a card towards him. The whip-crack sound of it leaving the deck was lost in another payout from the slots behind them. The card landed face up. A seven. "Stick."

"Dealer takes one," she said without missing a beat. She turned the card face up. A six. Eighteen total. "Dealer pays nineteen."

The player turned his remaining two cards over: Queen of Hearts and Three of Clubs.

"Player wins," Alice said, sweeping the cards off the table.

She turned over another forty-seven hands before her shift ended. The house won thirty-five of them, more than breaking even. The job had a ritualistic nature, the repetition of the same actions over and over, the exchange of tokens in offering and the fervent wishes of the players worshiping at her green baize altar. She wasn't sure if that made her a priestess or a sacrifice.

Her replacement brought her own decks and chips to the table. There were three players now, all men, all losers, both financially and in life. Alice left them with a smile and a "Bon courage," each one as fake as the other.

She went through to the staff quarters to change out of her uniform. She had a change of clothes in her locker—a sweatshirt, ripped jeans and a pair of white leather pumps. As she put her right leg into the empty leg of her jeans Archer appeared in the doorway with a little black dress slung over one arm. "Put this on," he said. No pleasantries.

She did as she was told. She wasn't stupid. If Samuel Archer told you to do something, you did it. That was just one of the irrefutable laws of her universe.

He watched her undress. There was nothing lascivious about his scrutiny. And yet it left her feeling like a piece of meat. He made her skin crawl.

"Nice dress, but I can hardly wear these with it." She held up her battered white pumps. Archer produced a box with a brand new pair of sling-backs in her size. He had all the answers. He always had all the answers.

She stepped into the sling-backs. They chaffed a little around the heel but she wasn't about to complain. She'd seen what Archer did to girls who complained.

"Ready?" he asked.

"Good to go," she replied.

Alice could still hear all of the noise and chatter from the gaming floor as he led her down the gangplank back onto dry land. A black Escalade with blacker windows waited for them on the shore.

"What's the job?" she asked as Archer opened the rear passenger side door.

"You'll find out when you get there," he said, which was enough to tell her that it was the kind of job she really didn't want on her résumé. He closed the door on her.

They didn't speak during the forty-mile journey back into the city. Archer wasn't a chitchat kind of guy. Alice watched the world go by outside her window.

The roads were deserted this early in the morning. The streetlights gave Chicago an otherworldly glow. It would be a few hours before the moon gave up the city to the light, so for now it was a warren of shadows and dark places that came together to offer a distinctly apocalyptic feel only broken by the sight of sanitation workers doing their best to make the place look respectable come morning. *The city is a different kind of monster at night*, she thought. That was when it showed its dark side both literally and metaphorically. In her experience the worst things always happened under the cover of darkness, as if the perpetrators couldn't bear to be seen when they released their inner monsters.

She hated the night.

They parked up outside a small boutique hotel in the South Loop. Once upon a time the stretch from Van Buren to 22nd had been so rotten and riddled with vice the locals had called it Satan's Mile, and it had deserved the name. Now it was all luxury high-rises and multi-million-dollar townhouses. The old slum had been well and truly gentrified. Ironically, the hotel with its huge plate-glass windows offered a glimpse of what looked like a tart's boudoir, as though the façade was a window into the past. The boudoir was actually an intimate little restaurant offering fine dining in seductive surroundings to the hotel's clientele.

Alice waited for Archer to come around the side of the car and open her door, and then slipped out gracefully into the bracing wind. He took her arm and steered her up the short flight of steps and through the glass doors—which a dour-faced doorman held open for them—into the hotel foyer.

They were expected, which, at 3 a.m., wasn't a comforting thought.

Inside everything was plush, red and gold, velvety and excessive as it tried desperately to capture the charm of a lost Art Nouveau world. To the left Alice saw two large Alphonse Mucha lithographs, and beneath them a Bechstein piano with wonderful detailing of a dancing sprite trapped in the lacquer, her dress flowing across the body and legs of the instrument. The low light from Tiffany lamps rendered everything beautiful in a soft formless sort of way. Archer shook hands with the night manager, who palmed the folded up notes the big man offered for his discretion.

They crossed to the single elevator and rode up to the seventh floor. As the doors parted, a sensual voice breathed a very disconcerting, "Seventh floor." It was obviously meant to enhance the boudoir feel of the place, but it just sounded creepy. Archer echoed the promise in the thirty seconds it took to reach the door to room 702. "There are five men in there, one a very lucky young gentleman who has just been called up to the Show. He's the golden boy right now. What he wants, he gets, you understand? You do everything he asks you to do. He's paying a lot of money for tonight. Make sure he isn't disappointed." She knew exactly what he meant. "I'll introduce you as Mystique, then I'll leave you to it. You know what to do. Don't let me down. If you need me I'll be waiting out here. All you have to do is scream and I'll come running," which wasn't reassuring.

Archer knocked once on the door and opened it to a wall of nineties electronica beats and a thick smoky haze. There were five men inside, four sprawled out languidly across the horseshoe of supple leather couches that enclosed the recessed floor. They were weighed down with the ostentatious gold chains and tattooed sleeves that young sportsmen had adopted as their uniform. Or maybe it was their armor?

The fifth man closed the door behind her.

"You took your time," the young ball player said. She didn't remember his name, but she'd seen his face plastered all over the town for the last week or so like he was the Second Coming. The kid was supposed to have a wicked-fast pitching arm complete with unnerving accuracy and a gift for making the ball move in the air—a genuine triple threat. She'd read somewhere that his throwing arm was insured for fifty million. Crazy money. Spread out on the couch, legs wide, he looked like a kid playing dress-up.

There were six nice neat lines of coke on the glass table in front of him, and beside them the platinum credit card he'd used to cut it and a pile of twenties still in cashier's blocks. There must have been twenty grand there. That was some serious bank. Considerably more than the two she cost. The baseball player was clearly grandstanding.

"Don't be a dick." Archer looked toward the bills. "I assume that is for me?"

"Not all of it," the player said, a gold-capped tooth monetizing his smile. He separated two thousand dollars from the stack and pushed it towards Archer. "But I've got to say, from here, I'm a little disappointed, man. She looks like a boy."

"If you looked that good in a dress I'd fuck you myself," Archer said without missing a beat. A couple of the other guys sniggered like they were back in high school, which was probably a couple of weeks' worth of time travel.

Alice resisted the temptation to bite. There was nothing to be gained by showing off the full range of her vocabulary. Alongside the coke were two nearly empty Absolut Vodka bottles and a cluster of smaller—empty—green bottles of imported beer. There was also a bottle of Cava that was open but still half full. Champagne money didn't extend to champagne tastes.

"What am I getting for my money?"

"What you see is what you get: a beautiful companion to help you boys party. Don't fuck me off, sunshine. I'll be right outside that door and if you get it into your heads to play Big Daddy Long Dick."

"Hear that, boys? The Chief's banging his chest like a fuckin' gorilla. Okay, old man, take your money and fuck off."

Archer leaned down to collect the smaller of the two stacks very slowly and deliberately. As he straightened up, one of the entourage spoke up. "How much would it cost to watch you fuck her, Chief?"

"I'm not your performing monkey."

"Another two grand? Think what you could do with that. A grand a minute for sticking the Little Chief in that boyish snatch? Got to be tempting, right?"

"No."

"You sure about that, Chief? I'm sure a big bastard like you would split her in two."

"I'd pay good money to see that," the player said, flashing his gold-toothed grin.

Archer ignored him. He turned to Alice. "I'll be right outside," he promised, and then left her alone with the wolves.

"I want you to dance for me," the player said as soon as the door closed.

The music changed around them, slower now, with a sensual undertone.

"Sure, honey," Alice said, starting to slowly sway in place. She contemplated her reflection in the glass as she moved. The combination of her pale skin and the little black dress made her look like a viper.

All eyes were on Alice, watching, hypnotized by the simplest of movements.

She stepped slowly towards the couch, straddling the player's thighs and reaching out for one of the gold chains around his neck to play with while she ground up against him, every movement in time with the music. He took hold of her hips, intent on transforming the provocative dance into something immediately more vulgar. She gave him what he wanted, because he was paying. All she wanted to do was go home.

He reached around her for the neck of one of the bottles on the table and raised it to his lips while she rode him. It would have been funny if it wasn't so uncomfortable. There was nothing remotely sexy about it. The dance was mechanical and dull, and it was painfully obvious he felt the same way. He pushed her away with a grunt, so she moved on to the next in line while the player hunched over the table to snort coke up his nose.

The second guy was all hands, taking advantage of the cover of her dress to reach up under the fabric and brush his fingers over her thigh and brush up against the lacy barrier of her panties. He pushed them aside, reveling in her gasp at his invasion. "Dance for me," he breathed like something out of a shit porno.

Alice moved away from him only to feel the player grab a tangle of her hair and yank her head back. "You heard my boy. Dance."

She almost called out to Archer, not liking the way things were going, but she knew the kind of beating she'd take if she did, so she kept her mouth shut.

The player kept her head back, forcing Alice to gaze up at him in mock adoration. This was his territory. His kingdom. Two grand in cold hard cash paid for that entitlement.

She opened her mouth to offer some semi-seductive dirty talk to try and make the whole charade feel more real, only for him to backhand her across the face before she could start with the come-ons.

The atmosphere in the room changed with that stinging blow. She could taste the danger in the air and knew she was out of her depth. This was more than just partying hard. Two of the player's friends crouched on their hands and knees, worshiping at the altar of coke. One after the other they snorted up their lines, shaking their heads and gasping at the sting. Only one of them, the youngest of the crew by the looks of his baby-faced complexion, wasn't playing. He looked decidedly uncomfortable and increasingly anxious.

"Take it off," the player said. "Let's see if you've got a cock hidden away down there before we get all excited."

Alice did as she was told. She turned her head, not meeting his contemptuous gaze, and slipped the little black dress up over her head. She tried to keep moving, the gentle sway now more of a pained lurch. He took the dress from her, stepping in close as if for a kiss, then reached down to cup her between the legs. "No cock," he said, almost sounding disappointed.

Alice pushed his hand away and backed off, looking for the source of the music. "Let's have something a little more sultry," she said. "I can't dance to this."

"Fuck that, that's just window dressing. I've not paid a small fucking fortune to watch you dance."

"Don't be a dick, Aitch," the guy by the door said. It was the first time any of the entourage had gone against the whims of the player. Aitch. Horace. That was it. Not exactly a hero's name. Alice offered him a slight smile in thanks, finding an ally in the room. There was always one in any group, one guy who was still at least mostly human and saw her as a woman not as a whore to be fucked and thrown away. A little kindness, like his smile, reaffirmed her humanity. It didn't take much. "What do you want to listen to?" he asked, holding up his cellphone.

"Surprise me," she said, and he did, selecting the Thievery Corporation's "Lebanese Blonde" with its shimmering tom toms and ethereal synth mimicking a snake charmer's flute. She found herself moving easily in time with it, her hands reaching up behind her back to unclasp her bra. She teased it out, taking her time to turn away from them, so that their first glance at her nakedness came through the reflection in the window.

The men watched her.

She couldn't describe their expressions—sometimes there were no words. Not hunger. Not lust. Those words were both far too basic. There was desire in there, of course, and ownership, but most of all she realized, loathing. The player—Horace—stopped watching her. He hunched forward over the table to snort the last line of coke. Shaking his head like a diver coming up for air, he straightened up, and wiped a finger under his nose. She didn't like the way he was smiling. That look was feral.

"Okay, enough of this shit, I want to watch what I paid for. Charlie," he said to her ally, "it's your lucky day."

7

ARCHER LEANED BACK AGAINST the door, listening to what was happening on the other side for much longer than necessary.

He could have intervened long before he did; it was obvious that things had turned nasty, but Horace Greene had paid his money and that, in the world of self-entitled pricks like Greene, gave him carte blanche to do whatever the fuck he wanted, immune to the consequences. So Archer let him have his fun, trying not to picture what was happening to Alice. But with each passing minute it became harder and harder to ignore her distress. It wasn't conscience that forced his hand though; it was possession. She was no good to him broken.

As her cries escalated, filling with genuine fear, Archer walked away.

He wasn't abandoning her. He was saving her.

He rode the elevator down to the lobby. His tame night

manager looked up from behind the reception desk. There was a moment of confusion as he realized Archer was alone, but that didn't last long. He was a smart guy. He needed to be to be good at his job, which was essentially being able to spot all the myriad varieties of trouble coming his way and head them off at the pass. Archer was trouble.

The big man crossed the lobby, and as he reached the desk, leaned in conspiratorially. "I need you to make me a keycard to Horace Greene's suite. Now."

"I can't do that. It's more than my job's worth. People expect a certain level of discretion. We can't have it getting out that they're not safe to play here. You understand?"

Archer repeated the request a little more forcefully this time, as though all it would take to remedy the night manager's lack of comprehension was an extra semitone.

"I can't," the man said again, genuinely distressed this time.

"Let me offer you a little incentive. Think of this as the carrot," Archer said, taking the bundle of notes out of his pocket and peeling away a hundred from the stack. He put it on the counter. "A couple of seconds to code a card, or we go to my other incentive, which is more of the stick variety. I don't think we want to go that way, do we, Stephen?"

The man didn't move to pocket the money.

"Take it. It's yours," Archer said. "You're giving me a keycard whether you pocket the bonus or not. Might as well profit from the transaction."

When the night manager still didn't move to take it, Archer

sighed and shook his head. "Don't say I didn't try to do this without blood." Archer reached out for the man's black tie, coiled it around his fist and yanked down hard, unbalancing him. As he tried to straighten up, Archer lashed out with his other hand and slammed the man's face into the glossy surface of the desk before he could pull away.

The impact was sickening.

Archer released his grip.

Stephen lifted his head up, bloody. Dazed, he reached for the reception desk to keep himself upright, only for Archer to snatch up a lamp and drive the base down across his fingers. "Don't make me hurt you anymore, Stephen. Give me what I want and I'll go away."

Mumbling, "Okay, okay," between bloody lips, the man did what he was told.

The entire encounter was over in less than a minute.

It took less than three between leaving Alice alone up there and opening the door to play savior.

Archer entered the room hot, not wasting precious seconds to gauge the level of shit he was wading into. It was all about shock and awe. There were five men in there. Whether they were high or not, those weren't great odds. He needed to minimize the risk he faced, making sure things didn't escalate beyond his ability to control, which meant evening up those odds pretty fucking quickly.

He hit the first guy like a linebacker sacking a quarterback with his pants down. It wasn't pretty, but it was effective. The guy went down badly, feet tangling in the puddle of baggy denim around his ankles as he tried to fight Archer off. It was the worst thing he could have done. He went down hard, cracking his skull on the corner of the glass table. There was blood and broken glass.

He didn't move.

Archer didn't waste time worrying about whether he was alive or not. He rose, roaring, and drove double-fists into the face of the second of the player's entourage. The man's head snapped back, and as he wobbled, Archer brought both clubbing fists together on the side of his head, stopping him cold. The man stood there stupidly, his erection pointing at Archer even as his knees buckled and he collapsed.

Three against one was much better, especially when the three in question were naked, coked up and bewildered by the ferocity of his attack. It's hard to fight naked, no matter how much of a tough guy you think you are. Naked and hard, apparently preparing for a gangbang, you're not expecting to have to fight for your life.

Alice lay curled up on the floor at Horace Greene's feet. Archer stepped over her, going for the player.

"I told you, no Big Daddy Long Dick, Horace."

The player looked at him. He looked ludicrous with his cock in his hand, staring slack-jawed at Archer. He looked about twelve sat there on the leather couch. As Horace reached out to block what he thought was a punch, he offered Archer exactly what he wanted: his fifty-million-dollar arm. There was a moment of horrific realization, followed by the sound of tearing muscle as Archer wrenched it so hard the ball joint of his shoulder tore out of its socket. Looking Horace Greene in the eye, Archer broke his pitching arm over his knee.

One arm wasn't enough.

He wanted both.

When he'd ended the golden boy's glittering career before it had even started, Archer took the rest of the cash from the table, gathered Alice up in his arms, and carried her out of there.

8

"THIS TWEAKER'S TRYING TO rob your fucking bank, Rickie," the black man said. "What you gonna do about it? You gonna let that happen?"

"Okay, okay," the manager said, holding his hands up. "Let's not do anything we're going to live to regret, eh? Nice and easy, just put the gun down and we can all walk out of here like nothing's happened. It doesn't have to end badly."

"You should listen to Rickie," the large man said. "He's a smart guy. Take the stack. I'm sure this lovely lady here—" he turned to the second teller "—will chip in with a nice stack of her own. That's a score. That's not to be sniffed at, man. Take it and fuck off out of here before you get yourself hurt."

"I can't do that," Adam repeated, shaking his head, willing them to understand and hating the desperation in his voice. It wasn't supposed to go down like this. It would have been so much easier if she could have just put the thumbdrive into the port.

Adam took a deep breath, concentrating on his treacherous right hand. "I don't think you are in any sort of position to start dictating terms here."

"You haven't got a clue who you're dealing with. Believe me, you really don't wanna fuck with me. But look, I'm prepared to give you a pass. What do you say? What's your name, man?"

"Adam." He shouldn't have said that. He really shouldn't. It just came out. He wasn't thinking like a bank robber. All he was doing was laying down a breadcrumb trail for the police to follow back to him.

"I'm Archer. Adam, you've got no idea what you are getting yourself in the middle of, but believe me, you couldn't have picked a worse place. We're talking one fucked-up confluence of events. Take the money and run. Fuck, if it'll get you out of here, I've got about twenty grand I'll put in your pocket right now. You'll clear thirty-six."

"I don't care," Adam said stubbornly. "All I want is for Sasha here to put the thumbdrive into a computer and run the program. It'll take a couple of minutes to do what it's got to do. We all go home happy. No one needs to get hurt."

"I told you," she said, "I can't."

Adam caught sight of the security guard's reflection in one of the glass partitions behind Archer. It was nothing more than a flicker of movement in his peripheral vision, a dark shape ghosting between the potted plants as the guard tried to work his way around the wall to get closer to Adam.

He swung around quickly, the barrel of his 9mm veering wildly as he tried to aim it at the guard.

"Don't come any closer," he warned, hearing his anxiety in his voice. It wasn't just the gun in his hand that had a hair trigger. "The last thing I want to do is shoot, but that's what I'll have to do if you try to be a hero." It all sounded so very reasonable to Adam's ears.

The guard, an old head, mercifully not some trigger happy rent-a-cop, held his hands up, palms out.

"Good, that's good. I want you to very slowly reach down and unfasten your belt, then put it on the floor and slide the gun over to me. Can you do that?"

The guard did as he was told.

9

THEO MONK WAS LIVING a stranger's life.

It wasn't meant to be like this. A decade ago he'd had it all. He'd been the golden boy, the department's shining light. Everyone knew it. He was the rising star. And then he wasn't.

One case ruined everything.

He'd found a thread, and that thread went from Chicago PD to the Organized Crime Bureau at Justice via City Hall and the mayor's office. He couldn't help himself. He had to pull it. That was who he was.

He had been investigating a construction outfit that was aggressively buying up the old projects, tearing them down and flipping the lots as multi-million-dollar residences, making a killing in the process. The whisper was they were paying the residents off with pennies on the dollar, and if they didn't want to trade their homes for the bright new future the city was promising someone else with the bank balance to grab it, then strong-arm tactics came into play. These people were being terrorized out of their own homes.

It had culminated in the deaths of forty-seven people; the tragedy was reported as the inevitable failing of a building that should have been condemned long ago, laying the blame at the door of non-code appliances and faulty wiring.

Theo Monk knew different.

The first time he heard the name "Saul Bonavechio" was six months before the fire. His partner, Charlie Coltrane, warned him off pretty hard. That should have been a clue that things weren't exactly on the level with the guy, but Theo was too trusting. They were partners. It was a character flaw that would eventually be his undoing, but in his world being partners meant something. It was hard being a righteous man in a world of corruption and lies.

Saul Bonavechio owned the loyalty of a lot of men in the high towers around the city. He made a lot of money for a lot of very important people. That meant they were inclined to turn a blind eye when his interests skirted right along the fringes of dubious legality. He was their bald-headed second-generation Italian goose laying shiny golden eggs. So what if a few people way down the social order got hurt? It wasn't as though their voices would be heard when they screamed blue murder. That was the reality of this particularly virulent strand of the American Dream. Those with money always found a way to position themselves on the side of the angels, even when they were making ordinary, decent people homeless.

The problem was he couldn't prove it.

Theo had been encouraged to stop pulling at that thread. No one went as far as to say he wouldn't like what he found at the other end, but the message was clear. Charlie set up the meet, though he hadn't realized what it was at the time. They were responding to a complaint from a dear old soul, half-blind, mostly deaf, infirm and incontinent, who barely knew her own mind most of the time. The old woman's nurse greeted them at the door. She warned the detectives that Esme wasn't having a good day, but they were welcome to come inside. The old woman sat in her wheelchair by the window, skirt hiked up to her knees, a tongue two sizes too big for her mouth protruding between her lips as she wrestled with a pudding cup. Esme wore a plastic bib. There was an empty jar of baby food on the tray in front of her. Most of the food was on the bib. It was already patently obvious that Esme hadn't made any call to the stationhouse.

Dust danced in the air. The net curtains had yellowed to the point of stiffness from tobacco smoke. He would never forget the pudding cup. The old woman couldn't peel the foil lid away. Eventually, frustrated with her own failings, she stabbed through the lid with her spoon.

She was still eating when the doorbell chimed again. The nurse hurried out to answer, and didn't return. A big black brute of a man introduced himself as Samuel Archer, and without any preamble laid his boss's cash out on the table. "Mister B is a very generous man. He's good to his friends, and he wants to be your friend, Theo. May I call you Theo? He wants to see that you have a good life. That you want for nothing. So this is what he's offering, it's a lot of money. Take it or leave it. I'd very strongly advise you to take it, Theo. Take it and enjoy it."

He left it.

There was no second offer. It wasn't a game of bluff and counter bluff. Bonavechio had offered him a golden hello as a welcome to the family and he'd refused it. But you didn't say no to a man like Saul Bonavechio. Six days later Internal Affairs had come knocking. They trawled through his life, through all of his old cases, finding evidence that shouldn't have been there. The money he'd left on Esme's table was in his gym bag at the back of his locker. Charlie Coltrane had stitched him up for Bonavechio.

Despite the fact that IA were never conclusively able to prove that he was on the take, Theo was let go. His reputation couldn't survive the job Charlie had done on him. As Theo had walked out of the stationhouse for the last time, he saw Samuel Archer in a car parked across the six lanes of blacktop.

He'd never forgotten the look on that bastard's face: the smug satisfaction of a job well done.

Archer tipped him a salute.

If they hadn't taken his gun from him Theo would have broken the Sixth Commandment then and there.

A lot of shit could happen in a decade.

A life—a good life—could unravel. Marriage vows broken,

leases terminated, prospects dried up, all of those dreams and hopes burned on the funeral pyre of his career. Theo was a different man now, living a stranger's life, doing a crappy job as a security guard in a small neighborhood bank. Somewhere, in some parallel universe, another Theo was living the life that was supposed to have been his.

But that Theo would have missed out on this glorious chance for retribution. Of all the gin joints in all the towns in all the world, Archer just had to walk into the one under his protection. It was fate. Kismet. Karma.

He had recognized Archer the moment he'd set foot inside the bank. How could he not? This was the man who had destroyed his life. That recognition didn't go both ways. He could tell that Archer didn't have a clue who he was or what he'd done to him ten years ago. Why should he? It wasn't like Theo's was the first life he'd ruined, or the last, he was just one in a long line of victims. He'd thought twice about intervening—about putting himself in the line of fire for that bastard—he could have just sat there in his comfortable chair by the door, listening to the piped music and watched it all play out like some sort of Greek tragedy, but that wasn't who he was. Even if he wasn't the man he had been a decade ago, he was better than that.

I deserve this, he thought, creeping around the credenza, eyes fixed firmly on the guy with the gun. Theo, once with a glittering career, didn't like the way his hand was trembling.

"Don't come any closer," the gunman said, looking straight

at him. “The last thing I want to do is shoot, but that’s what I’ll have to do if you try to be a hero.”

Theo wasn’t stupid. He wasn’t bulletproof either. The guy was on edge. If he pulled the trigger, Theo was going down. He held up his hands, palms out, showing he wasn’t a threat.

He tried desperately to remember his training, but it was such a long time ago, and there was so much adrenalin coursing through his system. It wasn’t like riding a bike. All he could do was go along with the gunman’s demands as he said, “Good. That’s good. I want you to very slowly reach down and unfasten your belt, then put it on the floor and slide the gun over to me. Can you do that?”

He unbuckled his belt and slowly lowered it to the floor, one hand still in the air.

He pushed it with his foot, looking beyond the gunman at Archer.

With the guy looking the wrong way, he saw Archer make his play.

It was a stupid move.

10

THERE'S A COMMON MISCONCEPTION that bullets are all about stopping power. Hollywood has perpetuated the myth with victims punched off their feet by the impact. The reality is governed by Newton's third law: if the recoil isn't hurling the shooter from their feet, the impact from the bullet isn't punching the victim from theirs. It's all about the mutual interaction of forces.

There are only three physical reasons why a person who has been shot becomes incapacitated: skeletal damage—a bullet shattering the spine, for instance; nervous system disruption; or blood loss. A lot of what happened to a gunshot victim after the bullet hits is psychological.

Adam Shaw knew all of this, but until that moment the knowledge had been purely theoretical. The reality of pulling the trigger was different. It had all escalated so quickly. The sheer amount of adrenalin pulsing through his system interfered with his Zanaflex, making it damned near impossible to control his traitorous hands. It had always been a risk, but he'd wanted to believe the plan would work. He'd been living in a fairy tale. A grim one with no happy ending.

He never meant to pull the trigger.

He wasn't thinking about stopping power or shot placement—at least, not consciously. He saw the big man take a couple of unsteady steps toward him, still raging even as confusion and the realization he'd been hit set in.

Adam looked down at the blood-red rose blossoming in the center of Archer's white shirt, variables and statistics flooding through his mind.

That was just the way his brain was wired.

Even without knowing all of the parameters in play inside these four walls, never mind the variables from outside, he knew enough to make assumptions about the situation and come out with the maximum-likelihood estimation for what would happen next.

Of course, the stresses involved were asymptomatic. There was no standard set of procedures to follow when you accidentally shot a guy in the middle of trying unsuccessfully to rob a bank, making it difficult to draw reliable conclusions based on past observations. There was always de Finetti's theorem of exchangeable variables, but right here, right now, all the statistics, probability levels and confidences didn't matter: he was fucked.

Adam stared at the blood.

Someone was screaming. A woman. Sasha. No. The other teller. The middle-aged woman with pale skin.

Archer reached up to press his left hand across the growing red stain as though trying to stem the relentless flow of blood pumping out of his chest.

"What the fuck have you done?" he said, staggering back a step, then another. He reached out, trying to grab hold of anything he could to keep himself on his feet. His hand hit the counter. Slapped on it and slipped off it. He took another backward step before his knees buckled. He went down hard, colliding with one of the floral room dividers balanced between two huge planters.

There was a lot more blood now, even just a few seconds after the shot had silenced the lobby. More than Adam would have expected from a single 9mm wound. The bullet had hit something vital.

Archer repeated his question. "What the fuck have you done?" Shock had replaced the anger in his voice.

Adam stared down at the gun in his hand.

There was no wisp of smoke from the muzzle, no gunslinger's curl to betray what had just happened. *Guns don't kill people*, he thought hysterically.

"I didn't mean to do it… oh God… I didn't mean to shoot."

The blood in the middle of Archer's chest was more like a handprint than a blossoming flower, and it was spreading down over his stomach. The man's skin had taken on an ashen texture. He kept reaching up to the wound, and for one sickening second Adam thought he was about to root around inside the bloody hole and pluck the bullet out of his chest.

"Jesus, Jesus, Jesus," someone invoked, as if by saying his name three times their savior might intervene. It was a man's voice. The bank manager. Adam looked at the man's nametag. Richard Rhodes. The name suited him.

"We've got to call 911," someone else said. This time it was Sasha, the teller. "He needs medical attention. Look at him. He's bleeding badly. You've got to do something or he's going to die." Though whether she was demanding action from her boss or Adam, he couldn't tell.

"No," Adam said, not exactly sure who he was talking to. "No one touches a phone. You." He turned toward the security guard. "Lock the front doors. No one gets in or out." That was a start. "You," he said to the manager, "get everyone together, sit them down in the middle of the room, here, on the floor where I can see them. Cellphones off, all of them." He pointed at a spot on the carpet with the gun. *Control the scene.* "Don't try to do anything stupid like hit the alarm or call for help. I just need her—" this time he pointed the gun at Sasha "—to run the program on the thumbdrive, that's all, then we can all go home. Please. Just do what I'm asking you to do. It's really the easiest way out of here. I don't want to hurt anyone."

"Else," Sasha said. "You've already hurt someone." Her eyes flickered toward Archer slumped on the floor a few feet away.

"It was an accident. You saw that. I know you did."

"I saw you pull the trigger."

"That's not what happened." But it was, of course it was. Just because he hadn't been in control of his hands when it happened didn't change what these people had seen or what the CCTV had recorded. These were the witnesses who would put him away for life. He was done. It didn't matter how things played out now. "Please, just stop arguing with me and do what I've asked you to do." He sounded hysterical to his own ears. Christ alone knew what he sounded like to the rest of them. His hand was shaking badly. It was still a couple of hours before he was due another dose of Zanaflex. He had one extra dose in his wallet; he thought about taking it to try to stave off the worst of the shakes, but in the circumstances, over-medicating was every bit as bad as under-medicating.

"I'm not lying to you," Sasha said. "I can't help you from here. It won't work."

He was in trouble.

He looked around.

There were no friendly faces.

11

MARGOT MOORE HAD A secret. She was in love with a man she had never met, and almost certainly never would. The fact that she was in love was only the half of it. Who the object of her affections was and how he'd come into her life, that was the really interesting part. That was the part that made it a secret worth keeping.

He was her guardian angel.

He was her reason for getting up in the morning.

For a while it had been dark, really dark; then he had come into her life like some kind of caped superhero. He called himself Nero, but that wasn't his real name. She didn't know what his real name was.

Margot would be sixty-three on her next birthday, making her the oldest of the bank's staff by almost a decade, and old enough to know better when it came to matters of the heart. But sometimes it was just a case of the heart wanting what the heart wanted however ridiculous that desire was.

They all thought she was so together, so ordinary. They had no idea what was going on inside her, or how it felt to have lost everything that mattered during six hellish months that had started out with confidence that together they'd beat it, that had become niggling arguments where she kept saying to Johnny she wished he'd put up more of a fight, that he'd just act like he wanted to live even though they both knew the non-Hodgkin lymphoma was eating him alive. It was already too late at that point. It had started out as an aching shoulder months before, then a raspy cough that he just couldn't shift, and even the week before they got the news that his liver and spleen were riddled with aggressive tumors, Johnny Joe Moore had been given the all clear from the oncologist as they searched for the root cause of his symptoms. The CT scan only covered the area around his throat down to his armpits and thyroid, ruling out lymphoma. She'd tortured herself for months wondering if those lost days might have been the death of her husband, cursing a health-care system that valued saving a few dollars on a scan over saving a man's life. Thinking like that was a killer. It led down very dark paths in the lonely hours of the night. For a month she hadn't washed the sheets because they smelled of him. For two more months she hadn't moved his sweater off the balustrade at the top of the staircase because that was where he always kept his sweaters and every time she walked past it she ran her fingers over the wool. It was the closest she came to prayer.

Everyone around her said the right things, asked the right questions and worried about her, but that didn't help because they weren't her; they weren't inside her head living with that new-found emptiness. And instead of getting easier with time it just got harder. That was a truth no one ever talked about. At the start she'd just been numb trying to deal with all of the paperwork and red tape involved in closing out a man's life; then there had been those long days of firsts: the first time she'd been to the farmer's market without him, the first time she'd watched his favorite show without him, the first day she'd not gone to the mailbox to collect his newspaper, the first time she'd gone to bed alone, all of those little things that had been so much a part of their life together that had suddenly become little landmarks to the man she'd lost. That was so much worse than the finality of the registrar and the death certificate with the word "pneumonia" going down as the official cause of death.

Coming out on the other side of the firsts didn't make living any easier. She'd been clinging to the notion that it would. All she could do was put on her bravest face and there was a limit to how long that particular trick would last—which was how she'd wound up taking the call from Nero that saved her life.

It was a culmination of so many small and seemingly unimportant events that led her up to the roof that night, the cold winds that earned the city its name blowing hard. She wasn't dressed for killing herself. It was a crazy thing to think, but she remembered that moment vividly, even now. The flat roof of the apartment building was six stories from the ground. Standing on the edge, looking down, the drop was dizzying. There wasn't a star in the sky. They didn't get many stars, even on clear nights, because of the constant glow of the city. She missed the stars. She'd grown up with them there every night, and just like with her Johnny, taken for granted that they'd always be there. She wrapped her arms around herself, not looking down. She could hear the low engine rumble of a plane coming in to land at O'Hare. She didn't want that to be the last thing she heard in this life, so she waited. It wouldn't be long before the dawn chorus broke out. Dying to a soundtrack of birdsong wasn't such a bad thing, was it? She could wait for that.

The buildings on either side of her rooftop were considerably higher, one fourteen more floors, the other even taller. In the movies whenever they showed someone standing alone on a rooftop they were invariably the heroes, guardians of a vulnerable city watching over its streets. Margot wasn't even the hero of her own life, never mind Chicago's. See, it wasn't all perfect with Johnny. It hadn't been for a long time before he'd died. He'd screwed some desperate housewife, for one thing, back when they were younger and dumber, before HRT had cut her giant-sized temper down to something approaching normal. She'd hated him for that, but then she'd forgiven him and they'd moved on. It had been twenty two years between his infidelity and his death and during those wonderful years they'd fallen in love all over again, getting to know each other properly and realizing that they genuinely liked each other and wanted to grow old together. Margot had always thought that was the most romantic thing Johnny had ever said to her, that day a few months after it had all gone to hell, when he held her hand and asked for the chance to earn her trust back, and maybe one day her forgiveness, because he wanted to watch life write itself slowly across her face.

She had forgiven him—or thought that she had—but after he died it all came flooding back and she hated him all over again for betraying her like that, the pain of it so fresh. She didn't know where the anger came from, but maybe it was easier to hate him for that than it was to accept that he was gone. She'd tried to forgive him again but it had been so much more difficult second time around.

She felt her cellphone vibrate in her pocket. Let it ring through to voicemail. They rang again. She didn't answer. The caller was persistent. They rang a third time and when she didn't pick up, a fourth and a fifth. Whoever it was, they really wanted to talk to her. The caller ID was blocked. Sixth time was the charm.

"This isn't a good time," she said.

"On the contrary, I'd say it was the perfect time," the voice on the other end of the line said.

"Whatever it is you're selling, I'm not buying."

"I'm not selling anything."

"Why don't I believe you?"

"Because you've been conditioned to think the worst of the world," he said.

"So you're selling God? Is that it? Want to save my soul? It's a bit late for that."

"No," he said again. "I promise you, no religion. No micro loans. No insurance. I'm not from a collection agency, either."

"Then what are you?"

"You wouldn't believe me if I told you."

"Try me."

"What if I told you I knew where you were and what you were about to do?"

"I'd say you're full of bull crap, mister."

"There are over ten thousand surveillance cameras in the city, did you know that? Right now you're in full sight of three of them. I saw you. Honestly, I thought I was going to be too late. I needed to reverse trace the signal from your phone off the nearest cell towers to get your number before you took that one step off the top of the building into nothing. I've never been so glad someone has answered the phone when I've called them, believe me. My name is Nero, and I guess you could say I'm your guardian angel."

She turned around slowly in a full circle, looking for the cameras. She couldn't see them. "Tell me what I'm wearing," she said.

"A floral print dress. It looks thin. Too thin for the cold winds up there. You've been wrapping your arms around you to keep yourself warm, which, considering what you are about to do, is rather endearing, don't you think? You're about to end it all, but you're worried about being cold? You've got short gray hair, cropped in what we used to call a pixie cut when I was younger. I don't know if you've been crying, the image isn't that good, but I think you have. I think you've been thinking about whatever it is that has walked you up to this place, up to the edge, and you've been crying about it all over again."

That spooked her. "You're watching me? Right now?"

"Yes," he said. "Please, just step back from the edge. However bad it is right now, what you're doing, that's not the answer. I'm not going to come out with some trite platitudes about how things can always get better; they're just words and there's nothing to say they're true. I don't know what's going on in your life, it's none of my business—you could have a brain tumor and days to live, for all I know—but I wanted you to know you're not alone. I can see you."

She kept turning slowly in that circle. "Tell me when you can see my face. I want to look at you."

"Now," he said a moment later.

"You can see me? My face?"

"Yes."

"Good. Now, look at me and listen to what I am about to tell you. I want to die," she said. "It's as simple as that. I want it over. It's my choice. Not yours. You don't get to call me on the phone and rob me of that choice. Do you understand me?"

"I do," he said.

"Have you heard the saying that if you save a life, you are responsible for every act that person commits from the time you saved it?"

"Yes."

"You don't want to become responsible for my life."

He laughed at that. That was the last thing she'd expected, genuine laughter. "Maybe I do. Maybe that's exactly what I want. Maybe it's what I *need*."

"What's your real name?" Margot asked, staring out over the rooftops. "Because it's not Nero. No mother would be that cruel."

He laughed again. She liked the way he really gave in to the sound, laughing all the way down to his belly. "Maybe I'll tell you when we know each other better. How's that sound?"

"Like you're trying to get me to make promises I can't keep."

"I think I like you."

"You don't even know me."

"True. How about we fix that?"

"Again with the promises? What's the next line, 'just step away from the edge, everything will be all right'?"

"Nah, I'm not that transparent. How about we play a game?"

That threw her. She scanned the reflected city in the windows beside her, looking for some hint of him. All she saw were the endless empty streets. There was probably some sort of symbolism in that. "What sort of game?" Margot asked, surprising herself.

"I'll tell you something no one else knows about me, then it's your turn. We'll start nice and easy. I haven't felt the rain on my skin in five years. Your turn."

"Can we ask questions?"

"Not yet. Later. Got to have something to look forward to."

"I used to have a crush on the manager at the bank where I work."

"Used to?"

"No questions. Your rule," she said, smiling to herself.

"You got me. My turn. I have this recurring dream where I'm naked flying like Superman across the rooftops of Chicago. I always shout 'Geronimo' when I take off."

"That probably means something," she said.

"Undoubtedly," Nero agreed. "But I'm not sure I want to know what."

"I fell in love with my husband because of his ass."

"I broke up with the woman of my dreams because I didn't think she was pretty enough for me. I actually gave the 'it's not you, it's me' excuse."

"Oh God. Seriously?"

"We're still not at the question part of our show," Nero chided.

"Fine." Margot smiled despite herself, forgetting just for a moment where she was and what she'd been planning to do. "Beat this: when I was seventeen I gave my daughter away." She couldn't believe she'd told a complete stranger her deepest, darkest secret, nor that it had come so readily to her lips in this game of truth with no consequences.

"I think I can do that," Nero said with absolute confidence. "I lost my legs five years ago. It was a car bomb. I'm lucky to be alive. Or unlucky, depending how you want to look at it. Half of my body is covered in a mesh of scar tissue from the burns. The right side of my face is ruined. It's like there's a sheet of melted plastic stuck to it."

He was right.

He won.

She didn't feel like playing anymore. But she had one last confession to make to the caller. She couldn't go through with killing herself, she realized, not in the face of Nero's pain. There was always someone worse off, wasn't that what they said? He'd lost his legs and his looks and still he was trying to save her life; that made him pretty special in her eyes. How could she admit that loneliness—nothing more than that, though surely that was enough, wasn't it?—had driven her to this edge? She felt stupid when she admitted, "I feel so alone," but that was actually her great secret, not the fact she used to have a crush on Richard Rhodes or that she had an affair of her own as revenge for Johnny's infidelity, or that she'd loved his ass before she loved him. No, the fact that she was so desperately lonely was the one thing no one knew about Margot Moore, because she hid it well.

"I can see you," Nero told her. "I might not be there with you, but you're not alone. Or you don't have to be."

And that was the beginning of their love story, the disabled shut-in and the suicidal grandmother. They talked every day, playing the same game of confession on the phone and over email, learning more and more about each other without ever once suggesting that they change the dynamic of their relationship and meet up. Each of them was happy to have the other in their life; why risk ruining what was working so well by changing things?

Nero had offered to help her find her daughter. That was the conversation where she knew the dynamic of their unlikely friendship had changed. He promised he could do it from the comfort of his apartment—he still hadn't said where he lived, but that would have been easy enough to work out if she'd really wanted to. She had his cellphone number and his email address. Everything was out there on the Internet if you knew where to look, that was what he'd said. But she didn't want that. Some things were better left in the past. She wasn't sure he understood. She wasn't even sure she understood herself, to be honest.

She'd talked to him that morning, telling him about the dreadful chat-up line she'd heard on the way in to work. That was the kind of thing they talked about now. They covered everything in pages-long emails and hours-long late-night chats, both finding comfort in the bond that was forming between them.

Last night he'd shocked her, confessing that the last time he'd tried to have sex he had used an escort service, but even though the woman was a professional and had been warned about his injuries, he couldn't go through with it. Instead the woman had talked to him all night, just lying beside him until sunrise. It was a different kind of intimacy, but even at a couple of hundred bucks an hour it had felt genuine. He needed to believe that it was. He might as well have been talking about her life, Margot had realized as she hung up.

Suddenly she was ready to fall in love again, even if it was with someone she'd never met and almost certainly never would. What no one would have been able to understand, without having gone through it themselves, was that this was every bit as powerful a connection as the first time she'd fallen head over heels all the way back when she was sixteen.

When the gun went off, Margot's first thought was that she didn't want to die before she knew Nero's real name. When the shooter turned his attention on her, she was resigned to the fact that she would.

12

"You." Adam turned towards the ghost-pale woman in the starched white blouse. "What's your name?"

"Margot," the woman said, though it was little more than a stammer.

"I want you to do something, Margot. I want you to help him."

She shook her head, and for a moment he thought she was refusing, but looking into her eyes he saw the panic. He needed to put her at ease. Everything was escalating. He hated not being in control. He breathed deeply, trying to center himself. "Don't think about the reality of what you're doing. This isn't about saving his life. Keep it simple. Get something to staunch the blood. You can do that, can't you?" She nodded. "Good. That's good." Adam nodded towards the manager, who stood there like a lemon—that was the phrase his mother had always used: *Don't just stand there like a lemon, make yourself useful.* That put a smile on his face, which he realized must have made it look like he was enjoying himself. "Press down on the wound and keep pressing as hard as you can." She nodded again. "Good. See, that's not too difficult, now, is it? Don't think about trying to use the landline, you pick up the receiver I'll see the line light up. That happens, someone will get hurt."

Margot nodded again and went in search of something to staunch the blood.

He looked over at the female customer with the bruised face—she, at least, wasn't causing any trouble, was keeping her head down. It was easy to forget she was there. He turned to the bank manager, Richard Rhodes. "I told you to get everyone together." Rhodes stared at the gun in his hand. It might as well have been the head of Medusa. "How many people work in the branch, Rickie?" That was what Archer had called him, not Richard. Rickie. If it was good enough for him it was good enough for Adam. He was thinking about all of the movies he'd seen from the cops' perspective. They all said the same thing: establish a rapport. So Rickie it was. "Don't lie. I'll know if you're lying. How many?"

The man blinked hard. "Today? Four tellers, plus me and Theo." He indicated the guard.

"So six people." Rhodes nodded, but Adam wasn't asking him, he was asking Sasha. She inclined her head slightly, which he took as confirmation. "Okay, you've got two minutes, get them all together. Same goes for you, resist temptation. I see the light on the phone right there, I'll shoot her, and if you're not back in two minutes I'll shoot her anyway." He nodded towards Sasha. He was trying to stay cool, but lines from old bank robbery movies kept ringing in his ears, the voices of all of those actors sounding utterly hollow against the reality of holding someone at gunpoint. It was easy to say something cool, delivering a line of Tarantino's dialogue in a dispassionate deadpan. Those lines were meant to be cool. It was much more difficult to just talk to people like a human being and get them to understand without them thinking that you were weak and they could walk all over you, gun or not. Adam had no intention of shooting anyone, but these people didn't know that.

As soon as the bank manager was gone, Adam leaned in towards Sasha and said, "I know you've got no reason to believe me, but I promise you, I'm not going to shoot you. I just said it to get him moving."

"Because you need me."

"Yes. I do. But really all I need you to do is believe me."

"Why should I believe you? You're holding a gun. That's not exactly a great way to inspire confidence." She smiled, just a slight twitch of the lips. "This is the part where you tell me you're one of the good guys."

"I know you don't believe that."

"But *you* do, don't you?"

"Everyone thinks they're the hero of their own life," Adam said.

"See, I don't think a bad guy would say something like that. That," she said, "and the fact that you're shaking. At first I thought you were just cranked up, but that's not it, is it?"

He nodded.

"So what is it? Parkinson's?"

"ALS." Most of his fellow Americans had at least heard the name thanks to the Ice Bucket Challenge. He saw the pity in her eyes. She obviously knew just how big a disease that little acronym represented. "I never meant to shoot. I shouldn't have put bullets in the gun." He didn't look Archer's way. He couldn't. He needed to build rapport with Sasha. She was his only hope. That flicker of sympathy could build to understanding.

"Then why did you?"

"Because I didn't think I'd ever need to take it out of the bag," he admitted, laughing bitterly at his own naïveté. It wasn't really an answer to her question. "But the way he came at me, the stress, even with the meds I'm symptomatic." He held out a hand, letting her see the extent of the shakes. "If you'd just put that thumbdrive into your terminal, I'd have been walking out of your life in a few minutes and he wouldn't be dying."

"It doesn't matter what the question is, this, robbing a bank like this, can never be the answer."

"It's for my son—" he began, but then Margot returned.

"I found this." She held up a towel and a first-aid kit. She crouched down in front of Archer, who winced as she pressed the towel against the wound. “I know it hurts,” she said, “but it’s that or—”

“Or I die,” the big man grunted.

“Tell me about your son,” Sasha said, so quietly Adam wasn’t sure if he’d imagined it. For the fraction of time between one heartbeat and the next, Adam convinced himself that he had an ally.

13

RICHARD RHODES WAS TAKING his life in his hands.

Seeing the croupier—Alice—in the bank had stopped him dead in his tracks. Her face was even more bruised than his own. Payback for his stupid stunt at the casino? At least now he had a chance to be a hero, as unlikely as that was. It was also his chance to stop his entire world going to shit.

One shot. That was all he had. And he wasn't a good bet. He moved quickly through the back rooms to the loan department.

He was gambling that the robber wouldn't miss him for a couple of extra minutes. His first thought was to run—out the back and away, look after number one. He wasn't proud of it, but that was the direction his panic raced, all the same. But if he started running, he couldn't stop. Ever. Everything would be out of his control.

Richard was shaking, and not because a man had just waved a gun in his face. He was staring down the links of a chain reaction that ended in questions from head office and answers from an inevitable audit that would expose his own Robin Hood crimes.

He almost wished the robber—Adam, he'd said his name was Adam—had shot him instead of that bastard Archer.

He leaned against the wall and closed his eyes. His world narrowed focus until all that existed was the silence between ragged breaths. Inhale. Exhale. Repeat.

He was screwed.

It was bad enough the way Sasha Sumner had looked at him. She knew something was wrong, the way she'd goaded him about his story, poking holes in it. He'd been an idiot to pretend the bruises were from a mugging. He couldn't even begin to understand what he'd been thinking—he obviously hadn't been. Any kind of violence against a member of the bank's staff had to be reported to the police. Stupid. Stupid. But at least she hadn't sold him out to the robber when he'd lied about how many people worked in the bank. The magic number was seven, not six like he'd said. That meant he had one person who could play Bruce Willis and sneak around inside the bank without Adam suspecting anything. His ace in the hole.

The truth was like the jaws of a vise slowly tightening around him.

Running might be stupid, but no more stupid than sticking around to be caught robbing his own bank. Even if he got away with it today, how long would it be before his own transactions came to light? A day, a week, a month? It didn't feel like a matter of *if* anymore, just *when*.

Secrets didn't want to stay secret, it was against their nature. His helplessness left him feeling bitter. Was what he'd done so wrong? Helping people who couldn't help themselves? Surely that made him the good guy, didn't it?

He'd been gone for a full minute.

He thought about trying to get a metaphorical message in a bottle into the hands of the right someone, but every time he pictured a stranger reading the message: WE ARE BEING HELD HOSTAGE. Unless Steven Seagal happened to be walking by, there was only one possible response and that was to dial 911, assuming that Victoria, Beth or Ellie hadn't done that already. For Rhodes that phone call meant *go to jail, do not pass go, do not collect two hundred dollars.*

Adam had only given him a couple of minutes to wrangle the bank staff and get them out into the lobby where he could see them and he'd already wasted one of them leaning against the wall feeling sorry for himself.

It crossed his mind that he could double back around the lobby, come in from the other side and take Adam by surprise, but that itchy trigger finger of his was frankly fucking terrifying. He didn't look like he had any sort of control over it. The fact the guy had turned down two blocks of cash, about sixteen thousand dollars, meant he wasn't some strung out tweaker looking to support his habit. It wasn't enough; that's what Adam had said. He wasn't leaving without making a big score.

"Fuck," Richard muttered.

There wasn't going to be a happy ending to this. It'd be just his luck to get his brains blown out trying to do the right thing. He really didn't want to die heroically. There was a certain inescapable irony to the whole fucking mess.

Of course the other option was to double down on the insanity and help the guy rob his bank and get him out of there before the cops showed up, then worry about covering his tracks after the event.

He was already covering up one theft, why not two?

For a moment he actually considered it, but it was absolutely fucking insane to go there. He pictured himself walking back out into the lobby with his best customer service smile plastered in place, arms spread wide, asking the guy to trust him. Then reality came crashing back with a bullet and a body. He couldn't nice guy his way out of this mess.

He needed a good old-fashioned miracle, and right now this Adam was fucking with any chance of divine intervention.

He looked across at Ellie Mason, sitting behind the small plaque that promised she was a LOAN EXPERT. A touch under six feet, long black hair—obviously dyed to make her more interesting, like the addition of the "ie" to her name instead of the "en" she'd been born with—and a twist of purple which he liked to think meant she had a bit of the rebel about her. She'd been in the job all of six months and out of college the same time. She was hardly old enough to be considered an expert in anything but right now she was his lifeline, because she was young, athletic and she liked him, he was sure of it. Even so, he wasn't sure he could ask her to do what he needed. It was a lot. More than a lot. It was insane.

It didn't help that she looked badly frightened. The gunshot might not have been heard around the world, but it had certainly made it back here. And that meant she must have tripped the silent alarm. It was drilled in to everyone until it became second nature, muscle memory, even if you assumed it would never happen to you.

Richard Rhodes had never prayed so hard for just a little bit of incompetence from his staff. Just this once.

She reached for the phone, but he stopped her.

"Ellie." If she picked up that handset the line would light up red on every other phone in the bank, including the one on Sasha's desk. "Don't."

She froze, her hand resting on the phone. "What's happening out there? That was a gunshot, wasn't it?"

If he was too blunt with his answer it'd spook the woman and he needed her calm, or as calm as she could be under the circumstances.

"We've got a situation," he said, like it was the most natural thing in the world. What he wanted to say was give me your cellphone, call 911, get us out of this mess. But if they called in a robbery there would be a full forensic accounting, his own creative book keeping would come out and his life would be over. So what he actually said was, "No one's been hurt." It surprised him how easily the lie came to his lips. "And if

I have my way, no one will be. Do you trust me, Ellie?" She nodded. He offered her a tired smile. "Good. That's good. I need you to listen to me, Ellie, because I'm putting my trust in you."

"Okay."

"He's on his own out there. Just one man and a gun. He sent me back here to round up everyone and bring them through to the lobby. He asked me how many people work here and I lied, I told him there were six of us, not seven. He doesn't know about you, Ellie. You're my John McClane." She looked at him like he'd lost his mind. "*Die Hard.* Nakatomi Plaza? East German terrorists take over the building, but they've got no idea Bruce Willis is hiding out inside. He picks them off one by one."

He might as well have been speaking a foreign language.

Then she mouthed, "Yippee-ki-yay, motherfucker," and he loved her just a little bit more as she reached into her pocket for an elasticated hairband and put her hair up in a ponytail, like she was making herself combat ready.

"I'm going to find Vicky. You stay hidden, okay? Don't make a sound. As long as he doesn't know you're in here we've got a chance of getting out of this in one piece."

"I tripped the silent alarm as soon as I heard the gunshot," she said. "The police are coming."

"Good," he said, hating the sound of the word. "We've just got to wait it out, but even if they get here in the next couple of minutes, they're not going to come storming in. They're on the outside. They've got their own way of doing things. They'll look to establish contact, find out what the guy wants and try to negotiate our release. You're the backup in case things go sideways. Better safe than sorry." He was speaking in platitudes and clichés ripped straight from prime time.

She nodded. She'd likely seen it enough times on TV. That was the joy of the modern world. Everyone had seen pretty much everything at least once. That meant they could buy into anything, even if they weren't in Kansas anymore. "What about the back doors? He doesn't know I'm in here, I could make a run for it."

Richard shook his head, looking for another lie as to why it wasn't the sensible option. "The windows can't be opened. The doors are alarmed, you know that. As soon as you push down on the bar and break the circuit that siren's going off. He's still got bullets in his gun. It puts everyone at risk."

She nodded again.

"Just be patient," he said. "Wait for the right opportunity. It'll come. As long as he doesn't know about you he'll be relaxed. He'll think he's in control. He won't have a clue."

"One question," Ellie Mason said.

"Shoot."

"Why me? Why not Vicky?"

14

Ellie Mason was twenty-three and as far as the rest of the world was concerned had her shit together. It was all an illusion. Put the right face on it and the world will believe up is down and black is white, or in this case that she wasn't a walking disaster.

She'd graduated college six months ago and walked straight into a job at Chicago Liberty thanks to family connections. Her father's old golfing buddy to be precise. He just happened to be on the board of directors and put a word in, fast-tracking her application. The appropriate wheels greased, she'd sailed through the interview process and joined the management program. Three years learning the different aspects of the job with her own branch waiting for her at the end of it. She was three months into her loan officer rotation. If only the rest of life were this easy.

Days before she'd started at Liberty, her world had

shattered as a driver plowed into the side of her father's Prius, ending his life instantly. Ryan Mason's passengers took longer to die. Her mother died at the roadside, thrown from the vehicle because she hadn't been wearing her seatbelt. Ellie's sister, Megan, made it twenty-two hours. The other driver hadn't been drunk, he'd been texting. *Happy just came on. I fucking love this song.* Four people died because Bryan Dikes had to tell his girlfriend he loved the song playing on the radio.

She'd gone through the next week in a daze. There was so much paperwork involved in death. People never talked about that. It was the dirty little bureaucratic secret of life. It wasn't just inheritances and estates, it was the practicalities of removing someone from existence, all of the phone calls and the polite sympathy on the other end of the line as she explained that Ryan, Katerina and Megan Mason were no longer with us, and yes, yes it was a tragedy and thank you so much for your kind words. The second week hadn't been much better, because that had been about her parents' secrets and no one deserves to know those. She'd found an old shoebox at the back of her mother's walk-in closet, and inside it a stack of old letters tied lovingly in ribbons. They were addressed to her mother, but they weren't from her father. Or, more accurately, they *were* from her father, but they weren't from Ryan Mason. They were signed by someone called Johnny. Not John. Johnny. No surname. No sender's address. They were incredibly intimate, snapshots of an illicit affair frozen in time. Not once in all of her life had she heard her parents mention anyone called Johnny.

The box contained both sides of the correspondence. Johnny had returned her letters along with his last one, saying goodbye.

That was the first thread that, when she pulled it, unraveled everything she'd thought she could take for granted about her life. There were thirty-seven letters dated between 1989 and 1994; the last one dated just a few weeks after her first birthday was heartbreaking. It was in answer to her mother's begging that Johnny walk away, and not try to see his baby girl again. She couldn't jeopardize her family or risk hurting the man she loved. But she promised him she had no regrets—how could she have with her gorgeous Ellen to show for their five years of secrecy? If she had her time over she'd do it all again.

He was obviously considerably older; it was in the way he expressed himself. He talked about regret and responsibility and wanting to do right by his daughter even as her mother begged him to just walk away.

In the end he had done just that, giving her what she wanted because he loved her.

There was an entire second life in those letters. She sat up all night reading them, then reading them again, then imagining. They were a glimpse of a life she'd never had, but one that by rights should have been hers.

All she had was a first name, Johnny, and occasional references to places they'd gone, places they'd stayed while her father was away for work. They even joked about checking in under movie stars' names to hide their infidelity, enjoying the knowing looks from the clerks behind the reception desk. They'd been everyone from Mel Gibson and Richard Gere to Julia Roberts and Helen Hunt. The one thing they'd never been was themselves.

The day after she'd discovered the box, Ellie had made her first trip to the gym. She'd done a free one-hour session with a personal trainer that had left her feeling so sick she'd lain on her back on the benches in the changing room while the room spun around like something out of a Looney Tunes cartoon. An hour later she'd gone to Dwane Reed and bought a bottle of hair dye, determined to go from blonde to black. She didn't. She went purple.

Ellen Mason had been strawberry blonde all of her life. After the initial shock at seeing a different person looking back at her from the mirror she realized she quite liked the idea of not being herself for a while. She made a second trip to the pharmacy and doubled down, buying another bottle of dye to turn the purple black. With a head full of chemical wash she decided to keep a single lock of the purple as a reminder, like those semi-colon tattoos some people who'd tried to kill themselves had. Life goes on. That was how Ellen became Ellie.

Over the next month, while she was facing down the reality of being alone, Ellie lost herself in the gym, punishing her body with grueling routines to build physical strength, agility, dexterity, and endurance. After six weeks she barely recognized herself. After seven she realized it wasn't enough. She signed up for a martial arts course, but didn't enjoy it. It was too disciplined. She wanted something explosive. She wanted to blow off steam. She tried CrossFit, and found she could lose herself in the grueling routines. Her world narrowed down to the panting of her breath and the burn of her muscles and for a while she could forget about her mother's secrets.

She started running, too. It was only when she was out on the open road, with the wind in her dyed hair, that she realized the real reason why she was putting herself through this punishment. It was a very real transformation. A metamorphosis. She'd walked into that gym all those weeks ago as Daddy's little girl, soft and trusting. She'd emerge from this cocoon of workouts and training eventually as something else entirely. She'd be a different woman. Her own woman. Whoever that was.

Bryan Dikes was lucky that he was dead, but that didn't stop her imagining what she'd like to do to him—and always to a soundtrack of that damned "Happy" song.

Last month she'd hired a private detective, Elias Barker, showing him the letters and asking him to find Johnny. Money wasn't an issue anymore, not thanks to the insurance policies for Ryan, Katerina and Megan Mason. She was a rich woman. She had absolutely no need to work, but had turned up that first day at the bank because the job felt like a last gift from her father. That was the real irony of what was happening. The death of the man she'd thought was her father was paying for her hunt to find the real one.

That morning, she'd had a message on her voicemail from Elias asking her to call him, saying it was important. That was why she was reaching for the phone as she looked up to see Richard Rhodes looming over her desk.

The conversation that followed was nothing short of surreal.

"One question."

"Shoot," Rhodes said.

"Why me? Why not Vicky?"

"Honestly? Look at yourself. I've got to get back out there. I'm trusting you, Ellie. We all are."

"No pressure, then," she said, but she was already pushing her chair back and thinking about the layout of the bank. She felt trapped; the walls seemed closer than usual. There were places she could hide, of course, and not just the janitor's closet or under desks. The old building was a labyrinth fit for the Minotaur. The basic layout was a horseshoe with banks of offices down each wing—one for corporate, the other for personal banking, their windows looking onto each other across a neatly manicured lawn—and the main lobby area occupying the middle span. If you didn't know the building you'd think it was impossible to move from one wing to the other without going outside, and going outside, from what Richard had just told her, meant triggering alarms.

But appearances could be deceptive. As much of the bank was underground as it was above. The vault itself occupied the area under the lawn, the passageways from both wings connecting with it. There was a smaller anteroom outside the safety-deposit storage vault, which was set in concrete so thick that the room had been a designated fallout shelter during the cold war hysteria. The bank housed close to four hundred security boxes. That was the world they lived in now. If you valued something you couldn't risk keeping it at home.

Across from the vault was the old mainframe server room from back when dino-puters had roamed the earth. Some of the empty rooms had become a repository for all the crap from the day-to-day running of the bank that no one knew what to do with. Two entire rooms were filled floor-to-ceiling with old paper duplicates of account transactions, time capsules filled with the organized chaos-in-triplicate that banking used to be. She didn't know half the stuff that was lying about down there.

Like every old building, the bank had its secret places, too. Down in the sub-basement the passageways were lined by pipes and draped with cables that fed into maintenance tunnels and a whole subterranean world no one knew about. That was just Chicago. There were places in the city that were built on top of streets complete with buildings that were still virtually intact after the great earthquake and the rebuilding that followed.

Ellie looked at the phone again.

She'd done all she could by tripping the alarm. She had to keep her head down now, stay out of trouble.

15

ARCHER WAS IN PAIN.

He could feel the bullet moving about inside him.

He knew it was phantom pain, like a ghost limb, and that he couldn't really feel it moving, but that didn't stop him from thinking he could. There was a massive difference between knowing something on a rational level and knowing it on a primitive one—and that was where pain resided. He grunted in pain as the woman pressed down on the wound, wittering on about how it was for his own good. He wasn't stupid. He was losing a lot of blood, and losing it fast. He'd dealt with this kind of wound before, from the other side. He knew better than anyone else in the lobby just how much trouble he was in if they didn't stem the blood loss soon.

"Give me that," he said, snatching the strip of gauze out of her hand. He fumbled with the paper wrapping, his blood-covered fingers making it difficult to get any sort of purchase on the sterile packing. He tore it open with his teeth, more blood spilling out of him with each heartbeat.

He could feel himself slowing down, already groggy and light-headed, with the cold stealing into his fingertips first and working its way down into his bones.

There was so much blood on the floor; too much.

He wasn't an idiot. This was his world. He knew the deck was stacked against him.

There must have been two, maybe three pints already spilled. It was so difficult to tell once it spread. Four pints was when things started going bad. Archer knew what was going to happen to him. He'd seen it happen often enough. This was different though. Now he was on the receiving end. The creeping cold was the first sign that his body was going into shock. It wouldn't be long before he wouldn't even realize he was dying.

Trembling almost as badly as the bastard that shot him, Samuel Archer wadded up the gauze and forced it inside the wound, packing it as the blood oozed out around his fingers. The woman stared at him in disbelief as he opened himself wider, forcing the edges of the bullet hole apart to press more gauze in.

"Give me another one," he rasped through clenched teeth, repeating the procedure even as he threatened to black out.

He pressed a white terrycloth towel over the wound while the woman fumbled with a bandage and tape, only lifting it for a few seconds for her to get at the wound when she was ready. The terrycloth peeled away, heavy with blood.

She folded the bandage up until it was almost an inch thick, then pressed it over the gauze-packed hole. “Keep it in place,” she told him, tearing off a strip of medical tape with her teeth and taping down one side of the bandage. Before she'd secured three sides a bloody red Rorschach blot had begun to spread across the square of bandage, and despite the wad of gauze, was growing with alarming speed.

Looking down at it, Samuel Archer saw the Reaper's gaunt face spreading out through the bloody stain.

He didn't need a psychologist to tell him just how fucked he was.

16

ELLIE MASON RUSHED DOWN the narrow flight of steps. Her heels clacked on the stone, the echo swelling around her until it sounded like a dozen angry dwarfs going at it hammer and tongs. She told herself that no one else could hear it, that in reality the sound was nowhere near as loud as it sounded to her, but ultimately she couldn't risk the chance that the gunman would hear it in the silence of the lobby. She slipped her shoes off and descended the rest of the way down to the vault level barefoot.

Pipes banged. Someone up above had flushed a toilet. The sudden rush of sound spooked her but she didn't slow down until she reached the second set of stairs parallel with the ones she'd descended and started climbing.

On tiptoes she crept up towards the door at the top, then waited, listening through the wood for signs of movement on the other side. Satisfied there wasn't a nasty surprise waiting for her, Ellie opened the door.

She checked left and right to make sure the coast was clear, then scuttled down the passageway, past the open plan hospitality area and the glassed-off private meeting rooms, past the water cooler and the kitchen with its gas range and fridge freezer.

The silence was eerie. What should have been a hive of hustle and bustle was a ghost town.

Much worse was the sudden rush of raised voices coming from the lobby. There was no mistaking the fear.

She tried to shut out the clamor, refusing to think about what it meant.

Ellie ducked into the last office and closed the door behind her. She didn't want her voice carrying back to the lobby. With her back pressed against the door, she slipped her cellphone out of her pocket and brought up her contacts. Her mother, father, and sister were still the first three names listed. Just seeing them there in black and white brought another swell of grief with it.

She swallowed it down and dialed 911.

"I'm in the Glenview branch of Chicago Liberty Bank. There's a gunman in the lobby. I've heard a single shot."

"What's your name?" the female dispatcher said.

"It doesn't matter."

"I need to call you something."

She paused, worrying what would happen if she got caught. Then she remembered what Richard Rhodes had called her.

"You can call me McClane."

"Okay… we've received an alarm call from your location in the last few minutes."

"That was me."

"Okay. Are you safe?"

"Enough."

"Good. Please stay where you are, we don't want you taking any unnecessary risks."

"I'm not going to."

"Do you know how many gunmen are in the building?"

"One," she said, remembering what Richard had said.

"You're doing great. Can you stay on the line without putting yourself in danger?"

"I'm not sure."

"There are cars on their way to your location right now. Does the gunman know where you are?"

"No."

"Try and keep it that way. You said you heard a shot. Do you know if anyone's been hurt?"

"No."

"Officers are less than two blocks from you. They'll be with you any second."

"I have to go," Ellie said, hanging up even as the woman said, "No, don't."

Staying on the line wouldn't change anything, and Ellie had seen enough cop dramas to know that one of the first things the police would do was kill cell reception. If she was going to die in here, she wasn't going to do it in ignorance. She rang Elias Barker.

He answered on the fourth ring. "This is Barker. What can I do you for?"

"It's Ellie Mason," she said, barely above a whisper. "I got your message."

There was a moment's hesitation on the other end of the line, as the private detective placed her name, and then genuine warmth as he said, "Ah, Ellie, good that you called back so quickly. I've got some good news for you, my dear, and alas some not so good."

She liked the way he talked. He sounded old for his years, world-weary, and exactly like she imagined a good PI should sound.

"Give me the good news first," she said.

"I found him." He was quiet for a moment, letting those three words sink in. She couldn't process them, not on top of everything else. That adage about life going on had never been more apt. "John Joseph Moore, more commonly known as Johnny." She had a name. A proper name. "Grew up around Portage Park to a good white-collar family. Nothing remarkable about the guy, really. No criminal record, no newspaper reports of heroics, nothing to indicate a life well—or poorly—lived. Outside the fact that he led a secret life for five years there's nothing to suggest he was anything other than a normal guy."

"Okay," she said, still trying to take it all in.

"It was easier than I expected, to be honest. The modern world's all about the paper trail, everything is electronic, recorded in bits and bytes, but it wasn't like that twenty-five years ago. That was a world where cash was king."

He was clearly fishing for her to ask how he'd done it so that he could impress her with his ingenuity. Ellie didn't have the time or inclination. "So that's the good news. The bad?"

"John Joseph Moore died a little over eighteen months ago. Non-Hodgkin lymphoma." She knew what he was about to say. Even so, she felt the bottom fall out of her world. "His wife's still alive. Her name is—"

"Margot Moore," she finished for him, looking out of the window at a pair of cardinals squabbling over the fallout from a feeder.

He didn't ask her how she knew.

Mind reeling, she hung up without telling him what was happening just down the hallway. What was she going to do, walk up to Margot and say, "Hey, did you know your dead husband's my dad? I guess that makes you like my mother-in-infidelity or something..."

17

ADAM LOOKED AT THE woman with the bruised face. She had her head in her hands. She hadn't said a word or moved a muscle since he'd pulled the gun.

"Put the flash drive in," he said again, as though by his demanding it often enough the terminal would suddenly grow a USB connection.

"Where?" Sasha's voice spiraled. "Where do you suggest I put it in? I keep telling you it's a dumb terminal, not a real computer. There aren't any ports. There's nowhere I *can* plug it in. Don't you think I would if I could? Jesus Christ, you need to plug it into one of the main computers. The one in the manager's office..."

That stopped him cold.

"Where is he?" Adam said, panicked, his sudden change of focus confusing Sasha. "Rhodes? Where is he? He should be back by now."

Her gaze flickered and he realized she was looking at the phone, or more specifically the bank of LEDs that indicated any lines that were in use. They were all dim, but the fact that he'd sent the man out there to wrangle his workers just went to show how out of his depth Adam Shaw was right now.

And I'm drowning, he thought.

There was no way this was going to work.

He couldn't hold so many people hostage in a building like this. It was insane. There were too many rooms he didn't know about. In his head it had all been so straightforward. Now he was supposed to trust these people to behave themselves just because he had a gun? Like that was going to happen.

Someone was always going to try to be a hero.

Even as he thought it, Adam looked across at where Margot was working hard to staunch Archer's blood loss.

The man was in a bad way. Adam had never seen so much blood. The sloppy-wet sound when he lifted up his shirt made Adam feel sick, but that was nothing like the way he felt watching the man push pieces of gauze inside his own body.

Faint strains of Daryl Hall's ghostly voice shimmered through the lobby. It clawed away at Adam's skin with its absolute blandness. "Can someone turn that shit off?" he asked.

"I like it," Margot said, then seemed to remember who she was talking to and bit her lower lip, averting her eyes.

"I didn't ask if anyone liked it," he grumbled. "I can't think with that damn music on." Which wasn't true, not really. It was the unwanted memories the song brought with it. Hall & Oates had been one of Lily's favorite bands. She used to sing "Rich Girl" in the shower. It wasn't Daryl Hall he heard, it was his wife.

He'd spent a long time trying to get her out of his head, but she was every bit as stubborn in death as she had been in life.

Margot got up a little unsteadily, and went around to the back of the bank of desks, reaching down.

A second later, silence.

"Better," he said, as Richard walked into the lobby, followed by the two female members of staff he'd been sent to find. "Over there." He pointed with the gun, indicating a bank of chairs. The first woman, who was somewhere between Margot and Sasha in terms of age, wore an expensively tailored trouser-suit, which put her somewhere higher up the bank's hierarchy, and had a feathered pixie cut that framed her face. She took the seat furthest from Adam. He couldn't read her name badge, so he asked.

"Beth," she said.

"Okay, Beth, just sit tight. With a bit of luck we'll all be going home in a few minutes."

He could tell she didn't believe him. "I will pray for you," she said in a soft Southern accent, and as she took her place did just that.

"No need, but if you've got a cellphone, turn it off."

She did as she was told.

Victoria, the second woman through the door, looked to be Beth's senior by a couple of years, but she was not as well dressed. She sat as close to Beth as was humanly possible. She looked like she was about to throw up. There was nothing he could say to put her at her ease; not when there was a man bleeding to death a few feet away.

"Don't," he said to the praying Beth. "Don't do that." But she continued to mumble entreaties to her god.

Beside her, Victoria, not above offending the divine, nudged her out of her prayer before she reached the "Amen" with an elbow and a sharp, "Shut up, Beth. Can't you see he's got a gun?"

"Precisely why we should pray for his soul," the other woman said, as if it was the most obvious thing in the world.

"Don't," Adam said again. "Don't pray for me. I'm going to hell. I already know that."

"It's not too late," Beth assured him. "Those who are truly repentant are always welcome in His house."

He didn't feel like counting the ways she was wrong.

"Oh for fuck's sake, shut up, woman!" Richard barked. "Can't you see that no one gives a fuck about your god? Right now *he*—" he nodded towards Adam "—is holding our lives in his hands, that makes him the only god we need to be worried about."

That was when Adam saw the dark stain spreading over Victoria's thighs, soaking into the fabric of the chair beneath her and realized that she'd wet herself. Rhodes continued railing at Beth, but Adam ignored him, crossing to where Victoria sat hunched up on the chair. He crouched down in front of her and reached out to put a reassuring hand on her knee, but saw the way the damn thing trembled and stopped himself a couple of inches short.

"I'm not going to hurt you, I promise," he said when she looked up at him. "Now, why don't you go and clean yourself up?"

She didn't move, clearly waiting for the other shoe to drop. "Sasha," he said. "Can you take Victoria here to the bathroom?"

He was struggling. He didn't want to let any of them out of his sight, but it wasn't as if he could lock them all in the open plan lobby. If he left them alone the chances were at least one of them would make a break for it. And he couldn't simply send Sasha into the manager's office with the thumbdrive in case she smashed the thing and left him out of options. It was all Adam could do to focus on one thing at a time, and he knew he was making mistakes. Lots of them.

He knew it was stupid to let the two of them out of his sight, but this mess didn't have to be any more unpleasant than it already was.

"Of course," Sasha said, coming around from behind the counter. She offered Victoria her hand. "Come on, Vicky. Let's go get you sorted out."

The other woman rose slowly, in a daze, took her hand and followed her.

For the longest time, no one said a word.

Richard broke the silence. "Adam—it is Adam, right? You and me, we should go into my office and have a chat."

"I can't do that," Adam said, looking at the people who had somehow become his hostages. If ever there'd been a case of wrong place, wrong time, this was it.

"They're not going anywhere, the doors are locked." To the guard he said, "Theo, give him the keys." He turned back to Adam. "There's no other way out. You've got to face it, you can't do it by yourself. So, you've got to make a decision on who you can trust—if anyone. I'll put my cards on the table: I've got one endgame in mind here, that's you, me and everyone else here walking out of here and going on with our lives. The last thing I want is for some shootout on the doorstep. You keep talking about that thumbdrive; the only place it's going to work is in my office. So you need to be in there with or without me. You keep telling us you don't want to hurt anyone, that what happened to him—" he nodded towards Archer "—was an accident. And I believe you. So why don't you explain to me what *your* win is here? Maybe I can help."

"I don't see how," Adam said. And he didn't. He really didn't.

"You'd be surprised," the bank manager told him. "We're all losers, Adam. Ask anyone here, they'll tell you I've got an invisible L painted on my forehead."

"He's not lying," Archer grunted. "Rickie's the biggest

fucking loser I've ever met. No offense, Rickie."

"So what do you say, Adam? You and me? Let's find a way out of this."

18

Richard Rhodes saw an opportunity.

He ignored Archer's jibe. Right now Saul Bonavechio's man was irrelevant. It wasn't often you could say that. At this moment, the world really only needed two people in it to function properly—Richard Rhodes and Adam.

He didn't even realize he was looking at Alice until she smiled at him. He drew courage from that and said, "So, who are you, Adam? Really? Because you're not a bank robber. Did you fall on hard times? Lose your job? There are loads of good reasons to be angry with a faceless bank, but in here it's got a face. Lots of them. Mine. Sasha's, Vicky's, Beth's, Margot's—" He caught himself before he named Ellie and gave her away. "Let me help you. What I don't want is for this to become a news story. What do you say?"

It was a decent gambit; get the bad guy on side. Maybe it'd be enough to get them all out of here alive. He looked at Archer slowly bleeding out and thought, darkly, that one casualty would be acceptable, then couldn't believe he'd thought that. But it was true, wasn't it? Archer was here to ruin his life. He'd fucked up last night, acting like an idiot at the casino and now Saul Bonavechio's man was here to own him. So, yeah, one casualty wouldn't be so bad if it was Archer.

If there was one thing Richard Rhodes liked to think that he was good at, it was putting desperate people at ease. It was a massive part of the job and had become bigger every passing year since the subprime mortgage collapse. It was his super power. People came to his office to throw themselves upon his mercy. "Look," he said with a *we're-in-this-together* shrug. He leaned in closer to show he wasn't scared. "Let's go to my office, you can do your thing with the thumbdrive and go, just run before the cops arrive. You're running out of time. I know you feel like you need to watch everyone, to be on top of things. I'd be the same. But what are you going to do? Come with me. You can tell me why sixteen thousand dollars wasn't enough to make you walk out of here."

Adam thought about it for a moment, then nodded.

"Good. Great. That's the smartest decision you've made today, Adam. Theo," he called to the security guard who was hovering uncertainly on the periphery. "You heard the man," though he hadn't, of course he hadn't, Adam hadn't said a word. "Make sure no one does anything stupid out here. Okay, Adam. I'm going to get up and walk slowly over to my office. It's at the back of the lobby, over there. You follow me.

I'll sit on this side of the desk, with my back to the glass doors; you'll be able to see everyone over my shoulder and you'll have the computer screen right in front of you. No one's going to do anything stupid, are you?" That was for the rest of the people in the lobby. There were murmured promises.

Richard Rhodes walked into his office, which was more of a glass cage than an actual room, feeling the eyes on him as he sat.

Adam didn't sit.

He stood behind the desk, setting the gun down beside the keyboard, and put the thumbdrive into a USB port without a word. Richard couldn't see what was happening, but could read the man's face well enough to know that it wasn't what he'd expected.

19

THE SCREEN FLICKERED, A line of static rippling across the various open windows, and settled. He had imagined it would be some sort of rapid flurry of activity marking the thefts, a digital tracker keeping score, but there was nothing to indicate any sort of back channel activity. Adam hit the space bar, then the enter key, beginning to panic.

And then something happened.

He stared at the screen in disbelief as what appeared to be a stripper gyrated against a pole of As before turning her back to him and bending over as the message: YOU'VE BEEN PWNED. ENJOY LIFE IN PRISON ASSHOLE scrolled from left to right across the bottom of the screen and mocking laughter brayed out of the tinny speakers. The stripper's ass was replaced on the screen by a crudely drawn, mocking troll's face.

Adam couldn't look away.

He felt sick.

He was going to prison, and he was going empty-handed. Even if, by some miracle, he escaped there was no encrypted hard drive waiting for him at Union Station. If he ran now he might just get out, but getting away was an entirely different prospect. In a post 9/11 world it was impossible to believe someone hadn't heard the gunshot and called the cops. Either of the two women the manager had brought from the back offices could have—would have, surely. More mistakes.

He'd been an idiot on so many levels. He'd put his faith in this program, that it would do what he needed it to do, choosing to believe he'd made a deal with money launderers, while instead he'd been played by some anonymous hackers looking to amuse themselves for a few hours while they destroyed his life. He should have known it wasn't a two-and-a-half-million-dollar job. He was an idiot.

He was done. It was all over.

He closed his eyes.

When he opened them again he was crying.

20

THE MAN LEANT AGAINST the desk. There were tears on his cheeks. It was impossible for Richard not to notice the way his fingers twitched. He had absolutely no motor control over them. The motion was erratic, not like someone nervously playing an invisible piano. There was something seriously wrong with him. Maybe it was really true that he'd never meant to pull the trigger. There was every chance that Adam was the most frightened man in Chicago Liberty Bank right now. That was a twist of fate Richard hadn't expected.

It didn't change how he had to play this, though. It wasn't any easier to calm a frightened man than it was to placate an angry one.

"What's happening here, Adam? Let me help you."

Silence.

"You've got to give me something."

Adam looked over Richard's shoulder. Richard craned

round and realized he was looking at the security camera watching them.

"If not for me, for them, the people who are going to watch this later and wonder what the fuck went wrong. What's your story?"

That seemed to work.

"I'm dying," the other man said, still not looking at him.

That was pretty much the last thing Richard had expected to hear. What was he supposed to do with that information? It changed everything, because suddenly he was sitting down with a man who had nothing to lose, and more immediately worrying, nothing to win. "I don't know what to say," he said.

"Well, at least you didn't say sorry. People usually say sorry, as if it's all their fault."

He studied the man, really looking at him this time, but the only thing that stood out as even slightly remarkable was the way his hand trembled. "What is it, some sort of wasting disease?"

"ALS," Adam said. "Lou Gehrig's disease."

"Shit, man, that's harsh."

Adam laughed, a sharp bitter bark of a laugh.

"That it is," he agreed.

"So that's why you need the money? To pay for treatment? The insurance company fucked you over?" Richard's mind raced to a bunch of inevitable conclusions that really should have meant Adam and his gun had turned up on the insurance company's doorstep, not his. "I get it," he said. "But sixteen grand would have paid for a lot of care, wouldn't it? You could still walk out of here with that in your pocket, no recriminations. I'll let you go. I really hate to kick a man when he's down."

"It doesn't matter anymore. It didn't work. It wasn't even for me."

"Who was it for, then?"

"My son."

It was all beginning to become clear. "How old is he?"

"Eleven."

"How long have you got?"

"I won't see him turn twelve."

"Mum?"

"Dead."

"Jesus."

"Jake's got Down's Syndrome. He's only expected to live into his mid-thirties. Do you know how much it costs to raise a child, Rickie?" Rhodes winced at the use of Archer's mocking nickname but didn't contradict Adam. He shook his head, but of course he knew. It was a significant factor in mortgage-lending calculations.

"A lot," he said.

"Somewhere close to four hundred thousand dollars. That's a normal, healthy kid. My son won't leave childhood, not really, that's the level of care he's going to need when I'm gone. I need to find two and a half million dollars before I die."

"And you've come in here carrying this baggage? Fuck me. Man. I'll be honest, I'm surprised you haven't blown your brains out." It was a stupid thing to say to a man on the edge, but maybe he'd just shoot himself and be done with it.

"I've thought about it," Adam admitted. "But that wouldn't change anything."

"I see why you couldn't just walk out with a bundle of cash. But two and a half million? You can't just steal that and expect to give it to your kid."

"I wasn't going to," Adam said, and outlined the deal he'd made, the money transfers offshore, how there were supposed to be Bitcoins waiting for him, how the corporations targeted wouldn't even notice because the individual sums were so small they would have been written off as shrinkage.

Richard recognized the arguments. They were compelling. Who wouldn't want to help some kid with Down's who'd been orphaned because life was, when it came right down to it, a bastard?

It was as close to a victimless crime as you could get when you were talking about the theft of two and a half million bucks, and if he hadn't already been doing something eerily similar to the corporate accounts under his control he would have been tempted to help the man. But two and a half million, no matter if it was stolen one cent at a time, spread across every corporate account Chicago Liberty handled worldwide, it would leave a big hole somewhere, the kind of hole that a decent auditor would be unable to resist delving into. And then when they went digging everything else would be brought up to the light. He couldn't let that happen.

"So," Adam said, still looking up at the security camera even though his testimony was complete. The tremors in his gun-hand were worse now than they had been a couple of minutes ago. "Now you know. Will you help me?"

Before Richard Rhodes could answer, a phone rang.

21

It took Archer a moment to realize the ringtone was his.

He didn't really hurt anymore, which was a bad thing. He was in shock, and now it was the not-so slow countdown to the euphoria of blood loss and the chemical cocktail that would kill him. He'd be damned if he was going to beg for his life. Closing his eyes, he reached for the cellphone in his pocket. He fumbled with the thing, trying to hit the spot that would pick up the incoming call, but with his thumb slick with blood the screen didn't register the touch.

People were looking at him. He didn't care. That cunt Adam looked terrified.

"I told you to hand that in!" Adam yelled, an edge of hysteria creeping into his voice.

"I don't take orders from shit like you."

Archer wiped the cellphone on his trouser leg then jabbed at the screen again. He raised it to his ear. Archer smiled through the pain and said, "Mister B."

"Samuel," the voice on the other end of the line growled. "Where the fuck have you been?"

"Right here," Archer said, giving nothing away.

"I got the message you flagged up, some joker called Milo supposedly representing a consortium from Vegas looking to muscle in? Talk to me, Samuel. Do I need to be concerned?"

"It's sorted," Archer assured him. It was difficult to focus. He felt himself slipping. Gritting his teeth, he tried to push himself back up until he was closer to sitting than lying. The blood all around him looked like some infernal lake glistening with all the pains he'd ever dished out in this life come back to haunt him.

"Is it?"

"He was all mouth. Believe me," he said, looking at Rickie Rhodes trying to play hostage negotiator. There were black spots across his vision, and a blacker frame around the world as he saw it, his world narrowing as he lost the fight. "Nothing to worry about there."

"Good. That's one less thing to worry about today then. You know how important today is, Samuel. We can't afford for there to be any fuck-ups."

"It's all good," Archer said, closing his eyes.

He felt his grip, tenuous as it was, slipping.

"Are you okay, Samuel? You sound strange."

"Been better, Mister B."

"Should I be worrying about you, Samuel?"

"Not really. Got some stuff I need to take care of, that's all. Personal business. You know me, Mister B."

"I do, Samuel. Indeed I do. Which is why I think you're lying to me."

"Why would I do that?"

"Because you're in trouble and you're trying to protect me. Is that it, Samuel? Are you trying to protect me from something?"

"Nah," Archer barely vocalized his denial. "Just been a rough day."

"I don't like it when people lie to me, Samuel. It makes me nervous."

"It's all good," Archer said again.

"It clearly isn't," Saul Bonavechio said. "Don't disappoint me, Samuel. I'm counting on you today."

"You can trust me, Mister B," Archer lied, his voice getting weaker. "I'll make it to the warehouse on time, it's all good." He was fading. He could feel it. The world around him was growing soft around the edges. He wasn't getting out of here. It was bitterly ironic: Samuel Archer, the great Samuel Archer, the red right hand of the king of Chicago, undone by a cripple's twitch. The gods laugh while idiots make plans.

"Don't be late. Get whatever it is you need to do done. I don't want to have to send the Dane to clean up your mess, Samuel. Today of all days, I can't afford any fuck-ups."

"Understood." Archer ended the call. He wasn't going to be there, but what was Mister B going to do, drag him back from

Hell kicking and screaming just to kill him all over again?

It was the Dane's problem now, and he loathed that bastard, so let him sweat.

He didn't know much about the guy. He was six-five, snow-white hair, chiseled, and he was ice cold. The Dane was Saul Bonavechio's chosen hammer when someone needed to be terminated.

He dropped the phone.

His mind was gone, chasing random flutters of thought but unable to catch any of them. He felt himself slowly slump and there was nothing he could do to stop it.

A fire blazed inside him, chewing through everything that made Samuel Archer the man he was. He couldn't lift his arm. He tried, but his body refused to obey. He was in trouble.

Margot reached out to help him, but he was too heavy for her.

Alice didn't move. She was clearly waiting for him to die.

Breathing hard, his mind everywhere but inside the lobby of Chicago Liberty Bank, Samuel Archer broke his promise. "Pick up the phone… now," he told her. He didn't say please, he didn't beg. But he had asked for help. That was something he hadn't done since he was a kid back in the projects. It was too late, though. He knew that. "Alice, get the paramedics… You owe me… Fuck… just… pick up the phone. Please…" He trailed off, looking at the cellphone on the bloody carpet just a few inches away, the implication obvious; he didn't have the strength left.

The silence stretched out through five heartbeats, each successive one feeling a little weaker against his ribs as his pulse became thready.

Alice answered.

One word.

"No."

22

The fabric of Vicky's trousers was soaked with urine. This was not how Sasha had imagined the day going when she'd got out of bed this morning with her head full of man trouble and bad sex. She led her by the hand past the glassed-off conference rooms without a word. As they entered the bathroom she tried to reassure her. "It's going to be okay, Adam won't hurt us." Vicky didn't say anything. The hydraulic arm drew the bathroom door slowly closed behind them.

Sasha had thought that Vicky's silence was due to shame. Her eyes were red with tears as she crossed over to the row of basins.

She was wrong.

As soon as the bathroom door closed behind them, Vicky became a different woman. She rubbed at her eyes with the back of her right hand, then twisted the faucet until steaming hot water ran from it. She splashed her face until it was red.

When she looked at Vicky in the mirror Sasha was surprised to see her determination. There was rage in her eyes, not fear. She pulled at the belt fastening her soaked trousers, unbuckling it and peeling them down and stepping out of them.

"We haven't got long," she said. "I've got a pair of jeans in my gym bag. Will you go and get them while I clean myself up?"

Sasha nodded. "Are you okay?"

"Of course I'm okay. Oh, these?" She bundled the trousers up and stuffed them in the trash. "Now he thinks I'm so scared of him I pissed my pants. He's not going to know what's hit him."

"You pissed yourself on purpose?" Sasha couldn't quite believe she'd misjudged her co-worker so completely. This woman was a fucking Amazon, not some timid little mouse. "I can't even begin—"

"There's stuff you don't know about me," Vicky said. "I wasn't always a corporate drone. Two tours in the original Gulf action. It's been a long time, and I've gone soft, but I can handle a prick like that with one arm tied behind my back."

"Jesus."

"He wasn't there." Vicky smiled. "That man is going to wish he walked into a different bank to pull this shit."

Until a couple of minutes ago Victoria Mann had been just another colleague in her rumpled off-the-rack suit, the wrong side of middle age, probably looking toward a comfortable retirement in a nice house down by a lake somewhere. Sasha tried to think of the last conversation they'd had, but couldn't.

She shook her head. The things you didn't know about people.

"What are you going to do?"

"Neutralize the guy, put an end to the threat. And you're going to help me. He trusts you."

"He's dying," Sasha said.

"Only if there's no alternative," the other woman said.

That took a moment to filter through, then she realized the implications. "No, I mean he's dying. You see him shaking? He's got ALS."

"Sucks to be him, then."

"Is that all you've got to say?"

Vicky turned away from the mirror and met her gaze full on. Sasha had never really thought about how intimidating the banker was, but she saw it now, even stripped down to her piss-soaked panties. The woman was a force of nature. "What do you expect me to say? That I feel sorry for a man who's come in here and shot a customer point blank? Yeah I'm heartbroken that he's having a bad time, kiddo."

"It was an accident."

"You march into a bank waving a gun, you don't have accidents, you have consequences, and you have to expect to take your licks. I don't care if you're dying, there are always going to be consequences. He can plead his case before a judge. The rest isn't my problem, Sasha. As long as he's got a gun and hostages *that* is my problem.

"He didn't have to come in here. Remember that. He didn't have to walk up to your counter. He didn't have to do any of those things when he found out he was dying. He chose to do them because that's who he really is when he's stripped of everything else."

"What are you going to do?"

"First, make sure word has got out to the cops. When he sees the cordon of blue lights and realizes there's no way out, then with luck he'll do the smart thing. But I'm not going to bet my life on it. So we prepare for the worst. Now, do me a favor, go get those jeans. I don't intend to face down a gunman in my panties. That's a bit too Ripley, even for me."

Sasha laughed despite herself. That was the last thing she'd expected to come out of Vicky's mouth, but then, she hadn't really known her until about thirty seconds ago, had she?

"And if you see Ellie skulking about out there, tell her to come here. She's got a role to play in what happens next."

Sasha had completely forgotten about Ellie, but Vicky was dead right: she hadn't been out in the lobby when Richard had assembled the staff. She'd heard him lie to Adam about how many people worked in the bank; now she knew why. Ellie was the element of the unknown he was banking on to save them. She still didn't trust him, but maybe he wasn't an idiot after all.

23

Alice spoke.

One word.

"No."

All eyes turned to Alice Fisher, the croupier. She realized that it was the first thing she'd said since Adam had pulled his gun on the teller.

The rest of them had forgotten she was even there.

She wasn't supposed to be. After he'd got her out of that hotel room Archer had taken her to the ER—it wasn't about caring; he didn't like his property being damaged. She'd tried to tell him she wasn't insured, but he wasn't having any of it. She'd overheard him giving his name as "Victor LaSalle" as he checked her in, filling out the registration forms and showing a fake driver's license. "She's on my insurance," he said, handing it over. "Alice LaSalle."

The triage nurse had studied her expression as Archer

explained she'd been attacked coming out of a club. Alice assumed she was being given a way out, a chance to say she was the victim of domestic abuse. She gave nothing away. Most of the damage Horace Greene had inflicted was down her left side, and therefore hidden by her clothes. The only obvious injuries were the beginnings of a black eye and some minor swelling around her cheekbone. She wasn't going to be able to work for a while. They waited through the night and well into the next day before she was finally seen and given the all clear. Archer said he would drive her home, but he had to swing by the bank first.

Now that it came to the fate of Samuel Archer she found her voice. "Let him die. He deserves it."

Beth looked up from her prayers, hands still clutched together, clearly about to chastise her when Archer shuddered, his arm flailing out and knocking one of the planters from its pedestal. The pot shattered on impact. Archer's body bucked twice, his mouth open, twisted as he tried to say something, but his words faded to nothing. His other hand clawed at his chest.

For an impossibly long second that seemed to stretch out for minutes, no one moved. They stared at Archer as he appeared to choke on the air he couldn't breathe. His fingers curled into a claw, his jaw hung slackly, and spittle dribbled down his chin.

"Oh Christ," Margot said, breaking the spell the simple act of dying had woven over the room. "He's having a heart attack."

Alice watched Margot push herself up from her crouch beside the stricken man and run flat-footed across the carpeted floor. The woman ignored Adam—who stood in the door of the manager's office, watching, gun in hand—as she dove behind the counter to where a one-shot defibrillator hung on the wall.

She had the container open and was already peeling the non-conductive film away from the two paddles as she fell to her knees in the pool of blood that had spread out around Archer. She twisted the dial to charge the machine, then fumbled around inside the box for the gel she needed to smear across the metal plates.

Archer wasn't breathing.

Alice watched as the woman tore his shirt all the way open. Archer was absolutely still; the absence of life had a stillness all of its own. Grasping the paddles in both hands, Margot trembled violently. Alice willed her to fail. If there was one person in this world who didn't deserve a miracle it was Samuel Archer.

Less than sixty seconds had passed from the moment the planter had shattered.

"Stay back!" Margot cried, even though there was no one within twenty feet of her as she delivered the shock. Archer's body bucked under the charge, left hand slapping weakly in the blood, and for a moment it looked as though there was something there. *Stay dead,* Alice thought, in direct counterpoint to Margot's words of "Come on, come on."

It wasn't happening.

Margot rested two fingers against his throat, feeling for a pulse that clearly wasn't there. She interlaced her fingers, forming a single fist out of both hands, and beat on Archer's chest three times—hard—in rapid succession, trying to drive the life back into him with the full force of her fists.

Nothing.

Margot put her mouth to his and repeated the pattern, three short breaths before she broke off to pump at his chest again, then three more breaths. Nothing. But she refused to give up.

While everyone's attention was on Margot and Archer, Alice slipped across the room to where Archer's jacket had been draped over the back of a chair. There was blood on it. His blood. She didn't care. Alice slipped a hand inside the folds of expensive material, her fingers finding the envelope he'd taken from the ball player to pay for her. There was a lot of money in the envelope. *So what if I'm stealing from a dead man?* she thought. *I've earned every cent.*

She stuffed the envelope into her bag, barely managing to close it before Margot looked up, locking eyes with her across the room, and said, "You got your wish."

"Good," Alice said, and she meant it. She had a chance to get her life back. Adam had given her that. Samuel Archer's last act of cruelty would finance a clean start. In that, at least, some good would come out of the hell of last night. "You don't know who he was. You don't know what he did to me."

“I know all I need to know,” Margot told her. “Someone will mourn his loss.”

Alice shook her head. “He caused nothing but pain.” There was no emotion in her voice; it was as dead as the man on the floor. She nodded at Adam in the doorway. “Believe me, the guy over there is my hero. He saved my life. The only way today could have been better would have been if I’d been the one to pull the trigger.”

24

IT WAS ALL ON camera.

The death of the man called Archer. They'd play it in court at his trial and he'd be damned by it. There were no circumstances in the world that could ever be extenuating enough to save him. Adam's mind raced: did Illinois have the death penalty? Did it even matter? His own body would execute him long before the state ever could.

He lurched into the foyer. "Get away from him. Just... get back. Move. Over there," he waved the gun towards the chairs. No one moved. "I'm serious. Just fucking *move*." There was an edge of hysteria in his voice.

That did it. The woman, Alice, who had just called him her hero, spat on Archer's corpse before she took a seat again. Adam didn't know their history, but it was obvious she hated the dead man. Not that it helped him.

"You're going to prison," Margot told him.

"Tell me something I don't know," Adam said bitterly. How to contain this mess? How to escape? What would Jake do when he didn't come home?

What would happen to Jake?

"Look, this is all a mistake. All of it. I don't expect any of you to believe me—or to care, but it's the truth. I came in here because I'm dying, because my son is disabled and he's going to be left to fend for himself when I'm gone. I didn't want to hurt anybody." He looked around the room, his gaze settling on Beth, who was already praying for his immortal soul. "I'm not looking for sympathy. I'm not trying to be anyone's hero. I just wanted to pay for my son's care after I've gone. No one should have been hurt. It was a tiny thing—"

"Two and a half million tiny things," Richard said.

"Why don't you go? Just get up and walk out the door. All of you. Go. I won't stop you."

The bank manager shook his head. "No."

Adam felt like a beaten man. "You can all go. I'll just wait for the cops."

"I can't," Richard said. "This place is my responsibility. It's more than my job's worth."

"Bullshit," Sasha said. She stood in the mouth of the corridor that led to the back offices. He couldn't see Victoria. He had no idea how long she'd been standing there. "You're up to something. That story about being mugged? I can't be the only one who thinks it stinks. The only reason you're not running out of here is because you can't—"

"Which is what I just said," Richard protested.

"—but not because of any sort of duty. If you could you'd be halfway down the block already. So whatever's stopping you from leaving, it's all about you."

"Don't look at me like *I* just killed someone. That was him," Richard said with surprising vehemence. "I'm not the villain here." But even as he said it, his hand went up to touch the bruises around the side of his face. He looked guilty.

"Really? Want to explain how you knew him?" Sasha nodded towards Archer's body. "Because he sure as shit knew you, *Rickie*, and acted like he *owned* you."

"It's not what you think."

"I think you're up to your neck in it, that's what I think."

Richard shook his head.

Adam watched him floundering for the words to deny it. Before he could, Alice spoke up. "You're not trying to protest your innocence, are you?"

"What the fuck are you talking about? I have no idea who he was."

Alice clearly wasn't buying it. "I recognize you. You called yourself Milo last night. Milo Rockwell, right? Like the painter. You said you came from the West Coast, bragging about how you were in town to check out the competition, like you were mobbed up. Pathetic. I don't know how you explained the bruises—" she touched her own bruised cheek reflexively "—but I can tell everyone *exactly* how you got them. Do you want me to do that?"

"That's not necessary," Richard said, sounding lost.

"What, you don't want your staff knowing what you did last night? Archer did that to him. He beat the living shit out of him as a lesson that you don't fuck about with Saul Bonavechio. And Archer wasn't here to check up on your injuries, was he? He's not thoughtful like that. He had something he wanted you to do. That's how he does it. Once he finds his way in, he owns people."

The bank manager looked like he wanted to curl up into a ball.

"Well, isn't that interesting," Sasha said. "I'm sure there must be a policy against that kind of thing, Richard. Or should I call you Milo?" She shook her head, like she couldn't believe how dumb he'd been.

"What are you trying to do?" Richard muttered finally. "This is so wrong. Jesus. I'm not the one in here robbing the bank. I didn't kill anyone. But you're still trying to make *me* out to be the bad guy. I don't know what I ever did to you. I don't deserve this."

"Then answer me one question. Convince me. If you haven't done anything wrong why haven't you called the police?"

Richard stared at her. "I have," he said, the gap between question and answer a moment longer than was reasonable for the truth. "I triggered the alarm when I went out to round the others up."

"Really?" Sasha said, obviously not believing him. "Maybe

I've got you all wrong, boss. Theo, take a look out of the window, tell me what you see."

The security guard did as he was told, clambering onto a chair to get a better view of the street. "Not much," he reported back a few seconds later. "Couple of kids at the end of the block, a decent-sized line at the food truck, other than that, all quiet."

"Any cops? The place should be swarming with them by now if our fearless leader isn't full of shit."

Theo pressed his face to the glass, raising his right hand as though taking an oath as he shielded his eyes from the glare. "None that I can see. No. Wait. Two. It's your admirer, Officer Jaeger and his partner."

"Andy's outside?"

Theo nodded. "Looking as dashing as ever. I think he dresses up just for you, Sash."

"Shut up, Theo. Okay, okay. I need to think. That doesn't mean he's going to come in. He doesn't drop by every day."

"Only most."

She turned to Adam. "It's not too late for you to run. There's a fire exit at the end of the corridor."

"And what then? It's all on camera. They'll just come and find me."

"Better that than getting yourself shot here," she said, which it was, infinitely, but it still wasn't a life worth living.

"Why are you helping me?" It was a fair question, but it wasn't like they had time to debate her answer. Not unless he intended to turn this into a proper hostage situation, and the minute that happened he wasn't getting out of here alive. He was a numbers guy. He knew the statistics. There were over five thousand bank robberies during the last year, two hundred involved acts of violence, seventy the discharge of firearms. There had been eighty-eight injuries and thirteen deaths. Ten of the thirteen killed were the perpetrators. He looked at Archer. The numbers would be different this year.

"Because I believe you. You aren't a monster. You're not even the worst person in the room," Sasha said.

"But I'm the only murderer in it," Adam said.

"It wasn't murder," Sasha said, and he desperately wanted to believe her.

"Semantics," Adam said, and it was. Of course it was. Murder One. Murder Two. Voluntary manslaughter. Involuntary manslaughter. They all had one thing in common: a victim lying on the coroner's slab. Everything else was for the lawyers to argue.

"You're wasting time. Go. Run."

It occurred to him to ask where the other woman was, the one Sasha had taken to the bathroom. He'd forgotten her name. Before he could, Theo said, "Here they come."

"Kill the lights," Adam said, thinking on his feet. It was too late to run now, but he could at least try to hide.

It wasn't much, but it meant that prying eyes wouldn't be able to see too deeply into the bank's interior. Lights out, locked door, maybe the cops would think—

He had to stop thinking that way. They knew. The silent alarm had been triggered.

“We’re out of time,” Theo said, ducking away from the window.

A moment later the front door rattled. A couple of seconds later it rattled again. It was followed by the sound of a fist pounding on the glass.

25

THE KID ON THE corner serenaded the food truck with her ukulele, telling everyone in the line their hearts belonged to her.

Andreas Jaeger smiled to himself. He was comfortably in love for the first time in years. Of course, the object of his affections had no idea. They had never kissed. Never held hands or been on anything resembling a date, which, all things considered, was a drawback in terms of Happily Ever After.

He just needed to man up. What could she say apart from no?

The skyscrapers in the distance looked like a pen and ink sketch, each outline and shadow stark in the sun. He loved this city and all of its sharp geography. There was no sight in the world to rival the skyline and the million lights that lit up the night, but daytime in the canyons of the city ran a close second.

It promised to be a beautiful day and nothing—absolutely nothing—was going to ruin his good mood. The birds might as well have been circling his head tweeting out a chorus of love songs. It was that kind of day.

"Let's shake it up a bit," his partner, Leigh Parrish, said to the smiling cook behind the food truck counter.

"You mean no *bánh mì*?" the man said incredulously.

"I mean no *bánh mì*," Leigh said. "What's good?"

The cook waved towards the griddle with his spatula. "C'mon Officer P., it's all good."

"Of course it is, but you know what I mean: what's irresistible? We're talking real fan favorite."

"The *bánh mì*."

"Funny man."

"I try. Okay, you leave it to me. I'll whip up something special just for you guys."

"Sounds good, just remember Buttercup is lactose intolerant and I have to share a squad car with him." He pinched his nostrils closed to emphasize the point.

Andy just shook his head. He had no such dietary problems. Leigh could be a complete prick if he thought it'd win him a laugh from the audience. That was just the price of their partnership, you took the good with the bad.

"Two lunchbox specials coming up, extra crispy," the cook said, and then over his shoulder to the next people in the line, "Okay folks, what can I do for you?"

Andy's radio crackled and he answered, "One-Adam-

Thirteen." He listened as the dispatcher ran through signal codes: 211S, robbery alarm silent, 1071, gunshots fired. He started when the dispatcher gave the location—it took him a moment to process what was happening just a few feet away in the Chicago Liberty Bank.

"Ten four."

He filled Leigh in, whose only answer was to reach for his weapon. "It'd be so much easier if you just asked that woman out instead of arranging a bank robbery so you can play the hero."

Andy ignored him and turned back towards the bank, studying the façade. It was a nice old building that had been converted from a municipal hall rather than custom built. There were a dozen windows on the ground floor, ornate black iron bars across them like something out of the Old West, a portico over the door and a creeper climbing up the corner of one wall, its roots wormed deep into the pointing. The rest was utterly corporate, plain and devoid of personality. He thought for a moment he caught a glimpse of a face up against the glass, peering out through the bars, but it was so dark inside the building it was impossible to tell. Probably just a shadow, he reasoned.

He stopped on the grass verge watching the bank for any signs of life.

Leigh was two steps behind him. "You should have bought flowers."

"I'm going to try the doors."

Leigh shook his head. “Negatory, we wait for backup.”

Ignoring him, Andy pushed against the doors. They were locked. He rattled the doors again, then banged three times on the glass. “Hello? Anyone home? Chicago PD. Make yourself known.”

Nothing.

He did it again.

Still nothing.

“I thought I saw someone in there before. You stay here,” he told his partner, “I’m going around the back to check things out.”

Leigh nodded.

Andy Jaeger moved fast, half-crouching, half-running along the front of the building, keeping below the level of the windows. He checked left and right, then went around the corner into a narrow alleyway. It was cramped, the paving slabs cracked by age and abuse, and lined with a bank of plastic trashcans that were filled to overflowing with pizza boxes and ripe garbage. A few windows looked out from the bank to the blank wall opposite. The alley ran the length of the bank, opening onto a small gravel parking lot that serviced both the bank and the neighboring buildings.

In the shade the temperature had dropped noticeably. Andy slowed halfway along the alleyway, moving cautiously now, aware of even the slightest noise as he lifted himself up a few inches and pressed his face up against a window to peer inside. He could see an office, but it was empty, and there was no sign of anyone through the glass partition wall that looked out over the bank's inner sanctum. That in itself wasn't so odd; it was a big building with a small staff.

He moved along to the next window and the next. Same situation.

He moved on to the final window. This time when he pulled himself up onto his toes he could have sworn he caught a glimpse of someone moving about in there, but they were gone too quickly for him to get a good look.

He tapped on the glass, hoping to draw them back.

He waited, counting silently to five, then tapped again. This time he counted to six and tapped again. *Tick-tick-tick.* The fifth time was the charm. He saw a woman creeping about inside the darkened interior. She saw his face at the window and pressed her finger up against her lips. She gestured right, then disappeared from sight.

He looked down the line of the building to the corner. Nothing. No fire exit, no other windows. He didn't waste his time tapping on the glass to try to lure her back. He scurried down the alley to the corner, pressed his back up against the wall, then spun around, ready to face God knew what.

He scanned the parking lot, looking for the wheelman. No one robbed a bank without a getaway plan in place.

He drew his service weapon. It was the first time he'd ever drawn his gun in the line of duty; that fact wasn't lost on him. He'd wondered about this moment, worried about it, but now that it was here he was absolutely calm.

There were security cameras watching over the lot. Each camera had one-seventy degree coverage, and they overlapped so almost all angles were covered. There was only one obvious blind spot, unless there was another camera he was missing. He scanned the cars. There were half a dozen in the lot, profiling a range of salaries and family situations. One obvious people carrier for a large family, two or three kids, one midlife crisis two-seater sports car, a couple of sensible sedans, and two practical station wagons. They all had local plates. They were all in good condition, no obvious damage. Either of the more bland vehicles would have served as a getaway car. A smart wheelman turned up in a car that was utterly unremarkable, the kind that would blend in. Any one of these parked cars could have done just that.

Andy moved quickly, going along the line of cars to be sure they were all empty, with no obvious signs of forced entry, and then turned his attention back to the bank.

There were more than a dozen windows looking out from either side of the horseshoe the building formed, overlooking a grassed garden. There were two obvious fire exits facing each other across the grass, and beside each a glass jar filled with water and floating cigarette butts. By the looks of it, this was where the staff snuck out for a quick cigarette.

He had to figure the woman had meant him to head towards the nearest fire exit, intending to meet him there. Andy crossed the lawn, painfully aware that it put him in full view of the windows and any gunman's cross hairs.

Before he reached safety his radio crackled, Leigh's voice scaring the life out of him. "You there, partner?"

He cupped his hand over the speaker, muffling the sound before he thumbed down the talk button. "I'm here. There's definitely something going down. Keep your eyes open. There are several ways out of this place and you're looking at the most obvious one."

"Just be careful back there, man. I've got the front covered. No one's getting out."

The woman appeared at the window.

He pointed towards the door, meaning she should let him in. She shook her head and pressed a piece of paper up against the glass. "Shit," Andy Jaeger said, reading the message: ONE GUNMAN. EIGHT OF US. HELP.

He repeated it to Leigh out front, then called it in.

"Control, this is One-Adam-Thirteen. Confirmation of robbery in progress."

"Roger that, One-Adam-Thirteen," the dispatcher's voice crackled back. "Secure the scene. Do not engage. Maintain safe distance until backup arrives. It's less than a minute out. We don't need any heroes, One-Adam-Thirteen."

"Least likely hero on the street. That's me."

"Just what we like to hear."

Backup would include a specialist crisis negotiation team and a SWAT team, ready to bring the curtain down as the last resort, if all avenues toward a peaceful resolution were exhausted.

When he looked up the woman was gone.

Unrequited love was the absolute last thing on his mind now.

26

THE BANGING CAME AGAIN and again, each time followed by the muffled voice.

And then it didn't. That was worse.

Adam paced in a tight circle. He left a single partial footprint in Archer's blood. Just the heel where he'd not been paying attention, then realized too late.

"What do I do? What do I do?" He wasn't asking anyone else, which was good because no one was answering. If there were police at the front of the building, then they'd surely be waiting at the back too. It was too late for him to run.

He looked at Beth, her hands clutched together in prayer. Why would one woman's god help out a sinner like him? The answer was obvious. He wouldn't.

Everything was different now.

He needed to think, but there was no time. He was losing himself.

"What's going on out there?" he said.

This time someone did answer. Theo, the security guard. He was still close to the window, but keeping back from the glass now.

"I can't see Officer Andy, but his partner's watching the door. There's no guarantee they're the only two out there."

Adam tried to visualize the street; there were two alleyways, both narrow, that ran either side of the bank, both opening out onto the same parking lot out back. There was the usual array of shops further up the street, where the idea of a village became more obvious, but down here it was more like a couple of strip malls side by side, with the bank at the center of them. There was higher ground across the street, with offices offering windows that looked down on the bank. Perfect for police marksmen to take up position at. He'd known it was a risk, but he'd run the numbers so many times, pushing all sorts of variables, and it had seemed so minimal as to be worth it. Now minimal was inevitable.

"He'll be checking the fire exits," Richard explained needlessly. Adam knew exactly what the cop would be doing. It was procedure. "There's no way you can secure the entire building."

He was right. It was too big. Too many points of entry. He'd need to barricade himself in here if it was going to get that far. But getting *that* far meant smoke canisters, concussion grenades, armed men swarming up both wings into the lobby. And mistakes. There were always mistakes when chaos was let loose, variables that couldn't be properly factored in, like bullets ricocheting. They could take him down, but with the kind of high-velocity weaponry at their disposal that bullet with his name on could feasibly go through-and-through, killing someone else too. Firing in an enclosed space full of people was a risk a trained shooter wouldn't ideally want to take. Smoke, confusion, shock and awe, they were better options if they could control the situation.

His risk assessment had gone out the window. Now it was all a matter of how lucky he felt.

Not even a little bit.

"What do I do?" Adam repeated.

This time Margot had the answer. "Give yourself up."

He closed his eyes, breathing deeply. Best-case scenario, he had minutes; then there would be a swarm of law enforcement outside. Worst-case scenario didn't bear thinking about. He needed to focus on why he'd come in here in the first place. That was his only win scenario. "I still need the money," he said. "That hasn't changed. I just don't know how to get it anymore. I can't walk out of here empty-handed."

"How the hell do you think you can get away with robbing the bank now?" Margot said.

"I don't know. I don't know. I don't know." He had to stop himself from saying it again and again.

"Don't do this." It was Beth. "Not yet. You can't let *him* win." Him being Adam. Her eyes darted from Sasha to Adam to Richard and the darkened opening of the corporate corridor, then back to Sasha, like she was looking for a miracle.

Adam looked around the lobby, trying to see whatever it was Beth saw, but all he saw were frightened faces.

Then he understood. An absence. Victoria hadn't returned from the washroom with Sasha. That was the miracle Beth was looking for, nothing divine. Fuck. He couldn't go after her. He couldn't leave the others in here. But he couldn't leave her to her own devices back there, either.

27

"What have you done?"

Vicky turned away from the window. The sunlight turned half of her face to gold. "Saved us," she said, balling up the sheet of copier paper in her hand. Only the word HOSTAGES showed through the creases. She tossed it, missing the trashcan. "You should go. Out through the fire doors while you still have a chance. The cops will be here soon. We'll be okay."

It was a test. She didn't know Ellie Mason all that well. She was still the new girl as far as Vicky was concerned, and probably would be for another couple of years. That was just the way she was with people. She was slow to trust them. But once they were through the barricades, she was fiercely loyal.

Ellie shook her head. "I'm not going anywhere."

"We're hostages. Also known as 'human shields.' You need to get out of here. It's one less body for him to hide behind."

"Save your breath. We're in this together." There was an

unexpected steel in her voice. There was something else going on here, but for now it didn't matter. Vicky could work with that steel.

"Okay, fine. Follow me." She took Ellie's hand, drawing her into the shadows. The bank was eerily quiet. It was hard to believe that only a few feet away a man was bleeding to death—if he wasn't already dead. She'd seen that kind of injury before. He wasn't going to make a miraculous recovery.

"You need to know what's going to happen here." Barely above a whisper, Vicky's words came in a rush. "Two of us gives us a chance. Not a great one, but better than it was a couple of minutes ago." She saw Ellie staring at her jeans. Vicky didn't waste her breath explaining. "There's a man back there with a gun and he has already shot someone. That means, first and foremost, our goal is to stay alive. We're not trying to stop him robbing the bank. Got that?" Ellie nodded again. She looked stubbornly determined.

"I know what you are thinking," Vicky said, despite the fact that she didn't have a clue what was going on in the other woman's head. The word choice was deliberate; it was all about making Ellie think she saw her as a fighter, another weapon, not just a liability to be mollycoddled. "You want to know how we're going to take him down, but we're not. He's got a gun. We're not bulletproof."

"But I thought—"

Vicky raised a finger. "I didn't say we weren't going to do anything. We've got to be smart. Smart isn't going to go face-to-face with his gun. Smart is using our heads. He's going to realize I'm missing soon, if he hasn't already, so I've got to go back in there because if I don't he's going to come looking for me, and then he'll find you too. Right now he's got no idea you even exist. Time's the key here. The cops are going to need time, plenty of it. They're out there now, but these things don't happen quickly. Once they're in place one of the first things they are going to do after making contact is take control of the utilities. They'll want to control his environment, so eventually they'll kill the power. The problem is we've got a backup generator. You're going to need to make sure that doesn't kick in."

Ellie nodded again. "I can do that."

"The heavy grade bolts on the exits aren't impenetrable, but they're going make things difficult for the cops. They're magnetically sealed, the magnets linked to the back up generator. By taking out the generator you give the cops a chance of getting in here without the chaos of a frontal assault. He'll have no idea what's about to hit him."

It was a simple plan. Simple was good.

Vicky was about to leave when she remembered her old commanding officer's favorite catch-all bit of wisdom: *Everyone has a plan until the shit hits the fan, then it goes straight out of the window.* That was usually when the first bullet was fired. They'd already had a first bullet fired, so in this instance chaos would kick in with the second shot. Vicky was fervently hoping they wouldn't reach that point, but like it or not plans had to adapt and if she couldn't get word to Ellie it could wind up getting one or both of them killed. "If the circumstances change or I need to get a message to you I'll leave it in the washroom. Second stall, on the back of the door. Don't expect anything, that's worst case. This could drag on. It's smart to have a way to communicate with each other. Likewise, if you need to get word to me, that's how to do it."

"I'll check on the hour," Ellie said.

"Make it every other. Every time you move increases the risk of being discovered. Find somewhere safe, preferably lit, so when the lights go out you'll know it's time to do your thing. Until then, keep your head down. Resist the temptation to creep about. He's not just going to give in because the cops have shown up. They're going to talk. They'll want to put him at his ease before they start negotiating, then get him to surrender; the last thing they want is to have SWAT storm the building. For him, it's going to feel like it's all happening too fast, like he can't control anything. And that means he's going to make mistakes. That's how we're going to get out of this, Ellie. Are you with me?"

Ellie nodded yet again. "Yes."

"When the power goes out, you'll have a couple of seconds grace. Don't screw this up."

28

THEO MONK HAD HAD a recurring dream for the worst part of a decade. He never thought he'd see it come to life in front of him. At most he'd thought he might pick up a copy of the *Tribune* and read a small piece beneath the fold about how the man who had ruined his life had died in some sort of gang-related shoot-out. But here he was, standing over the corpse of Samuel Archer. What the woman, Alice, had said went double for him. The only thing that would have made this moment sweeter was if he'd been the one to pull the trigger.

He'd fantasized about being there watching the life leak out of Archer's eyes, standing over him, telling him why he had to die. Archer knowing who had beaten him, understanding that karmic balance had been restored. Because that was how it always happened, wasn't it? There was a speech. The hero told the villain why he had to die.

Archer's corpse let out a slow gassy fart as the juices settled.

Theo walked back to the window, watching the street. The first responders were getting into place. He could see two radio cars parked at the side of the road, their wheels up on the sidewalk, forming a makeshift barricade. The engine blocks were bulletproof; standard issue nowadays. A third car came down the street, moving fast—no lights, no siren—and whipped around in a tight arc to form the short side of the L butted up against the others. The driver and his passenger were out of the car in a couple of seconds, moving fast to take up a position behind the barrier.

Now they knew there was a potentially active gunman in there, no one risked moving within range of the doors or windows.

One of the officers talked into his radio. Theo couldn't lip-read, but he could take a reasonable guess what the officer was saying, having been on that side of the glass before more than once.

He couldn't see Officer Andy, which meant he still had to be around the back, looking for an alternative way in. The bank wasn't exactly Fort Knox, but it wasn't vulnerable either. The vault and safety-deposit boxes necessitated a certain amount of security. Cutting the power wouldn't isolate the place completely; there was a back up generator that would kick in as soon as the power went out. That would keep minimal functionality going in there. They needed to work out exactly what that entailed before they went blundering in. For now, that, along with the knowledge that there were hostages, was all that was keeping them outside. That would change at some point over the next few hours.

"They're here," he said over his shoulder. The announcement was greeted by silence. He could hear Adam pacing back and forth.

"What do I do?" Adam said. It must have been the fourth or fifth time he'd asked.

He didn't know what to tell Adam, but part of him really wanted to say "thank you." *Thank you for doing what I've always fantasized about doing. Thank you for giving me my life back.* Because that's what it felt like now that the euphoria was beginning to fade and the reality of their circumstances was sinking in.

Adam was wretched, shaking badly. He held his right arm at the elbow as if he could somehow smother the tremors as they twisted his entire right side. It was a futile resistance. All the king's horses and all the king's men weren't going to put Adam together again. There was no happy ending to this story.

"They're going to try to make contact," Theo said. "They're going to want to know what you want."

"Money. That's the only thing I want. Nothing else matters," Adam told him.

"You need to start with something smaller, Adam, something they can do straight away. Going for the big demand makes you too dangerous for them. That's how they think. They're going to ask your name, and when you tell them it they're going to check out your life story, looking for a way in. Social Security, credit history, medical records, you name it. There's nothing they can't get their hands on, given time. Inside the hour they'll have someone reading your Facebook and Twitter feeds and trawling the Internet for every faux pas you ever made. So think, what are you going to say you want?"

"I told you," Adam said. "The money's all that matters."

"Okay, it's nearly lunch time: are you hungry? You should ask for food, it'll take them time to organize it, but it's something they can give you. It establishes a line of communication, but it also says you're not going to be rushed into doing anything you don't want to. That's important, too. They'll want something in return as a show of good faith. They'll want you to release one of us, but that's a big ask." He looked from Adam to Beth, whose hands were clasped together so tightly her fingers had gone white. "I think you should do that, one at a time, maybe twenty minutes apart, draw it out as long as possible. You've got eight of us to bargain with. We're your Kevlar vest at the moment. As long as you have us you've got to gamble that they won't start shooting. No one out there wants another Misty Holt-Singh situation if they can help, but there's only so long they'll allow this to drag on. When the time comes, give them Beth."

"Seven," Adam said.

"What?"

"Seven," Adam repeated. "You said eight, but there are only seven of you."

"Right, yeah," Theo said, thinking fast. "I was including the dead guy in the count. My bad. Seven hostages."

"I don't believe you."

"What?"

"I think you're lying to me."

There were two ways he could answer, pleading understanding or belligerence. He went for belligerence. "That's your prerogative. Doesn't change the theory though. One body more or less won't affect the big picture. They'll look to negotiate you into surrender, then you'll cop armed robbery, wire fraud, and murder all wrapped up in a set of charges you'd need to be immortal to see out. But you still don't get what you want."

A phone rang.

It took him a moment to realize the source of the sound: it was Samuel Archer's cellphone.

"What do I do?" Same words, different question completely.

Theo looked at the dead man.

"Leave it. No good's going to come from answering that call."

29

Samuel Archer didn't pick up.

He didn't like that.

They had an agreement. Archer was, if nothing else, a man of his word. That was an important quality in a man. One that Saul Bonavechio greatly valued. Archer wouldn't break his promise. It was out of character.

But there was no getting around the fact that he wasn't picking up.

Saul dialed again. This time it went straight to voicemail—which meant that Archer wasn't just ignoring his calls, he had turned his phone off.

Saul's clenched his fingers around the handset. He stared at some invisible point way off in the middle distance, then hurled the phone at it in a rage of frustration.

This *couldn't* be happening. Not now. Not with so much at stake.

The delivery had been made—he'd had the call from the guy in the warehouse. Everyone was waiting for Archer, and they were getting itchy.

Saul breathed deeply. Held his breath. Waited. Counted to eleven in his head, imagining with each number another layer of pain he would inflict upon Archer for fucking this up. This deal had been seven months in the making. Seven. Promises had been made. Reputations put on the line. He had left himself exposed here. He never left himself exposed. He was a cautious man. You didn't get to live the life he had without being cautious. It was too easy to fuck up, start thinking you were invulnerable, untouchable. He wasn't like that. He was smart. He thought things through, weighed things out, kept the checks and balances, and was above all, clean. With the eyes of the city watching him, just waiting for him to fuck up, he couldn't afford to be anything else.

But there was always a part of every deal where you were exposed. The trick was to minimize the risk to the point where it was acceptable. That was where Archer came in. He acted as a buffer.

In this case, with several factions who absolutely distrusted—and in one case actively detested—the others, everything was so finely balanced that a single misstep, even the faintest whiff of something off, could bring the whole thing tumbling down.

He didn't lose. That wasn't who he was. He wasn't about to start now.

Archer had assured him he had everything in hand, that he'd be at the warehouse. But he wasn't there; Saul's man had confirmed that colorfully, claiming they were left shittin' in the wind. Despite Archer's assurances, it obviously wasn't in hand.

Saul made a fist and pressed it to his temple, twisting it slowly, first to the left, then to the right until it felt as though the bridge of bone over his eye was about to collapse. When he took his hand away this time there was a single trickle of blood from where a too-long nail had dug deeply into his palm.

He watched it dry before he retrieved the phone and dialed the only number he had committed to memory. The world had changed a lot in a short span of time. Now everything was auto-dialed from contact lists and speed dials, no one remembered numbers. Apart from this one. It wasn't safe for this number to exist outside of Saul's head.

The Dane's number wasn't linked to a landline. It was out there in the ether, routed through countless servers and bounced from satellite to satellite on the way to true anonymity. Saul had always suspected the Dane had a man deep within the phone company covering his traces for vast amounts of cash. Normally they would make contact through a message board hidden deep in the Tor network where people like the Dane could move about in the darkness in relative safety. There were three kinds of site down that rabbit hole: pornography—the really sick stuff that didn't belong in the world above, like snuff and kiddie; crime—trafficking and drugs; and death—sites offering up a menu of services including assassination, for the right price. That was where he'd found the Dane.

As best he could ascertain, the Dane abandoned his fjord in the middle of his Nordic nowhere and relocated to Chicago a decade ago. He wasn't the guy you used to put the frighteners on a mook, he was two stages beyond that when you wanted to bury them. Saul used him two, three times a year tops.

The Dane could be relied upon.

But then, until a few moments ago he'd thought the same of Samuel Archer.

The Dane picked up on the first ring, like he'd been expecting the call. He didn't introduce himself. He didn't need to. Saul was the only person with this number. Other clients had their own dial-in. That was the way the Dane worked.

"Archer has dropped off the radar."

"Not ideal," the Dane said. His accent shone through in those three short syllables.

"I need you to step up. Find him. Deal with this before it becomes a situation. People are getting antsy."

"Do you trust your man?"

"I did."

"Past tense. Noted. Why the change of heart?"

"Circumstance. Something happened last night. A run-in with some muscle from the West Coast, a guy called Milo Rockwell. He assured me it was nothing. That it was handled. Now this."

"I will be in touch."

That was it, done. The Dane wasn't one for wasted words. And, most importantly, he didn't fail. He was that good.

Now he had to wait. He hated waiting almost as much as he hated the idea of losing control.

It took less than five minutes for the Dane to call back.

"Your man is in Glenview, in a branch of Chicago Liberty Bank, has been for a long time. Before that he was at a hospital. But anyone could trace his cellphone. So why me?"

"Who the fuck spends that long in a bank?"

"The staff," the Dane said.

"He doesn't work in a fucking bank," Saul said, perilously close to tipping over the edge. "Don't fuck with me. Sort this out."

"Whatever *this* is," the Dane said. "It will take me an hour to get there."

"Make it half an hour."

"Impossible."

"Make it work. An hour is too long. Half an hour. Not a minute more. Drive fast. Steal a fucking helicopter, I don't care. Think of it as a problem you have to solve."

That was greeted by silence on the other end of the line. He thought for a moment the Dane had killed the call, but then he heard the other man breathing.

"It is not ideal," the Dane said eventually.

"No shit. The whole thing is far from ideal."

"It is what it is," the Dane said.

"I'm not paying you for your philosophies, just deal with it."

This time the Dane did kill the call.

Saul placed the phone very carefully down on his desk, and pushed himself to his feet. He crossed the room to the only window, then braced himself on the sill, looking out over the city that was his and his alone, no matter what the politicos and the businessmen thought. He was the king in the most feudal definition of the word. Those people out there, scurrying about like ants down below, paid tribute to him.

In a warehouse on the waterfront, over five million dollars' worth of handguns, semi-automatics, automatics and ammunition was boxed up ready to hit the streets to the glory of the Second Amendment. All he had to do was close the deal. He had a network of straw men in place to make sure those weapons, untraceable by the time they made it to their final destinations, got to where they needed to be, tripling his investment in the process. Saul wouldn't normally use the Dane for a job like this. It was small fry; not worth his fee to get involved. It bit deeply into the bottom line, but if someone needed to die, no one did that kind of thing better than the Dane.

Unknown to him, one of the samples Archer had filtered out to his army of straw men to test the viability of the operation had ended up in the trembling hands of Adam Shaw, and the bullet inside Samuel Archer came from the very first box of ammo. Saul would have appreciated the irony, had he been aware of it.

All he could think was: *A bank? What the fuck is going on?*

It didn't make any sense.

30

THE DANE HAD LIED when he said it would take him an hour to get across the city. He was less than a dozen blocks away, in a chic little boho café with a jester's motley of stuffed seats and gaudy art in ridiculously heavy gilt frames. He was enjoying a double shot of espresso and a slice of artisanal cheesecake churned from the milk of virgin alpaca or some other inane claim meant to disguise the fact that it was mass-produced shit stuffed full of chemicals and preservatives.

That was just the way it was these days; nothing was straightforward. Chocolate couldn't just be chocolate, it had to be from hand-picked cacao beans, slow roasted over an open fire of imported timber from the deepest darkest rainforest.

He was one to talk. Born in Bremen to Slovakian refugees, he was hardly what he claimed to be. But then, he'd lived through seventy-six passports and identities over his fifty-nine years. It was hard to remember who he *had* been. In

Mogadishu he'd been Reinhardt Metzger, an investment banker. In Bogotá he'd been Kurt DeNardo, a securities trader. In Eritrea, Axel Kiel, an aid worker on a fresh water project. In Stockholm he had been Tomas Janko, an IT consultant who had been behind one of the biggest data breaches in the nation's history, embarrassing Säpo, the Swedish intelligence agency, and leading to publication of photographs of certain royals with gangland figures and prostitutes. Sometimes the job was to kill, sometimes it was simply to humiliate. The money came in just the same. London, three times, three different names, three different background stories spread across three decades: Jeff Sexton, Wilhelm Meikle, and Fredrick Anderson. Sexton had been in personal security in the wake of the Iran–Contra scandal; he'd helped move arms despite the embargo. He'd made a lot of money, enough to set himself up for life. The real payday had come after he'd destroyed a number of classified and damning documents before investigators from the Reagan administration could learn the truth. Of course, he had copies. They were his insurance policy even now, locked away in a safe in Geneva.

Later, as Meikle, he'd claimed to be an investigative journalist and had worked himself into a position of influence during the mid-1990s, close enough to the real powerbrokers to exert the influence his paymaster demanded. Several problems went away that year. Big ones. Ones that should have been plastered all over the tabloids.

As Anderson he had hovered around the art scene at the

turn of the millennium, a well-known face in several galleries for a while. That face hadn't been seen since the loss of several priceless works of art came to light, each replaced by a near-perfect forgery while the rest of the city partied like it was 1999.

Today it felt like every one of those fake lifetimes ago.

He sipped at the espresso while the barista chose some godawful New Age hippy-shit music for atmosphere. He watched her move about behind the counter. She had a good shape, though not the trendy athletic body type. On a scale of one to ten she was a six. She wasn't going to break any mirrors or any hearts. It was a good place to be. The Dane had made his fortune by being a six, by not standing out. But now that he was aging, his hair turning white instead of straw blonde, his close-cropped beard all salt, no pepper, it was becoming increasingly difficult not to stick in people's memories. Everyone noticed and remembered the white hair, but on the verge of his sixtieth birthday few people would look at the Dane and realize just how dangerous he was. He still had the raw physicality of youth, but the crags and fissures where he'd grown into and was now beginning to grow out of his face left them seeing an old man. So they saw him, but they underestimated him. He could live with that.

He took the old Linux-driven ThinkPad out of his messenger bag and powered it up. He preferred Linux to any of the commercial operating systems on the market, not least because Apple, Google and Microsoft filled theirs with a vast array of applications designed to track the user's tastes, preferences and digital footprint. Yes, they claimed to offer anonymous browsing and other security workarounds but he didn't trust any of them to keep their promises.

That Samuel Archer had spent the night in the hospital, suggested to the Dane that something was going down he wanted to know about. He watched through the window, waiting for the inevitable. It took less than ninety seconds for a police cruiser to drive by, fast, no lights, no siren, heading south. He noted down the number.

He liked the old ThinkPad because it came with a SIM-card reader that allowed him to use burner SIMs for Internet access. He broke a brand new SIM out of its blister pack and fitted it into the slot. He took another sip of espresso before opening the terminal and executing a series of shell commands that took him seamlessly into the mobile data terminal of the car that had just passed him. The MDT was hooked into the police national computer and was capable of calling up license details, offender records and incident logs. He scrolled quickly through the logs. He knew exactly what he was looking for: he'd heard a single gunshot a few minutes earlier. It had been faint; almost lost to the distance, but there's no sound like it in the world. Even across ten blocks it was unmistakable if you knew what you were listening to. He'd been close to death several times, delivering it, though twice he'd been the hunted rather than the hunter—in Mogadishu and Bogotá. In Mogadishu he'd woken to the soft rustle of bare feet on the old newspaper he'd laid out on the cold stone floor of the hotel room as a last line of defense. He'd barely had time to hurl himself off the mattress in a tangle of sheets, and rise naked, face-to-face with the man who would have killed him if he hadn't spent a buck on yesterday's news. He punched him in the throat so hard it ruptured something. In Bogotá it had been a car bomb that had left a piece of shrapnel the size of a compact disc buried deep in his side. It had done some serious tissue damage and still ached like a bastard in bad weather. But he was alive, and in his game that was a win.

He found the shorthand description of the calls between Dispatch and One-Adam-Thirteen, Officer Andreas Jaeger: *211S, 1071, confirmed hostages.* He could see that crisis response were already on their way. Three minutes out, headed by a crisis negotiator called Marcus Davenport. They'd follow set procedures, which meant he had plenty of time. He ran a quick search through the root files but couldn't find much on Davenport, suggesting he was a greenhorn. That would add its own layer of difficulty to the job; it was always more challenging to predict the actions of a newbie. Would Davenport go by the book or off message? Would he do anything to save the day? He'd find out soon enough.

Time to move the car.

He killed the connection, exiting the system. He still had about four hours' battery life left, which was more than enough for today's business.

The Dane finished his espresso and left a two-dollar tip on the table. He was halfway out the door when the barista called out. He turned to see her waving her thanks for the tip. He offered her a slight smile and raised a hand.

He was two blocks away by the time the first of the rest of the crisis response cars thundered past, their wheels drumming arrhythmically over the cracks in the concrete. He counted six cars and two larger mobile units—one marked SWAT, the other obviously the command unit—in the convoy.

In the seven minutes it took him to walk the rest of the way to the bank, the hostage negotiation team had secured the area, setting up a double barricade. One man stood apart from the rest, facing the bank's glass doors. He held a phone in his hand, no doubt waiting for word that a direct line into the bank had been secured. The Dane assumed it was Marcus Davenport.

Two uniforms stopped him at the first of the barricades.

The Dane showed them his ID and walked straight through.

31

"WHY ARE YOU HELPING me?"

It was a good question. Theo didn't have a great answer for it, only an honest one.

"Because that man ruined my life," he said. "I used to be a cop. A good one. Well, not a terrible one. An honest one. Which in this cesspit of a city is a pretty shit thing to be. I'd been working a case, forty-seven people dead in a fire in an apartment block. They blamed it on faulty wiring but something about it stank. The more I dug, the more it reeked. There was a construction company buying up then demolishing old projects, and selling the lots to developers. The residents who didn't accept the shitty deal for selling up were threatened. I knew what was going on, I just couldn't prove it.

"This city is corrupt, you just have to accept that. It always has been. Mob money. Bastards like Saul Bonavechio—the guy that asshole Archer worked for—have friends everywhere. They're untouchable. They find your weakness and they get dirt on you, then they own you. That's how they got my partner. He stitched me up. Planted money to make sure I took the fall. Like the lady said, Samuel Archer was a bastard. No one is going to cry over his death. That's why I'm helping you."

"Two wrongs don't make a right," Beth said disapprovingly.

"Which is why I said he should let you go first. Bank robberies depend on timing. In and out inside two minutes is best. If you're still inside the bank five minutes after that, you're fucked. This is only ending one way. That's the way they're thinking out there." He shrugged.

"It doesn't have to," said Alice, the woman who'd come in with Archer. She turned to Adam. "You're not alone," she said. "Like I said, today you're my hero. Samuel Archer ruined my life. He made his money off girls like me. You saved my life."

No one said anything for the longest time. Theo looked at her bruises and understood. There was only the ever-present hum of the air conditioning working in the background. There was a slight click to it every few seconds, like something was catching inside the mechanism.

"I'm sorry," Theo said eventually.

"Don't be. Today is better than Christmas as far as I'm concerned," Alice said. "You'd agree with that, wouldn't you?" She turned to Richard, "I mean, it must be a massive relief that he's gone. knowing he can't make you do what he wanted you to do."

The manager looked like he wanted to be anywhere other than here. He shuffled around in front of the seats. There was a guilty man if ever he'd seen one.

"I'm not unhappy with how things have worked out," Richard said, finally. Beth and Margot were obviously shocked by his admission, but not Sasha. She didn't look the least bit surprised by the revelation, Theo realized, which was interesting. But then, she'd been sniffing around Richard since the staff meeting that morning trying to work out what he was hiding. *She's got good instincts*, he thought. *She's wasted in this place.*

"What did he have on you?" Theo asked.

Richard rubbed at his mouth, then pinched the bridge of his nose, both actions too hard and a little too long. He was obviously gathering himself, deciding how much he was willing to admit. So, whatever he said, Theo figured you multiplied that by a factor of two. The weasels of the world had a habit of trying to make themselves look better than they really were.

"I was stupid," Richard said. He slumped. "Like you said, I met him in a casino. I was using a false name. That was all. He beat the crap out of me. I thought this," he touched his face, "was going to be the worst of it, but then he called me at home in the middle of the night. I don't know how he got my number. He told me what he was going to do to me if I didn't do exactly what he wanted—set up a fake account and clear a big transaction into it. Five point three million. There are laws about this stuff, we have to report big cash movements, but he wanted it to go through without being flagged. It doesn't sound like much, but it was worth millions, and it's wire fraud."

"So you were supposed to become his personal banker?" Theo mused. Money laundering. Mob money. He knew the kinds of sums they were talking about if Saul Bonavechio was involved—a not so small fortune. There was big money in cleaning cash. A dirty million became a clean three hundred grand. There were costs, cuts, percentages, and no doubt Archer would have skimmed his own cut off the top.

Theo turned to Adam, who right now was looking like the most innocent man in the room. "So, there, you see, three people in here have every reason to help you get out of this mess."

"Four," Sasha spoke up. He couldn't read her face. "If Richard will tell us the truth, all of it, because he's still hiding something."

"I'm not," Richard said, shaking his head. "Why would I?"

"Why did you lie before?"

"Isn't it obvious?"

"Not even remotely."

"Because he was blackmailing me."

"You know, I absolutely believe that, but is you being a dick at a casino enough dirt to get you to risk everything—including federal prison—to cover up? I don't think it is. Not even close. There's something else here. What did that man have on you?"

Richard drew in a deep, beaten, breath. "You know the truth."

"Do we?"

He looked at all of them in turn.

"Yes. But there's something else. I've been helping people." No explanation of what he meant. "Why do *you* want to help him?" Richard asked Sasha, his eyes widening. "Do you know Adam from outside? Isn't there normally an inside man on a bank job? That's how it works isn't it? That's why you want to help him. Jesus, I'm such an idiot, I didn't see it."

"Don't try and turn this back on me, *Rickie*," Sasha said. "Or should I call you Milo? I'm not the one who pretended to be some big swinging dick in a casino last night. For your information, I feel sorry for Adam." She said it as if it were the most obvious thing in the world. "I believe you," she said to Adam. "What you said about your son, about your illness. And whatever Beth says, in this case I think two wrongs might just make one right. Helping you is the Christian thing to do. So I'm in. But I don't know what I can do."

"Thank you," Adam said.

"Margot? Beth?" Theo asked.

"You know how I feel, Mr. Monk," Beth told him. "We're talking about murder. Robbery. I can't just turn a blind eye because he has a child. He should have thought about that before he walked in here with a gun. He has to be prepared to face the consequences."

"It wasn't murder," Theo argued. "Look at him. No jury in the land would convict this guy of murder. He's a physical wreck."

"He pulled the trigger," she argued.

"But he didn't. Pulling the trigger is a conscious act, an impulse goes from the brain to the finger telling it to squeeze. That didn't happen."

"Semantics."

"Look at him."

Adam held his right arm at the elbow with his left hand, trying to minimize the tremors. It looked like he was wrestling with a sack of eels. It wasn't just a finger twitch now. Theo figured the man needed his meds.

"Look at him," Theo insisted. "You're a good Christian woman, Beth. I know you. You buy bags of the day's unsold bread from the café across the street to give to the homeless. You care about people. Be compassionate. Leave the judgment for others."

Alice crossed the floor and knelt before the woman, cupping her hands around Beth's as though joining her in prayer. Theo watched as she looked up at the woman, the eye contact unflinching. "You said yourself, two wrongs don't make a right."

"Exactly, exactly that," Beth said, nodding her understanding.

"But," Alice went on smoothly, "when you see someone in distress, someone who can't help themselves, isn't it your Christian duty to try to help them?"

"He killed that man," Beth insisted.

"Yes he did. It was his gun. He put the bullet in the gun. But there was no malice. It wasn't planned. It was an accident."

"That doesn't change anything."

"Yes it does," Alice said, softly. "It changes everything. He doesn't deserve what's going to happen to him. And his boy, he's only got so many days left with his father." Her grip tightened around Beth's hands. "Would you deny his son those last days with him for the sake of a monster like Samuel Archer? Believe me, he was not a good man. He is not worth your prayers. There's only one place he's going."

"That doesn't change anything," Beth repeated. She looked down at her hands cupped in Alice's. It was the most intimate of gestures, and Theo thought he could see the cracks appearing in Beth's certainty. It wasn't just black and white, right and wrong, good men saved and bad men going to jail. Up was down and she was struggling to maintain the rigid path of righteousness in the face of it.

"Margot?" Theo asked, looking for another ally. "That only leaves you. Do you want to see him spend his last days locked up or with his son?"

"That's an emotionally fucked-up way of asking the question," a voice said from behind them. "I almost hate to crash the party but whatever she says, you're going to jail."

32

ADAM POINTED THE GUN at her.

If he pulled the trigger—deliberately or accidentally—there was a better than even chance he'd take out the computer beside her.

"I wouldn't shoot," Vicky said calmly. She looked different. Harder. There was no hint of the earlier fear that had made her piss herself. Either she'd done an amazing job of pulling herself together or he'd been played. A gambler would have bet the house on option two. "It's not like you get a two-for-one bonus or anything."

"Shut up. Just shut up." Adam tried to think. He'd lost track of the number of times he'd said the same thing. The words rolled constantly around inside his head. *Shut up shut up shut up* on a continuous loop.

"Take a look around you, you're screwed. Why don't you just put your hands up, march outside and hope they don't shoot?"

"Not helpful, Vicky," Sasha said.

"I wasn't aware we were supposed to help people rob a bank and get away with murder, Sash. Call me old-fashioned but I'm pretty sure that breaks at least a couple of commandments. Beth?"

"You don't have to be a complete bitch about it, Vicky."

"I really do. You all seem to have become pod people. This whole thing you've got going on in here is just fucking weird."

The entire exchange washed over Adam, the words like bees buzzing around inside his head. They stopped making sense. Then his hand was rock steady for the first time since he'd walked through the front door.

"Do you want to know a secret?" he asked Vicky, his voice low, almost conspiratorial. "I don't give a flying fuck. That's God's honest truth. I'm so far beyond caring it isn't funny. So, yeah, I'm going to jail. But I'm also going to die. Not in some distant unknowable future—we're talking about months, not years. So honestly your threat rings pretty hollow. How do you scare a man who has already lost everything?"

She looked at the gun in his hand, then at him, seeming to see the mess he was in for the first time. "Shit, you really don't look good." That wasn't sympathy in her eyes. It was too calculating. She was trying to work out if she could get the gun out of his hand before he pulled the trigger. This definitely wasn't the same woman who'd pissed herself.

But he'd been telling the truth, or at least a version of it. On one level it didn't matter anymore. Let her take the gun. Let her pull the fucking trigger for that matter.

The problem was that just because he didn't care what happened to him didn't mean he was ready to go, no matter what he'd said. He couldn't remember where he'd first come across the concept of a last good day, but the idea had resonated with him. Every day he did something with Jake, even something simple, was a good day, but there would come a day when these simple pleasures were denied him. There would be a last good day. On one level he didn't care what happened to him, but he so desperately wanted to live right up until that last good day.

"Shut up," he said again, but this time he walked towards the woman. The gun pointed the way, unwavering. He kept walking right up until the barrel pressed deep into her belly, and even then he kept walking, just an extra step to push her back.

She stumbled into the flimsy room divider and went sprawling.

Without taking his eyes off her, Adam said, "I need something to tie her up with. I don't care what. Just give me something."

For a moment there was silence. He'd reminded them all there was no romanticism to what was happening around them. He'd stopped being some tortured hero. There was a threat implicit in his presence, reinforced by the gun, but only made real by that shove.

"Will pantyhose work?" Sasha asked, breaking the silence.

Before he could decide if it would or not, Margot had her own suggestion. “No. Use the cat stranglers we use to secure the money pouches. They’re in the bottom draw of my desk.”

“Get them,” Adam said.

A few seconds later Margot pressed a handful of plastic ties into his free hand. There was complicity in both the suggestion and the gesture. There was a world of difference in trying to stop Archer bleeding to death and helping bind up one of your fellow hostages. She was willingly making herself an accomplice. Did she know that? Or was she just trying to diffuse the tension so they could all get out of the bank sooner rather than later? Being tied up was better than winding up dead.

“Get up,” he told Vicky.

She did as she was told. She was moving with less confidence now, clearly doing nothing to make him nervous or risk angering him. “Get a chair from over there,” Adam told her, nodding towards one of the uncomfortable metal-framed seats that customers were made to sit in after they were summoned from the comfy chairs to face the bankers. That was another part of the psychology of the bank: offer comfort while you wait then take it away as you prostrate yourself before the staff.

She moved the chair to the middle of the floor and sat. He walked around behind her, taking her right hand and pulling it back hard, pressing it against the metal frame and binding it so tightly the plastic tie sliced into her wrist. The way the ties worked, the more she struggled the worse it would get for her. She didn't fight it.

Adam used a second tie to bind her left hand to the other side of the metal frame, then stood up. For the first time in hours he felt like he was in control of something—which was the greatest illusion of all because he was in free fall.

"She can still cause problems," Theo said, behind him. The security guard had one of his socks in his hand and a roll of electrical tape in the other.

He didn't wait for Adam's approval.

He forced the woman's mouth open with his fingers and stuffed the sweaty sock in so deep she gagged. Before she could spit it out Theo tore off a strip of tape and slapped it across her mouth.

She stared up at him with pure unbridled hate in her eyes.

"Better," Theo said. "No offense, Vicky, but you need to cool down. We're all in this together. We need you on our side, not fighting us. One for all, or we all go to prison. And I don't know about anyone else, but I've got no intention of wasting away inside. So take a minute, gather yourself. Let me know when you're ready to be a team player." He offered Adam a crooked smile. "Okay, now where were we? That's right, we were working out a way to get away with murder." Adam winced at that, but it wasn't wrong. "I've got some questions for you, because we're going to need to think this stuff through."

"Okay," Adam said.

"How many times did you come here to stake out the place?"

"Twice. Why?"

"Because when the police scrub back through the footage on the security tapes, which goes back months, they're going to notice you. Today and twice more to be precise. And I'm willing to bet you didn't just take a number and wait over in the seats, did you? You wandered around because you were looking for things like cameras, right?" Adam nodded. "That's suspicious behavior. Normal customers don't do that. It means we're going to need to doctor more than just today's footage if we're going to make you disappear. You're all over the security system. It's going to take some doing but three times isn't an impossible fix."

Adam looked up at the camera in the corner. It would be the death of him, he thought, and almost lost it. The urge to giggle rose up uncontrollably. It was such an absurd thing to think, but it wasn't wrong.

"I know someone," Margot said.

For a moment he thought she was talking to herself. She'd been so quiet for the last few minutes. "A friend. He can do anything with computers."

"Are you sure?" Theo asked.

She nodded. "I've seen what he can do. He found me when I was at my lowest. When I thought I was done with living. I was wrong and he was there to make sure I knew it." It took Adam a moment to realize she was confessing to a suicide attempt. She didn't look the type, Adam thought, realizing just how ridiculous a notion that was even as the thought took shape. Who did?

"Okay that's good. That's something," Theo said, ignoring the revelation. "And we're going to have to do something about that—" he nodded at the corpse "—not just the body, the stains on the carpet have to go, too. That's going to take time. Even if we've got the stuff we need in the janitor's cupboard it's going to take work to get the carpet clean and then time to dry out."

"The one thing we've got is time," Sasha said. "They're not going to come storming in if there's a chance of a peaceful solution."

"True," Theo said. "So when they call, you need to give them something. Let them know you're open to negotiation. It doesn't have to end in violence."

"Like what?"

"I don't know. You'll have to improvise."

"I don't like the sound of that."

"I have an idea," Richard said.

Theo inclined his head, inviting the bank manager to talk.

"Okay, we're surrounded. No way in, no way out?"

"Pointing out the obvious isn't helping," Theo said.

"It is, if you think about it. There's one place they won't look. It won't even cross their minds because it's the *safest* place in the building."

"The vault," Sasha said.

Richard nodded. "We put the body in the vault, seal it up, then get it out of here when everything's blown over. There's a thirty-minute time delay on the lock, meaning we've got to set the process in motion before we can open the door. Given the fact it'll take a lot longer than that for us to clean up the blood I don't think that's a problem."

"That might work," Theo agreed, nodding. "It's flimsy, but if we can sell it to the cops that Archer was the robber and Adam's just another hostage. But we'd have to make it look like Archer escaped."

"Which is easier said than done. Look out of the windows. Any one of them, the view's the same. The building is surrounded."

Richard rubbed at his jaw. "Right, yeah. Okay... what if we fire another shot, and when they storm the place they find Archer's body and we tell them we overpowered him? The gun went off accidentally. It's not so far from the truth."

"That might work," Adam said.

Theo contradicted him. "No. For one thing, by the time we're out of here the body lividity won't match the supposed time of death; the blood's already beginning to settle around his back where he's been lying. That would tie in with the first shot. That inconsistency is going to start people asking questions. If they start digging around too much, we're fucked."

"Not *we*," Beth said, quietly, still not looking up. "Him. Just him. He's fucked. We go home."

Theo ignored her. "Okay, okay, we've got to face facts,

someone heard the actual shot that killed him. So let's assume they already know to look for one bullet—the one lodged in that bastard's body."

"Are you suggesting we go digging around inside him looking for it?" Richard asked. He sounded sickened.

"Fuck, no. The thing is, none of this works if one thing is wrong. We've got to get this absolutely right."

"We could come up with the most incredible plan to get out of this mess," Richard said, finishing the thought, "but one wrong word from someone in this room and we're fucked."

"Not *we*," Beth said again, making her position abundantly clear.

33

"YES, 'WE.'" SASHA CONTRADICTED Beth sharply. As the stress levels went up her willingness to humor Beth's acts of piety went way down. "We're all in this together. We have to be. It's the only way this works. If you want to unburden yourself later, find a priest. I'm sure he'll be only too happy to cleanse your soul with a few Hail Marys and maybe a healthy donation to the church." Before Beth could object, Sasha said, "Pass me his wallet," to Alice.

The woman had no problem rifling through the dead man's pockets. She found his wallet and tossed it to Sasha. Crossing the lobby, Sasha flicked through it, finding Samuel Archer's driver's license and another one in the name of "Victor LaSalle"—the photograph for that one was unmistakably that of Samuel Archer.

Sasha'd been wondering about his presence here for a while. She had questions of course, and Richard's confession only served to spark more questions and bigger doubts. There was still something he wasn't saying. She didn't trust the guy, but she had to put that aside for the moment. Right now he'd offered up the best suggestion so far, using the vault to hide the body or the bank robber, or both. She rattled off a quick search on the terminal in front of her, putting Archer's given name into the system: Samuel Jefferson Archer. Aside from his savings and checking account, fifteen other accounts came up where he was listed as signatory. The majority were linked to construction and other enterprises, one to the casino, and several other legit businesses around the city. There were some pretty hefty numbers in some of the accounts. It was the kind of money that made her head swim. If what Theo had said was true, they would probably all lead back one way or another to Saul Bonavechio.

She stopped at a Cympac Holdings account. The balance was zero—unusual against the rest of the accounts. She soon spotted the reason for the balance: a 5.3-million-dollar payment was in escrow pending clearance to the destination account.

She called up the transaction history. There were regular—weekly, sometimes bi-weekly—deposits being made into several accounts, including River North Project, South Loop Project and Magnificent Mile Project—all areas of the city undergoing rapid urban development. These were pies Saul Bonavechio had his sticky fingers in. It was almost impossible to follow all of the money, but she did notice payments from each to the same offshore account. Each one was a dollar or two below the ten-thousand-dollar reporting threshold, meaning they wouldn't come up on the IRS's radar and were unlikely to ping with Homeland Security or any other agency looking for suspicious activity. Of course, that kind of activity was exactly what they should have been looking for. In banking terms it was called structuring and was a crime. Alone those just-sub-ten-thousand-dollar transfers weren't significant enough to warrant attention, but together they represented substantial amounts of money flowing overseas. Sasha looked again at the Cympac account with its entire balance reserved against a pending transaction. Of course there was no obvious way of knowing who had instigated all of the overseas deposits, and if they were genuinely involved in money laundering or just theft, but the numbers didn't add up to her trained eye.

"You should see this," she called to Theo. The ex-cop was more naturally in control of the room than Adam. He was the one thinking on his feet. Adam came over with him. The pair of them looked at the numbers on the screen, but it was Adam who grasped the significance of the transfers into the offshore account quickest.

"He was stealing from Bonavechio. All those micro transactions, moving money just under the reporting threshold, funds going from one construction project to fill the holes in other projects where he's been skimming off the top..."

"It's what he did back when he stitched me up," Theo said. "Only back then it was small potatoes; he was subbing out materials for cheaper alternatives and pocketing the change."

She ran a second search, this one totaling the value of the transactions from the various project accounts into the offshore one. The search string returned a flood of transactions dating back over a decade. Just south of eighteen million dollars had flowed out of the accounts and ended up washing ashore on some island tax haven. The numbers stopped making sense. She thought about what Adam was going through and it just made her all the more determined to help him in any way she could.

"That's a lot of money," Theo said, looking at the grand total. "Pity it's lost to the world. It could have done some good."

That was hard to argue with. Eighteen million bucks could have changed a lot of lives.

"I wonder what Bonavechio would say if he saw those numbers?" Sasha said, and without even thinking about what she was doing printed off the transaction history. A soft hum preceded the whisper of paper feeding through the printer as it produced what would have been damning evidence if the man hadn't already been dead.

"Unless he was *asking* Archer to move the money for him," Adam suggested. He turned to Richard. "You said he was leaning on you to move a substantial amount of money without reporting it?"

Richard nodded. "But not offshore. And not to his checking account. I told you he'd asked me to set up a brand new account for him."

"It's not showing in the system," Sasha said.

"It wouldn't. It's not under his name. The account holder is Milo Rockwell. It's the account he asked me to set up."

Sasha ran another search. There was a single account registered to one Milo Rockwell. The current balance showed as zero, but there was a 5.3-million-dollar deposit in escrow pending from the Cympac Holdings account. "What the fuck are you mixed up in, Richard?" she said, looking up from the screen. She wasn't angry. She wasn't even all that shocked.

"I don't know," he admitted. She knew when he was lying; he had a tell. He averted his eyes, just a flicker, as though by breaking eye contact could save him from the blush and immediate grin that followed being found out.

"You're going to have to tell the truth sooner or later, you realize that, right?"

"I am. I swear I am. He just wanted me to move some money. He didn't want the IRS digging around in his business."

"Saul Bonavechio's business," Alice said from across the room. "Anything Archer did, it was with Bonavechio's blessing. Always. Even his own Best Little Whorehouse in Illinois. The old man knew about it all. It's the only way it could work. Archer liked to think he was the devil's right hand, but really he was just Bonavechio's bitch."

Moving some money gave Sasha an idea.

It was a seriously stupid idea, but more often than not they were her favorite sort, hence the fifty notches on the bedpost and counting.

The cash in Archer's named accounts was quite literally at

her fingertips but anything coming out of the account would have raised a huge red flag for the cops when they ran the dead guy's financials. But it was a safe bet that there was nothing to tie Victor LaSalle to Samuel Archer. Hence the second license; it was a clean ID. She ran a search on the name.

"Holy shit," she said. "Well, that changes things."

"What does?" Theo asked.

"Samuel Archer has banked some serious money, or rather Victor LaSalle has. And I mean *serious*."

She ran the numbers as she explained to the others about the second ID. Samuel Archer was dead and Victor LaSalle didn't exist. There was three million and change in Victor's account with no one to miss it. The cops would be all over Archer's accounts, including the ones he was a signatory on, but as long as she never turned over the fake ID there was every chance they'd have no idea about his alter ego, assuming Archer had firewalled the identity. That made Victor the answer to Adam's prayers. His way out of there with the money he needed, and even better, there was no need to move the money. "I need your address," she said to Adam, who looked confused but told her. Sasha altered Victor LaSalle's address to match, and triggered a request for a new ATM card and transaction book with withdrawal and paying-in slips to be sent "home." She also requested a new PIN which would give Adam full access to the account. She told him what she'd done. "The money you need is in there. You should have the card by the end of the week."

"I don't…" he said, and lapsing into silence.

"It's not like he's going to need it where he's gone," Sasha said, pushing the fake driver's license towards him. "Take it."

All Chicago Liberty employees had checking accounts with the bank. There were six of them in the lobby, meaning there'd be close to eighty-five grand apiece left after Adam had his two and a half million, give or take a dollar or cent. That was life-changing money. It was also complicity. A huge deposit like that, unreported, would tie them all together in this. No one would believe they weren't all involved to some degree or other.

She started by transferring the money from Victor LaSalle's account into theirs. Eighty-five thousand dollars at a time, Beth first. It took her less than five minutes to move all the money. Every aspect of it was routine, the same keystrokes she'd repeated a thousand times a day, apart from one: the fact that the money was going into the accounts of people she considered friends.

The others were arguing about what to do next, focusing on the vault and the fact that the cops were going to want concessions and how they could stop Beth fucking them over. She ignored them and concentrated on the numbers until there was only Alice's and her own slice of the pie left when she realized that she'd forgotten Ellie Mason in her calculations.

She pulled up Ellie's account details, looking at the transaction history. There were a number of payments to the Elias Barker Detective Agency. There was also a balance that, until a few moments ago, would have made her head hurt. Ellie was the one person here—alive and kicking—who absolutely didn't need a day job.

"Richard?" she called him over. On a scrap of paper she scribbled two words: *Where's Ellie?*

If Ellie was still in the bank she was a liability that threatened to unmask their lies before they'd even begun trying to sell them.

"I told Ellie to sit tight." Richard looked at Adam and shrugged a half-hearted sorry as Vicky snorted. It was the only sound she could make around the makeshift ball gag. "You were right, I lied to you about the numbers. You were the bad guy then."

"I'll find her," Margot said.

"Do that. Fast. Before she screws everything up," Theo said.

Sasha looked back at her screen, but didn't transfer a cut into Ellie's account. It would have ruined her numbers, and left Adam short. Worse, if anyone did look closely at their accounts the fact that Ellie was loaded would make it obvious they'd just been paid off. She didn't know how she was going to explain to everyone what she'd just done.

Honesty was the best policy. Pretty much the opposite of the Richard Rhodes school of management.

Sasha took a minute to print out the transaction history of the accounts she'd manipulated, then collected the sheets from the paper tray. She walked through the lobby, going from person to person, handing out their statements without explanation.

When she put Richard's into his hands, he stared at it with a frown. "What's this?"

"What does it look like?"

"It looks like I won the lottery," Richard said.

"Close enough. Samuel Archer, well, Victor LaSalle, was feeling generous."

That was when the others started to realize that they'd just robbed the dead man.

"I didn't know where to put your share," she told Alice. "It's still there. I'll open an account here for you. You'll need to give me an address to send the ATM card, but I needed you to know we're all in this together. The numbers don't lie."

"You can use my mother's address at the care home," Alice said.

34

YEARS AGO, HOSTAGE NEGOTIATION teams had served a single purpose—and it wasn't to resolve a crisis. It was to provide a distraction so that SWAT could get into position. They were like stage magicians pulling back the black cuffs on their suits to reveal the crisp white of the shirt beneath with a flourish. "Look, there's nothing up our sleeve." Only in this case the "nothing" was Special Weapons and Tactics. They resolved the crisis, their ordnance doing the talking for them. But the understanding of human behavior had changed; in modern-day hostage situations, the emphasis was on preventing a situation from developing into a crisis. It was all predicated on establishing good lines of communication, building trust and a rapport before, ultimately, talking the subject down from the edge.

Marcus Davenport knew the hostage negotiator's behavioral change stairway model inside out—he knew about active listening, empathy, rapport building; he knew that bringing his influence to bear on the small things like sending in food and listening to a guy rant about wanting a helicopter could lead to a bloodless surrender. And he knew that he could just as easily push a desperate man into doing something irreversible. What he couldn't tell the guy on the other end of the phone was that this was the first time he'd danced this particular dance. He'd spent six years studying a range of psychologies, how different narcotics screwed with thought processes, suicide intervention, de-escalation and how the best outcome, always, was nothing happening. It wasn't just about listening to the words; it was about listening to the emotion behind them. If the subject sounded frustrated, the trick was for Marcus to acknowledge it, say, "You sound frustrated," and ask them why. Everyone wants their side heard. No one is the villain in their own story. It was about mirroring their word choices, using emotion labeling. Lots of "I" statements, but minimal encouragers. Marcus had one job, to work towards safe ground and an agreement, and he couldn't rush it.

One wrong word could undo all the good work. There was no script because the man on the other side of those glass doors had no script. Beyond mistrust, it would be a struggle for dominance, the only thing between them a phone line. A lone gunman locked inside a bank with hostages was far from ideal. He didn't know the gunman's state of mind. Was he an addict? Was he ex-military? Suffering with some sort of posttraumatic stress disorder or other mental illness? What had made him desperate enough to lock himself inside a building with those hostages?

Marcus looked down the line of officers securing the inner perimeter. Every single one of the arrest team was on edge. The tension in their bodies was palpable. He looked up at the sky: clear blue, a beautiful summer's day. It was his job as crisis negotiator to make sure it didn't turn to shit. A bank of SWAT gathered behind the mobile command center that had rolled in a couple of minutes ago and was already up and running. They were getting their own instructions from the field commander, no doubt being told they needed to be ready to move fast; if things went south it was their job to pick up the pieces. On scene, Command's first task was always the same—secure the phone lines. No calls going in, no calls going out. It was vital to starve the subject of access to the outside world. Ideally they'd take down the utilities too. The subject wouldn't be calling family or friends, attorneys, or the press. Marcus and his team couldn't allow it to turn into a circus. It would be bad enough when the journalists arrived, which they would. Equally important though was to ensure that no one was dialing in to share intel on the police maneuvers outside. Command could also block cell reception in the vicinity, effectively turning the neighborhood into a dead zone. The next step was to assign a new number to one of the landlines inside the bank to serve as a direct line between the crisis unit and the subject.

Marcus got the okay from the officer on the steps of Command.

He dialed in to the bank.

He could hear the echo of the ringer loud in his ear. It rang and rang. "Come on, come on, pick up," he urged, all eyes on him.

It was all about first contact. That set the tone. Fuck this up, and someone was going home in a body bag.

The phone stopped ringing.

There was a moment of silence, no longer than that between heartbeats, and then he heard breathing.

"My name is Marcus Davenport," he said. "I'm here to make sure we find a way out of this peacefully. I'll need you to help me with that. How about we start with you telling me your name? How's that sound?"

"Samuel," said the voice at the other end of the line after a moment's hesitation, like the speaker was trying out the sound of it for the first time.

35

"SAMUEL," THEO SAID.

He nodded a couple of times, but didn't say anything else for a full twenty seconds, letting the man on the other end of the line talk. "I understand. Everyone's fine."

He stood away from the window, in the lobby's dark interior, out of sight of prying eyes. It was as good as a Kevlar vest. No one would risk shooting where they couldn't see. In less than thirty minutes it would be different, though; they'd have infrared optics in place, showing them exactly where people were inside the building. He'd cross that particularly rickety bridge when he came to it.

"I don't know if you can, Marcus." He used the negotiator's first name, knowing that the man was looking for signs of connection. He'd done all the same training courses. "That we have. But sometimes, everything isn't what it seems." He threw that out there, letting the guy ponder it for a moment.

"Well, let's just say that it's too easy to judge things on face value. You're talking to me, and you are thinking to yourself, *I've got to talk this guy out of what he's doing and convince him that he isn't going to jail*, when we both know there's no way out of this for me. It's just how it is."

He watched as Alice moved to sit beside Beth. It looked like a gesture of support, but in reality he knew she was making sure the other woman didn't betray them. "I don't believe you, Marcus. I want to, though. So that's something I suppose," he said. "So, tell me, how do you intend to help me?"

Beside Alice, Vicky didn't move. Her arms were pulled tight behind her back, the ties binding her to the swivel chair. She stared daggers at him, but with a dirty sock stuffed in her mouth, that was the limit of her interference. For now. They'd have to deal with her later. But that was a problem for the other side of this mess.

"I want a helicopter," he said. "I want guaranteed safe passage, a flight path cleared from here to a non-extradition country, and hell, throw in a hot night with the Bears' cheer squad. That ought to do it. Let's open negotiations, I'm flexible on a couple of my terms."

Unsurprisingly, the guy blew him off, but that was what he'd expected. What he'd wanted, actually. If Marcus had made any of those big promises all that would have proved was that he was full of shit. Theo couldn't work with that. He needed a straight man to play off. Someone predictable. "Let me ask." He covered the mouthpiece with his hand. "They want to know if we're hungry? I don't know about you, but I could eat."

A couple of the others nodded, but most of them looked as though food was the last thing on their minds. He took that as a majority decision and said, "Sure, we could go for pizza. Keep it simple, just cheese. Then we can talk properly, after we've all got full bellies. Hungry people make bad decisions."

The other man was on a fishing expedition. That was good. It meant they weren't looking to storm the place with SWAT yet. But they would come in eventually. They wouldn't let this drag on into some protracted siege; Marcus and Theo alike were buying time for their own side to come up with a plan.

"Samuel Archer," he told Marcus. "You've got people out there who can look me up; they'll tell you everything you need to know about me. I don't have a lot of secrets."

36

"All right, Samuel," Marcus Davenport said. "I work for Chicago PD, but I'm not a cop. I'm what we call a crisis negotiator. I don't like the word 'crisis,' though; I like to think of myself as a facilitator. I'm here to help you the best I can. I'm like a John in a massage parlor, all about the happy ending." No laugh. Not so much as a chuckle or the sharp intake of breath that might have been a snort. "Tough crowd."

It was easy to take the silence as an affirmative, but he needed to make Samuel talk to him.

He had a few simple yes/nos to help that along. "How are you feeling in there, Samuel?" Repeating the name was the smart move. "Tell me something, okay? Talk to me. Is everyone okay?" It was a better way of asking if anyone was hurt, especially as they'd had a report of gunshots fired. Gunshot, singular. He didn't want to mention that yet. Those kinds of questions backed the guy in there into a corner, and a man in a corner was more likely to lash out. "That's good. That's really good to hear, Samuel. Do you know why it's good? Because that means I *can* help you."

Marcus turned his back on the bank's row of glass doors, looking down the block, first towards Glenview and the boho cafés and little ma and pa stores, then the other way, to the glitter of the skyscraper skyline to the south. Two different worlds. He needed to establish quickly which one Samuel fit into.

Everyone was on edge. He could see the techs from Command working away feverishly through the half-open door of the mobile unit. Their screens were lit up like the Fourth of July in there, but from where he was it was all just pretty splashes of color.

The SWAT captain came towards him, pulling a Kevlar vest over his head. He had a spare one in his right hand, which he held out for Marcus to take.

He watched an imposing figure move across his line of sight; a comfortable six foot plus, two-twenty or more, with close-cropped white hair and a neat beard trimmed down to an eighth of an inch, and the deep worn lines of a life hard lived in the leathery skin. Some men carried age as if it really was nothing more than a number. It was obvious he was one of that breed. And there was a hardness about him; Marcus had seen men like him before. They all had one thing in common: they had done things people like him, normal people, never would. Under the white beard his features had a Slavic sharpness.

Marcus didn't recognize the man, but he had seen him show his ID before ducking under the police tape and moving into the hot zone unchallenged, meaning he had to be someone.

Cops talked about instincts a lot, about gut feelings and trusting them being the difference when it came to life and death situations. During their careers they amassed a wealth of circumstantial data, every eventuality of passion, fear, cold cunning and forethought played out before them. They might not remember it but it was all buried down in their minds, waiting for instinct to tap. He truly believed that nothing was ever forgotten. He didn't have the same lifetime in law enforcement to draw on as some of those men, and his gut wasn't exactly screaming that this guy was wrong, but there was definitely something *off* about him.

Maybe it was just the way he walked through the scene as if he owned it?

Marcus assumed he was something to do with the armed response officers, but their captain made no move to interact with him. They were the last resort. The nuclear option.

The man made eye contact. Marcus nodded, just a slight incline of the head, not offering any deference.

He didn't like him on sight.

"We've got ourselves into a bit of a situation here, haven't we? Okay you've got my attention, Samuel. Uh hunh. What do you mean by that?" He listened for a moment before contradicting the man on the other end of the line. "I'm not thinking that. I promise you. I know it's tempting to believe

I'm your enemy here, Samuel, that my sole purpose in this is to bring you in. But it isn't. I want to help everyone. My win here is everyone going home to their families tonight to enjoy a nice evening meal so they can piss and moan at the game later."

Samuel had his shit together. He wasn't a wreck. The appearance of the police outside hadn't thrown him. Or if it had he was recovering quickly. That made him interesting. Your average Joe didn't do that. On the back foot they started retreating or they got mad. But here was Samuel, offering him a third choice. "How can I help you? Normally it's me asking that question, Samuel, but sure, I guess we can start with you telling me what you're hoping to achieve here because we're way past the point of you walking away with a stack of bills. So what do you want? How can I make it happen?"

He laughed at the answer. He couldn't help himself. The guy had a sense of humor.

He'd asked for three impossible things. He was testing Marcus to see if he would promise any of them. If he did it was all over.

"I can't do that, my friend. As much as I'd love to sanction you getting jiggy with it, technically that's prostitution so I can't see the boss going for it. Sorry. And let's be brutally honest, there's not a prayer of a helicopter or an island getaway. That's movie stuff. And as good-looking as I'm sure you are, I doubt you're George Clooney and I'm certainly not Tom Cruise, so let's keep things in the realm of possibility.

You must be hungry? How about we start with something simple like pizza? That I *can* do."

He caught himself nodding as he watched the white-haired man move right up close to the barrier, then walk slowly along its length, never taking his eyes off the building. He was looking for something. He stopped on the farthest corner of the bank, looking down the line of garbage cans towards the parking lot out back. Marcus watched the guy rub at the white stubble of his close-cropped beard, then he took a cellphone out of his pocket.

"Cheese it is. I'll order them myself. It'll take a little while, but there's a place just down the street that looks pretty decent. So, while we wait, why don't you tell me a little about yourself, how you ended up here. Help me understand you."

All the while he didn't take his eyes off the white-haired man.

Something was wrong with the picture, but he wasn't sure what. Like one of those Chinese finger puzzles, the more he worried at it the more difficult it was to solve.

"How about you start with your real name, Samuel? Show a little goodwill. If you work with me, I can work with you."

There was a moment when he thought he'd blown it, pushed too hard, too fast. He knew he was supposed to tread softly, but they were real people in there and the longer this dragged out the more likely a tragic end became. He forced himself to stop talking. To wait. The link between them was such a fragile thing right now. One ill-thought-out word and the man would hang up, putting them back to somewhere south of square one and increasing the push for SWAT to take lead on what would then become a siege. No one won then, but plenty of people lost.

He noticed the white-haired guy looking at him curiously.

Marcus realized what was bugging him: the guy was on his own cell in direct contravention of hostage protocol. It was supposed to be a closed scene, the only active line belonging to the phone in his hand.

His first thought was that someone in Command had fucked up big time and forgotten to kill the cell reception in a five-block radius, meaning anyone on the inside could theoretically get word to an accomplice out here. And that set his mind racing. They only had the word of one of the hostages that Samuel was working alone in there.

A second perp on the inside would change everything.

The dynamics behind every decision they made would be off.

Right now, as he wasted his time trading pizzas, a different comms circuit could be in place, the gunman getting precious intel relayed back to him from a grizzled old white-haired accomplice on the outside. People misjudged old men. They took them for granted. He stared hard at the one in front of him, trying to read his lips. He couldn't.

He knew he was jumping at shadows. But the thing about shadows was they were compelling. That phone was working when it shouldn't be. The man was communicating with someone right now. That much was fact. It wasn't too big a stretch to imagine him orchestrating things. Marcus remembered Samuel's opening remark: *Sometimes everything isn't what it seems.* Was this what he meant? That he had a man on the outside? That this wasn't just a hold-up gone wrong but something more elaborate?

He didn't like it. It didn't feel right.

Then Samuel gave his full name.

Marcus Davenport gestured for one of the techs to come closer, ready to run the name back to the mobile command center so the officers in there could do their thing. "Samuel Archer," he mouthed.

The officer nodded that he'd got it, and disappeared into the truck.

The clock was ticking.

37

"WE'RE GOING TO HAVE to come up with a concession," Theo said. "We've got to give Davenport something. So how do we use this to our advantage?"

"Don't look at me," Richard said, shaking his head. "I used up my genius with the vault idea." He offered a wry smile, trying to be self-deprecating. Theo thought it just made him look like a dick. But he was right, the vault *was* a good idea. If he didn't come up with another useful contribution all day he'd still played his part.

Margot spoke up, surprising Theo. "We have to send someone out to him. It's a way of getting someone on the outside."

She was right. They were going to need someone on the outside. They couldn't just walk out of here with a dead body after the police had gone. They were going to need to put things into motion to not only cover their tracks but lay down an entirely false scent for the police to follow. And not just the police, Theo realized. A man like Saul Bonavechio wasn't going to just sit idly by while his right-hand bastard disappeared off the face of the earth. The odds were good that he'd see the disappearance as a personal attack, and the minute that happened he'd come looking.

Theo chewed on his bottom lip. It came down to two things: who they could trust and who would be more useful out there. The cops would see a message in whoever walked out of the bank. If he sent Alice out, it said Samuel Archer was keeping the bank staff together, holding them responsible for his plight; if he sent Margot, he was letting the oldest person leave, meaning he had some compassion; if he told Richard to go, he was getting rid of the obvious authority figure; if he sent Theo it was all about removing the physical threat he posed; and so on. Everyone was different, their release signifying a very different state of mind.

So what message did they want to send?

There was no obvious candidate, so he worked through it backwards. Who did he want to stay?

Sasha was an obvious choice; she was his strongest ally. Beth would betray them, he was absolutely sure of it, even after Sasha's mini heist-within-a-heist that had made the woman eighty-five thousand dollars richer. Richard he didn't trust. The man was a snake. Victoria was an obvious no, and *he* wasn't about to leave, not when he couldn't trust anyone else to run the negotiations. So that left Margot or Alice.

Of course, that wasn't the whole equation, was it? Like Sasha said, there was Ellie, out of sight somewhere in the building.

She was probably hiding in the back, not bound by the complicity Sasha had woven around them all. Margot would find her. They needed to bring her into the fold. Or get her out before she knew the truth. That was the other option.

He rubbed a tired hand across his eyes. It had been a brutally long day already, with no sign of any respite in sight. First things first he needed to tell Adam that he'd been lied to, on multiple occasions, by the one person he seemed to trust in here, and then he'd have to deal with the consequences. Maybe that would change who went out in the exchange.

"You need to know something," Theo said.

Adam seemed resigned to yet more bad news. "You mean the person you all lied about not being here?"

"Yeah. Look. You aren't going to like this, but I hope if I explain, you'll know you can trust us."

"And you're telling me the truth now?"

Theo nodded. "It might change decisions we have to make from now on. It might not. But it'd be stupid to ignore the fact that you're playing with a loaded deck. Ellie's back there. Richard didn't bring her in when you sent him to round people up."

Adam stood absolutely still for the longest time.

"Margot will find her," he said eventually.

"But it doesn't change anything," Theo said. "Not in terms

of the big picture. They'll still knock on the door with the food and Archer will still be expected to offer up someone in trade."

"I'm sure he doesn't care who gets to leave."

"I'm sure he doesn't. But we should. Because whoever goes out there needs to want Samuel Archer fucked all the way to Hell and back."

"I'm the natural candidate then," Alice said, pushing herself up to her feet. She'd been sitting cross-legged on the floor, staring at the dead man, not saying anything. He didn't want to know what was going through her mind. "None of you had a real reason to hate him, not like I did." She looked at Theo. "He might have destroyed your career," and at Richard, "and been holding you to ransom, but he turned me into a whore."

Theo agreed. She was the natural choice. "Any arguments? Anyone else think they should be the one to go out when the food arrives?"

"I could do it," Richard ventured.

"I don't think so," he said. "It sends the wrong sort of message. You're a man. You're young. This is your bank. It makes you look like a coward. And it makes Archer look like a prick. Women and children first. As I see it, it's either Margot or Alice. Margot fits the profile they'll be expecting. She's the oldest one in here. She's female. Sending her out is a sign that Archer knows how to play the game. Alternatively, Alice is the odd one out, in the wrong place at the wrong time and not part of this at all. She'd have a good excuse to go after she's given her statement. Margot would be expected to stick around because her friends are still in here. So, no, not you. You're not even second on the list."

Richard couldn't argue with his logic, but it was obvious he wanted to.

"Alice," Adam agreed.

"Okay, that's three votes for Alice. Show of hands, all in favor of sending Alice out when the time comes?"

Every hand that could went up. Even, surprisingly, Beth's. He'd expected her to abstain.

He wasn't sure what this meant; whether she was resigned to being a part of what happened from here on in, her Christian conscience bought and paid for by Archer's eighty-five grand, or Adam's plight had finally registered. Or she just wanted Alice gone because she was the one person in there with a genuine hatred of the dead man, meaning she would never back down far enough to see things from Beth's perspective. There was that, too.

He wasn't entirely sure her motivation made a difference.

"Alice it is," Theo said. "Now we need to work out a plan, because once you're through those doors we've got no way of communicating with you. We need somewhere to dump the body once this is all over."

"I've got an idea," Alice said.

38

"LET'S HEAR IT."

She looked around the lobby. It felt like they'd been in here for days. Everyone looked sweaty and exhausted, apart from Adam. He looked like the tweaker Archer had called him when this all kicked off. They were all looking at her with an expectation that bordered on, well, if not exactly fanaticism something incredibly close to desperation. It was strange how the same thing could look so different on so many people's faces. One person absolutely didn't want to hear her bright idea. Another was clinging to the hope that her four little words might get them out of here once and for all.

"He's got enemies," she said, pointing out the obvious. "You don't get to be who he was without alienating a lot of dangerous people. I think we should try to use them." She was looking at Adam as she said that, but Theo answered.

"We don't know who they are, so how are we supposed to do that?"

How *were* they supposed to do that? She wasn't entirely sure, but Archer had done something unforgivable to her last night. She wasn't about to forgive and forget, even if he was dead. She wanted *everyone* who had been in that hotel room to pay.

"I think we should use what happened to me last night."

"I'm not following you. What happened to you last night?" Theo said.

"You ever play cards? Sometimes winning isn't about the cards in your hand so much as how you lay them down. The hotel isn't far from here. Fifteen minutes on a clear road. That's one card. Archer hurt the night manager this morning. That's another. I *think* I can get him to help us."

"How?"

"Put our mysterious Milo Rockwell in one of the empty rooms last night and tonight. Maybe stretch the booking for a week so it looks like Milo was in town for a while. Between the money and the hotel reservations we've got a link between Archer and Milo Rockwell. If Sasha can move some cash from Archer's account into the one Richard set up for Milo today, there's another. Plenty of people saw Milo at the casino last night, too. He wasn't exactly shy about coming forward, and remember, you heard Archer on the phone, saying how 'the guy' wasn't a problem anymore? He must have been talking about Milo. So if the police question Bonavechio they're going to hear how he had a run-in with a Milo Rockwell the night before he died. It fits."

"It's pretty flimsy," Theo disagreed.

"You're missing the point. That's the beauty of it. We don't want it looking perfect. Anything too neat and tidy looks like a setup. We want the cops to feel like they're doing genuine detective work, following the money, letting it lead them to Samuel Archer and inevitably to Milo."

"And we've got the smoking gun. Literally," Sasha added. "We can use that hotel room, assuming you trust the night manager. If we can get the body out of here we can dump it in there, put the do not disturb sign up and let housekeeping find it in a week..." She trailed off. "It'll look like a falling out among thieves. Milo turned on Archer."

"I can't believe you're seriously thinking about moving a dead body, covering up a murder and a bank robbery, and stealing hundreds of thousands of dollars." Beth couldn't stop shaking her head. She was like one of those bobble-headed dolls with spring-loaded necks. "What the hell is wrong with you people?"

It was a good question. Alice didn't have a good answer. At least not one more compelling than the fact that plenty of the people in the lobby had very good reasons to hate Samuel Archer and celebrate the fact he was out of their lives. Normally that would have been enough; they'd have walked away. It wasn't as if Adam was an innocent, but weighing his desperation against Archer's malice made it an easy call.

Archer had died in the wrong place at the wrong time. The whole thing would have appealed to Archer's sense of humor. He had been a macabre fucker at the best of times.

"Works for me," Alice said. "We just have to spin it so it looks like Archer was trying to buy his life back from Milo, something like that. It could work."

"It has to," Theo said. "We don't get a second shot at this. Once the story is out there, it takes on a life of its own. We've got to sell it. And sell it well."

"So let me take the gun, get it out of here. I'll sort out the room. The hotel is across Highway 41 from the Shedd Aquarium, on the South Loop. It's a fancy little boutique place. Big plate-glass windows downstairs, with a restaurant, looks like a fancy whorehouse."

"I know it," Sasha said.

"Great. Okay. I'll stay the night so people in the neighboring rooms can hear someone moving about in there. I'll make sure I've got the television on annoyingly loud, and hope someone complains about me to reception. Let there be a record of room service, too. I'll just get them to leave it outside the door so they don't know there's a woman in the room. It also means you can reach me if you need to."

"Sounds like we've got the beginnings of a plan," Theo agreed. "We need to make a start. That means moving the body, but we can't do that until the vault's open, so get down there and start the process." Richard looked distinctly unenthusiastic at the prospect.

"We're going to need to clean the blood up, too."

"Sounds good. We can move him after we've eaten."

"I don't know about anyone else, but I really don't have much of an appetite," Richard said.

39

THE DANE HAD WHAT he needed. He'd overheard the negotiator repeating Samuel Archer's name. What he needed wasn't exactly what he wanted, though. It presented difficulties he was going to need to work around.

But that was what he did. It was the art of his job.

To some he was an assassin, to others a more general problem solver. A fixer. He'd read a book years ago about someone like him, a guy called Repairman Jack. He liked the idea. It sounded like someone you could trust, someone who fixed broken things. It was better than a "cleaner," which had been the go-to term for a few years after that Tarantino movie. If he was doing his job properly things didn't get that far.

If.

"I've found him," he said into his cellphone, turning his back on the negotiator and walking away. His phone was military grade, shielded from outside interference, operating on a different frequency to the police signal blocker.

"Problem?"

"You could say that."

"Okay, let's say that. Talk to me. I need to know what's happening."

"At this precise moment he is negotiating for pizza."

Silence at the other end of the line. A beat. Two. "What the *fuck* are you talking about?"

"You asked what was going on," the Dane said. He watched the only other man talking on a phone for a moment. He kept fiddling with his collar, like he was uncomfortable or hot. Nervous. It wasn't exactly unseasonably warm. Not enough to sweat a guy out. "That's what's going on."

"Stop trying to be clever."

"Your man is currently holed up inside the Glenview branch of Chicago Liberty Bank."

More silence, anger simmering just beneath the surface, hiding in the moments between breaths.

"What the Jesus fuck is he doing in there?"

"Robbing the place, by the looks of things, and badly. SWAT are on-scene with a hostage-negotiation team. Which explains why he isn't where you need him to be."

"There are hostages?"

"Hungry ones, hence the pizza."

A slow heavy breath. Bonavechio wasn't happy.

"What are you going to do?"

"What do you *want* me to do?" the Dane asked. Always

better to have the client make his demands, that way there could be no misunderstandings to come back and bite you on the ass. He knew exactly what Bonavechio was going to ask him to do. Men like Saul Bonavechio were predictable in that silence was always their preferred method of dealing with problems. Silence could be bought or enforced. It didn't matter to them either way.

Unlike Samuel Archer the Dane wasn't Bonavechio's man. Theirs was very much a temporary arrangement. That was the way he liked it.

"This is a mess," Saul Bonavechio said. The Dane wasn't going to dispute that. He walked to the edge of the police barrier, turned on his heel and stopped, peering into the shadows along the side of the bank, scoping out the options available to Archer. There was a parking lot at the far end of the alley, and if the floor plans he had checked out through the planning department's online archive were accurate, two alternative exits. That meant at least three different ways into the bank. He couldn't watch all three of them, and he'd rather not go inside. That meant improvising. It would be much cleaner to take up a vantage point in one of the skyscrapers nearby and use a high-velocity sniper rifle to take Archer out as he emerged from the bank, but men like Saul Bonavechio were hands-dirty kind of guys. They wanted their factors on the ground, right up close enough to taste the dead guy's sour breath as he crapped his pants and shuffled off to meet his maker.

"I can't risk him talking." And there it was, right on time. The kill order. "There is too much at stake."

"Understood."

"Is there any way you can get in there?"

"It's not impossible," the Dane said.

"Okay, so deal with it as quietly as you can. Whatever happens, do not let Archer walk away from that building."

"He's a dead man," the Dane agreed.

"Excellent. I don't care how you do it, just get it done. Bank robbery ends in tragedy blah blah, gunman takes his own life? Something like that."

"Something like that," the Dane agreed again.

Predictable.

40

"EXCUSE ME, SIR, WHO are you?"

The white-haired man turned away from his conversation as Marcus Davenport walked towards where he stood with Jaeger, the first officer on the scene. He arrived as the officer was giving him a detailed situation report.

"What seems to be the problem?"

"It was a simple enough question. Who are you?"

"Ah, right." The man reached into his pocket for his badge and offered it to Marcus. Marcus flipped it open to see FBI credentials. Field Agent Kage Salisbury. He handed the wallet back to the Fed.

"On what planet is this an FBI matter?"

"Oh, it isn't. I was just having a cappuccino in the café up the street when I saw all the excitement and thought I'd come down and see if there was anything I could do. Looks like you've got your hands full here?"

“We’ve got things under control.”

“I don’t doubt it,” Salisbury said smoothly. “Think of it more as a friendly offer of help to stop them steamrolling over the scene.” He nodded towards the SWAT vehicles. “What do we know about the guy?” The way he said it, *we*, like they were both in this together. Complicity. It was smooth.

“Not enough,” Marcus said, not giving anything away. “Who were you talking to before?”

“Sorry?”

“On the phone. I saw you talking. I’m curious, because reception is down for a five-block radius, which means I want—no, I *need*—to know who you were talking to. And how.”

Salisbury had the decency to look confused, then seemed to realize what he was being accused of and his entire demeanor changed. He laughed. He actually laughed. “I wasn’t talking to anyone. Well, that’s not strictly true. I was talking to myself.”

“Bullshit,” Marcus said.

The white-haired Fed reached into his pocket for his phone. He swiped and tapped into an app, a old-style singer’s mic appearing on the screen, and a moment later his own voice played back, describing the scene.

“Habit,” he explained. “I do my best thinking aloud. It’s amazing the amount of detail you see and forgot, things that might be important, so I like to get it all down. Besides, it makes it so much easier to type up the reports later. It’s all about the detail.” With another tap of the screen Salisbury killed the audio playback and pocketed the phone again. He offered a wry grin.

"I suppose you begin every memo with 'Diane'?" The guy didn't get the *Twin Peaks* reference. He had a bit of an accent—certainly not local, possibly not a native speaker, so maybe he had been under a cable-free rock where the show wasn't on permanent repeat every few months. "Well at least that coffee you like's coming back into style," he said, earning a nonplussed stare. "Okay, well, like I said, this isn't a Fed case, I'm running the scene. I can't have you wandering around."

"Couldn't agree more. This is your show. Too many cooks. And speaking of cooks, these are yours, I take it?" he said, indicating the delivery boy balancing half a dozen pizza boxes as he negotiated the barriers. "So, like I said, what do we know about what's going on inside? Talk to me, maybe I can help."

"Single suspect, identified as Samuel Archer. We're still unsure as to how many hostages he's got in there, but we're working on eight, based on intel. We've had unconfirmed reports of a shot fired, but Archer just assured me everyone's fine in there."

"Samuel Archer, huh? I know that name," Salisbury said, catching Marcus by surprise. "Are you *sure* that's who we're dealing with?" Again with the *we*, possessive.

"He's got no reason to lie," Marcus said.

"Actually, I'd say he had every reason to lie. Look around

you. But let's take his word for it. Samuel Archer isn't exactly unknown to the Bureau."

"I'm not going to like the direction this is going, am I?"

Salisbury shook his head. "No. We've come up against his name in a few cases over the last couple of years."

"With regard to?"

"An ongoing investigation."

"I've shown you mine, your turn to show me yours," Marcus said.

"Organized crime."

"Okay."

"He's one of Bonavechio's men."

"Bonavechio, as in the casino guy?"

"One and the same."

"Shit. Shit. That's just fucking peachy. Are you *sure*?"

"You don't forget a name like that."

"But why would Bonavechio risk it all robbing a bank? That's not his style, is it? He lives in the shadows."

"That he does. I can't imagine he'd be happy to find out his man is in there."

Marcus turned his back on Salisbury, staring at the bank's glass doors and trying to imagine what was happening on the other side. What he couldn't decide was if this new information meant that Archer had a man on the outside or if he was acting alone. A career criminal, one in the employ of one of the few genuinely untouchables, wouldn't be stupid enough to walk into a bank and get himself trapped like this.

It didn't make sense. There had to be a plan, an angle that he just wasn't seeing.

"Who am I supposed to give these to?" the delivery boy asked, looking at thirty possible customers. "It's the first time I've ever delivered to a bank robbery." He gave a wry grin.

"They're going inside," someone said.

"But I'm not," the guy said.

"Don't worry," Marcus called over. "Excuse me," he said to Salisbury. "I've got to deal with this."

"No worries."

Marcus took his wallet out to pay for the pizzas, and gave the kid a hefty tip. He waited until he was out of earshot, then called the bank. The phone rang only once this time before it was picked up. "Got your pizzas out here, Samuel," Marcus said.

"That's good news, Marcus. Now, I suppose this is the moment you tell me you want something in return, right? Like, how about I release someone as a show of good faith? Does that sound about right?"

"It does," Marcus said.

"So, what pays for those pizzas?"

"You've got more people in there than you need, Samuel. How about you send the hostages out? That sound like a fair trade?"

"Not remotely," the other man said. "But I know how this works, got to show willing. Send in the pizzas, I'll send someone out."

"That's good, Samuel. That's really good. Work with me and we might just get out of this mess."

"I'm banking on it, Marcus. My life's in your hands."

41

"I HATE THIS," BETH Jones said. "And I hate you. All of you. I hate what you are forcing me to do."

"I'm sorry," Adam told her. "I really am."

Margot still hadn't returned with Ellie.

Beth crossed herself, knowing that no amount of contrition would help this time. Some sins weren't absolvable with a few Hail Marys even if the Blessed Virgin really was filled with grace. Beth was going into a dark place filled with brimstone and sulfur. She could almost hear the cries of the lost rattling through the old air conditioning. But, and this was the one thing that she wouldn't have believed possible even yesterday, she was going there willingly. Her unshakable faith wasn't just cracked, it was broken. These were good people, people she knew and trusted. They weren't monsters.

And yet they were doing this?

She drew in a deep breath. She'd given up fighting them.

She tried to tell herself it wasn't about the money Sasha had deposited in her account, that she wasn't so cheaply bought, but it was hard to deny that it made a difference. Beth had never thought of herself as that sort of person, but it turned out she was. Once she'd let the numbers get inside her head they started doing strange things, taking on a life of their own, making promises of better things to come. *All you have to do,* those numbers whispered, *is keep quiet*. She could do that. She could even convince herself that silence wasn't the same thing as lying. And that surprised her.

But what was considerably more surprising to Beth Jones was that she found herself thinking about what they needed to do to cover up a murder.

Sasha had been right.

Eighty-five thousand dollars had bought her complicity.

"Archer and Bonavechio, they're different. They're dirty. Archer ran Bonavechio's legitimate business and he betrayed him. That's the story here, isn't it? Look at the money that Archer was moving into the Milo Rockwell account. He was stealing from his boss. If we want a narrative the police are going to believe, surely that is it?"

Theo shook his head again. "It's too much. We do something like that, we paint big targets on our backs. There's no way Saul Bonavechio takes being set up for murder lying down. He'll come after us."

"Milo Rockwell came to town to check out the competition, wasn't that what you said?" Beth turned to Alice. The other woman nodded. "And Bonavechio's the competition. It's still a dirty business. The cops will buy that. This fictitious Milo is just the identity of a hitman. That would explain why he doesn't have a birth certificate, license or passport. After the shakedown last night he's taken Archer out as a message to his boss. Doesn't that make more sense?"

It did. She was *sure* it did. Pin the target on the bigger fish. If you were going to lie, lie big. People were more willing to believe the big lies. A man like Saul Bonavechio? Everyone knew the kind of person he was, the kind of business he ran, even if they couldn't prove it. That made the lie believable.

"I don't know," Sasha said. "Isn't it easier to make it look like Milo and Archer were in this together?"

"I guess that makes sense. Keep it easy. But I really don't want to spend the rest of my life sleeping with one eye open, waiting for one of Bonavechio's *real* hitmen to come knocking. Best not to throw words like 'hitman' and 'assassin' around, so I vote no. But we're all in this together. So, Adam? Alice? Richard? Sash?" They couldn't poll Ellie or Margot, and Vicky wasn't going to give an inch regardless of what lie they decided to tell. "What do you want to do?"

It was Alice who answered. "I'm our star witness."

42

THE KNOCK ON THE door meant they didn't have time to discuss what she meant.

Adam's heart hammered wildly. There was so much room for things to go wrong. He didn't understand why Alice was staring at him like she expected him to do something. She held out her hand. He shook his head, still not understanding. "The gun," she said.

He hesitated, but it wasn't as though the gun conferred any power to him in this situation. Everyone was working to help without the threat it posed, so why should he be so fearful of handing it over?

"Give her the gun," Theo told him.

Adam looked at Sasha, who he still thought of as his one friend in here. She nodded, too. Just a slight inclination of the head.

Give her the gun. It was so much easier said than done. He looked down at it in his hand.

It felt so much heavier now than it had when he'd first taken it out, but it had taken a life now, hadn't it? That had to add extra weight. It was carrying a death. So why couldn't he let go?

Because it makes me helpless, he finally admitted to himself. But of course he'd always been helpless, long before he set foot inside the bank. A gun didn't change that. Surrendering it would make him stronger, at least in the eyes of these people, because without it they'd stop being his hostages and become his… what? Accomplices?

He surrendered the weapon with all the reverence of a ritual.

Alice didn't say anything as she popped the magazine out, and slipped both parts of the gun into her clutch bag. "Where did you get it?"

"I bought it."

"You mean properly? From a shop? Filled out the license applications and everything?"

"No. From a kid."

"That's good. I assume it's clean. I'll make sure there's nothing that connects back to you. I promise."

He heard the bolts going back on the main doors. "Thank you."

"No, thank you," she said. "Really. You saved my life. Maybe that's your karmic balance? A life for a life?" He didn't have an answer to that. "You can trust me, Adam. I won't let you down."

With that, Alice took a moment to gather herself, then turned her back on him and walked across the lobby. She paused beside Richard as he said something, just a couple of words, almost pitched too low for Adam to catch, "On the outside, do you think there's a chance? Me and you?"

"Ask me again when this is over," she said, and then Alice was through the front doors and walking away without a backwards glance.

The pizza boxes were stacked up on the sidewalk beside the entrance. Adam watched Richard pick them up, then return to the lobby. The door didn't close properly behind him. The hydraulic arm wasn't working. Richard had to put the boxes down so he could pull it closed, then slam the bolts into place.

The murder weapon was no longer inside the bank. Where it ended up was out of Adam's hands. But there was a chance, wasn't there?

Richard Rhodes stood there, silhouetted against the glass. He would have made an easy target for a SWAT sniper with an itchy trigger finger. He leaned back against the glass door. Adam could see the sweat matting his hair flat to his scalp. There were wet rings staining the fabric under his arms.

Something had changed.

It took Adam a moment to realize what was different; the ever-present hum of the air conditioning unit wasn't there. He hadn't noticed it happen, but it had been long enough for the air to become stifling. Between the electric arm and the air-con Adam had all the evidence he needed to know that the negotiator was following the exact blueprint Theo had laid out.

Richard carried the pizza boxes over to the counter. "Grub's up," he said, opening the lid of the first box, letting out the delicious aroma of melted cheese. He pulled apart the crust and teased out a slice, the topping sliding greasily through his fingers.

Adam said nothing, thinking hard. The air-con and the door's arm had to be on a different circuit to the lights, which was why the corridors were still illuminated. The bank would have different circuits for different functions, and a backup generator for the vault in the event of a complete blackout.

Seconds later there was a dull shunt as the power stopped flowing, followed by absolute stillness as the lights and computers died.

They had waited one minute for Alice to get clear of the building before they killed the power.

One minute.

A slice of light cut through the darkness, running from the main doors almost all the way to the counters. Richard stood half in, half out of the light. "Bastards couldn't even let us enjoy the food first," he muttered, holding the wedge of pizza up.

"Give with one hand, take away with another," Theo said. "It's all just power play. They're letting us know we're at their mercy, that they can pull the plug on this at any time." Adam knew what he meant; he wasn't talking about the power, he was talking about SWAT.

The phone started to ring.

Theo snatched it up. "Marcus, you bastard. You didn't have to do that. I did what you asked. I gave you the girl. I was ready to send someone else out. You fucked it up, man. You fucked it up big time. How am I supposed to trust you now?"

43

The Dane watched as the woman came out. She moved with her head down, shoulders slumped. Her hair hung over her eyes. Police officers came forward to swarm protectively around her.

Voices called out, “It’s okay, you’re safe, it’s all right,” blending into one.

She didn’t react or look up from the ground beneath her feet.

He was a decent judge of people; it was one of the many gifts he possessed that had kept him alive this long. Everybody was a book of flesh and blood just waiting to be read, if you knew how to pick up on the non-verbal cues: facial expressions, posture, gestures. Unlike words, they didn’t lie.

Of course it was different across cultures and faiths, but he was watching a relatively unremarkable woman emerge from the bank, thin, pretty enough, but showing none of the obvious signs of trauma, save for the fact she refused to look up. It was like she was afraid of being caught in a lie.

This wasn't someone who'd just been in fear of her life.

That was interesting.

The girl hadn't been in there very long, but how long was long enough? There should be signs of shock, of growing relief.

He watched as Davenport met her halfway between the doors and the barrier. The man swept the woman up into a protective embrace.

She shuddered at his touch.

It was almost imperceptible, but the Dane knew what to look for.

She was younger than he'd expected. Early twenties, certainly no more than twenty-five. So why send her out first? Normally it would have been the oldest, or the youngest if there were kids in there, a pregnant woman, an injured hostage needing treatment, not a perfectly fit and healthy twenty-something. The only thing that made sense was that Archer saw her as the weakest link.

Did that help him?

Was she someone he could use?

Davenport handed the woman off to one of his crisis team who would take care of the debrief, getting every last little thing—no matter how seemingly unimportant—about her experience without it ever feeling like an interrogation. They'd want her to feel safe, and to do that they'd look to bring her family here, someone to talk to. Ideally he'd have been a fly on the wall for that chat, but Davenport had come over all territorial when he'd shown his fake FBI credentials, making it painfully obvious he'd be kept on the outside. He was going to have to find another way in. The trick, as ever, was just acting as if he belonged. You could get away with murder as long as it looked like you had every right to be killing.

The good thing about the law was it didn't think for itself, it followed well-established procedures. That meant it was predictable. He could work with that. It would take time to get the family in place, so that was his window, somewhere between the first flurry of questions and the relief that she was out of there and one less thing for them to worry about.

The hostage was led towards the command center. He could hear a female officer promising the woman hot food and a chance to sit down just as soon as they'd had a medic check her out. She repeated the phrase, "You're safe now," half a dozen times until it became a meaningless platitude. The woman kept shaking her head, insisting she was fine and didn't need a doctor, she wanted to go home. The Dane knew that wasn't going to happen any time soon. She was their one good asset, they weren't about to let her go until they'd bled her dry of every last bit of intel.

The cop said as much. "All in good time, but we need to talk first. You know what's happening in there better than any of us. What's Archer's state of mind? How are the hostages holding up? As much as we'd like to, we can't just send you home yet. You're our best hope of making sure no one gets hurt. So why don't we sit down and have a chat, just you and me?" She was good, not great, but she kept her voice calm and reassuring, relying on an accelerated friendship brought on by the extremes of stress and circumstance. It would work. The woman would open up.

The Dane needed to hear what she was going to say.

He'd walked the perimeter twice since arriving at the bank, and noted a couple of decent vantage points—both now occupied by police snipers—counted off the doors and windows as possible points of egress and ingress, and watched the mobile Command techs set up three-hundred-and-sixty-degree surveillance on the bank. No one was getting in or out off camera.

That was going to make his job needlessly complicated.

Ideally, despite what he'd said to Bonavechio, he would have gone inside, killed Archer and liberated the hostages. Piggybacking SWAT was still an option. He could roll in with them and make sure a bullet found its way into Samuel Archer's brain before he could talk. Not ideal, but functional. It was better than pretending to have an itchy trigger finger as they led him out. Of course, it was always possible that Archer would recognize the Dane and panic, try to run. There would be enough firepower aimed at him that someone was certain to put him down. The official report would write it up as suicide by cop. Clean. Tidy.

"What's the mood like in there?" the female officer asked.

"Tense," the woman said. "He's on edge. But he's not jumpy.

He's eerily calm, actually. Like he's resigned to whatever happens next."

Not good, the Dane thought, and looking at the way she just brushed her fingertips across her lips, not true either. The woman was lying. Interesting.

Was this why she was the first out? To fashion the narrative?

Now he really was interested.

What was Archer playing at? What did he hope to achieve by spinning a web of lies given the fact that he was well and truly caught at the center no matter how inventive the story he tried to sell?

Saul Bonavechio hadn't sent him here to work out what was happening, though. He'd sent him to make sure Samuel Archer died today. That was the only thing he needed to concern himself with. The rest of it was just window dressing. As long as Archer was dead, Mister B would be content.

Then the woman said something that betrayed her. "It's so unlike him."

Four words that changed everything.

The Dane knew why Archer had sent her out. She was his accomplice in this debacle. He was getting her clear before things went south.

The Dane tried to think like Archer. He was trapped inside a prison of his own making. Three ways out, but none of them viable. At least not yet. So, ignore the idea of protection, he was trading a hostage, an asset, what did he stand to gain by sending her out now? How could he best cash that asset in? The most obvious thing—the most *selfish* thing—was misdirection. She'd been sent out to make sure everyone looked the wrong way while Archer made his move.

Pretending to dictate a fresh thought into his phone, the Dane took a surreptitious picture of the woman and sent it to Bonavechio.

Is she one of yours?

44

"How am I supposed to trust you now?"

"You're not."

"So much for common decency," Theo said.

"Just protocol, nothing personal," Marcus Davenport said. "The thing is, you were never going to trust me, were you, Samuel?"

He had a point.

"We're both men of the world, we know how this is going to go down. I don't see the point of lying to you. Sure, anyone listening in is probably shitting themselves right about now, but you and me, we're big boys, Samuel. We've been around this particular block. I've been reading up on you, you've had an interesting life."

"That I have," Theo agreed.

"So, enjoy the pizza while we talk about getting everyone out of there."

“Not going to happen. Call back in thirty minutes.”

“Then SWAT are coming in. Neither of us want that. I don’t want to lose any of the hostages to a stray bullet. You, I very much doubt, want to end up as another crime statistic, so let’s agree to never say never, eh?”

“You didn’t have to turn the lights out, man. That just wasn’t cool.”

Across from Theo, Sasha had turned on the flashlight app on her cellphone; the light lit up the underside of her face like a Halloween mask, all sharp angles and dark hollows. The others were reduced to shadows within shadows. The blood on the floor was black.

“Think of it as inspiration,” Marcus said. “And if that doesn’t work, as the seconds hand on a ticking clock. Things can’t stay like this indefinitely. Now it’s dark in there you know it’s only a matter of time before SWAT come through one of those three doors, and when that happens, well, not to put too fine a point on it, you know it isn’t going to end well for you.”

“Has anyone ever told you you’ve got quite a way with words, Marcus?”

“It has been said,” the negotiator agreed. Theo could hear the smile in his voice.

“You know, I had hoped we might become friends.”

“And grab a beer later? Yeah, I know you’re shitting with me, but keep that sentiment in mind. I’ll be in touch.”

The line went dead.

“Okay, they’re not playing now,” Theo told the others.

"Best guess, we've got a couple of hours, at worst, a lot less, so we've got to make things happen. Richard, you and me, we're moving the body. Beth, we need you to clean the carpet to get rid of any sign of blood. They're not going to blue-light the room, but it needs to be spotless. Sash, you need to trash the security footage." He turned to Adam, just visible in the darkness beyond the diffuse beam of Sasha's phone. "Adam, this is it, the moment of truth. You need to decide if you trust us. I hope we've done enough so far to earn it, but right now, from here on in, you're in our hands. This is what I'm thinking: you hide in the vault, take a couple of pizzas down with you in case you get hungry, and during the night two of us will come down to get Archer's body to move it to the hotel. It means you being locked in with him for a long time, which won't be much fun, but in the morning when everything has died down and this place is cordoned off with police tape, you just walk out of here with no one any the wiser. Can you do that?"

Adam's lips twitched. Theo could see he desperately wanted to say, *Sure, yes, absolutely, I can do that*, but the words wouldn't come. Finally he said, "Why? Surely I can just walk out the front door with you?"

"Honestly? I don't think you'll hold up under interrogation. They're talking to everyone out there, asking questions, trying to put together what's happening in here. Stress makes your symptoms worse, right? We send you out there and you blow it, we're all fucked. I don't want to risk my life on you not coming apart at the seams, so I vote you stay in here."

"He's right," Richard said. "It's going to be rough out there. It's better to make it look like you were never in here. Just keep your head down and let us help you."

"What about my son?"

"I can take care of him tonight," a disembodied voice assured him. Margot stepped into the light cast by Sasha's phone. "Just tell me where to pick him up, I'll take him back to my house and spoil him with junk food and movies."

"He's not good around strangers," Adam told her.

"Then I'll just have to make sure I'm not a stranger for very long. We'll be fine," she promised. "I managed to get two daughters to college, I think I can manage one night."

"Thank you." He told her the sitter's address. She scribbled it down, Sasha holding the light over the paper for her.

"That means you're next out, Margot," Theo said. He'd already been thinking about sending her out because of her friend, the one she'd said had the tech skills to hack into surveillance cameras across the city. He was going to be useful. "That makes sense. They'd expect us to send the women out first. No sign of Ellie?"

Margot shook her head. "If she's still in here she's determined to stay hidden."

Another cellphone lit up a different corner of the room as Richard took his out of his pocket and turned it back on.

"Save it," Theo said. "We're going to need those lights when we're cleaning up, so let's try and conserve the batteries. Use them one at a time."

Richard killed the light without protest, pocketing the phone.

With the lights out the atmosphere in the bank had changed. His own breathing was the only sound Theo heard for the next few seconds. He was angry with himself for not anticipating Marcus's next move. He'd naively expected to have a couple of hours of light before the police killed the power. There were so many things they needed to do if they were going to get away with covering up Archer's murder and moving that money about, and most of them depended on electricity.

They were going to have to improvise.

He didn't like that, but there wasn't a lot he could do about it.

"What about her?" Adam asked.

Her was the bound and gagged Victoria. His eyes had adjusted enough to the darkness to see that her head was down, chin resting on her chest, hair falling over her eyes. She didn't look up. He watched the steady shallow rise and fall of her chest. He'd been thinking of Vicky as a bridge they'd have to cross when they got to it, but now that moment, the point of no return, was rapidly approaching. He was going to have to decide what to do with her. The problem was that he couldn't be sure that money in her bank account was enough to buy her silence. It was fine in theory, it was a lot of money. Life-changing money. That ought to buy her complicity. The woman looked shrunk in on herself, reduced, broken, but he wasn't buying it. She'd been prepared to piss herself to be sure Adam underestimated her. She was perfectly capable of playing the victim if it suited her. They couldn't trust her.

He couldn't deal with her now. He'd have to do it when the others were gone.

Just him and her. It would be easier that way, with no one watching.

He'd give her one chance to plead her case. But whatever happened he wasn't going to let her send him to jail. That was one endgame he wasn't prepared to let play out.

"I'll take care of Vicky," he said.

45

RICHARD GRABBED THE DEAD man's ankles.

"On three," Theo said. There was no nonsense. They had a job to do, as unsavory as it was.

Richard tried not to think about what he was doing as he straightened his back, lifting the corpse.

The dead man farted as his bowels emptied.

"Ah fuck," Richard said, struggling not to heave at the wet sounds coming from the dead man's pants. "I really don't want to do this. Can't we just—"

"Suck it up," Theo said bluntly. "If we don't get him out of here, we're screwed. You get that, right? They're coming through those doors soon enough, and when they do, if he's still here, we're a magnitude of fucked that's not been defined yet. That's how fucked we are."

"Yeah, yeah, I know," the bank manager grumbled, struggling with Archer's corpse as he shuffled back a couple of steps.

Samuel Archer had been a big man in life, in death he was an uncooperative giant. Richard felt his grip slipping after a couple of seconds, and as he tried to adjust it the dead man's left foot slipped from his hand and slapped on the floor. Theo shook his head, the gesture caught in the beam of Adam's cellphone flashlight as he spun around to see what the noise was.

Richard's heart raced. His breathing was ragged.

Adam led the way, the beam from his phone juddering erratically ahead of them as his tremors intensified. They shuffled forward another dozen footsteps, their feet scuffing on the carpet.

"This bastard's heavy."

Theo ignored him. "Adam, the door's right ahead of you, a little to the left." The light paused, and then moved again as Adam opened the stairwell door.

They shuffled on another couple of steps in heavy silence, Theo's frame blocking out most of the cellphone light. The stifling near-darkness inside the bank made Archer's dead weight so much heavier. Their grunts and Richard's own increasingly labored breathing were the only sounds as they took the first couple of steps on the staircase that would lead them down to the vault.

Richard knew they must look ridiculous. He suddenly thought about the security cameras—the police would be able to see everything!—but quickly remembered that Archer had made him deactivate them before the dead man set foot inside the bank. That was one small mercy. There was no footage.

The stairwell was bare concrete and the echoes of their footfalls were loud as they descended. Three times, Richard nearly dropped the corpse, struggling with Archer's bulk and the slippery fabric. Countless other times he banged the dead man against the metal safety rail, sending a dull echo back up the stairwell. He couldn't stop thinking like he'd stumbled into an episode of *CSI*. His brain was firing off random lines he remembered from the endless repeats. There would be marks on the body from their moving it; that was unavoidable. The bleeding might stop with the heart, but every time they moved Archer they opened the wound a little more, and their head-up feet-up hold drained the blood toward the gaping hole meaning they left a trail that would have done Hansel and Gretel proud. They couldn't hope to clean it all up without proper light. The whole place was full of forensic evidence that would tell the real story. Everything hinged on the fact that the cops wouldn't be looking for blood or any other evidence in the stairwell—at least not at first, which was why it was so vital they got their ducks lined up.

He wished, and not for the first time, that he'd never tried to help anyone. It would have been so much easier if they could have just tripped the silent alarm and waited for Adam to commit suicide by cop. Instead it was all about trying to hide his own crime, and because he was trying to think three steps ahead of everyone else he kept making mistakes. He'd screwed everything up. Well, fuck it, there was nothing he could do about it now.

He shifted his grip, grabbing a hold of Archer's trouser cuff before the dead man's leg could slip through his fingers again.

"Hold on," he muttered, making a fist around the fabric.

"We're on the clock," Theo said.

"Do you want to leave a big bloody smear down the stairs? No. Then hold on a fucking minute." It was getting to him. The thin veneer of his slick salesman's façade had fractured over the last couple of hours. Underneath lay all the insecurities, doubts and fears of the bullied kid he'd been growing up; the same kid who had dreamed of becoming a modern-day Robin Hood.

Richard hated the blood on his hands, the stench in the stairwell, taking orders from a washed-up cop like Theo. He hated the way they'd manipulated Beth into turning her back on her faith because her beliefs were making *their* lives difficult. He hated the way he'd had to put his life in Alice's hands. Alice had hated Archer, that much was obvious. That was the only thing that might—just might—get him out of the shit. You could trust that kind of hate. If she came through, the cops would be looking elsewhere, in a hotel room halfway across the city.

His heel slipped on the blood.

Richard lurched backwards, instinctively letting go of the dead man to stop himself from falling. That put the entire burden on Theo, four steps below him, who wisely let go and allowed Archer to fall in a flail of limbs and sickening impacts. Richard heard the sound of bone snapping as Archer's weight carried the body to the bottom of the stairwell.

As the echo of the impacts faded he heard something else in the dark.

Footsteps.

46

SHE CAME OUT OF the shadows beneath the stairs and tore into the first face she saw, guided by the light of a cellphone, driving the heel of her hand into his nose with savage force. Even as he threw his arms up to try and fend her off, she cannoned into him with the full weight of her body, her momentum driving him back.

He went down awkwardly, the side of his head cracking off the balustrade with a sickening thud.

His cellphone skittered across the floor, extinguishing the one light source.

"What the fuck have you done?" A man's voice.

It took her a moment to realize it was the security guard, Theo. The man barely managed a grunt whenever they came into each other's orbits. She wasn't used to hearing complete sentences, never mind that kind of razor-wire accusation coming from his lips.

"What you should have done hours ago," she snapped back. "Now let's get out of here. Let the police do their job. This guy's not going anywhere. You can thank me later."

"*Thank* you?"

She could hear the sharp inhale-exhale of flared nostrils. Theo was seething.

"He's still breathing," Richard said, the relief in his voice evident even in the dark.

Why did he care?

"Thank God for that," Theo echoed the manager's sentiments a little more vehemently.

Something was happening here she didn't understand. From where she was standing it looked like Theo and Richard were on the same side as the robber.

"I think it's pretty safe to assume he's not down here with us," Richard mumbled. He sounded strange. Weirded out. As he picked up the robber's cellphone the light shone on the second—very dead—body at the bottom of the stairs.

Ellie took an instinctive step back, shaking her head as she tried to understand whatever was happening in this weird *Twilight Zone* episode she'd somehow stumbled into.

"Are you..." She struggled to find the word, and kept coming back to the same one, which she couldn't bring herself to say.

She didn't need to. Richard said it for her. "Corrupt? No. No, we're not. I promise you."

"Then what the hell's happening here?" That was greeted

by silence. "Please. Explain this to me, because I've got a really bad feeling about this," Ellie said. "Mr. Rhodes?"

"I need you to stay calm," Richard said, sounding anything but. "Can you do that for me, Ellie?"

"He's dead, isn't he?" she said, ignoring him.

"Yes," Richard said.

"Did *he* kill him?" She nodded at the unconscious man.

"Yes," Richard said again.

"Oh, God. Oh, God."

"It's not what you think."

"You're not trying to dispose of a dead body?" Ellie said before she could stop herself.

"Maybe it *is* what you think," Theo said wryly.

"Shut up." Richard bristled, obviously not appreciating the security guard's grim sense of humor. "I was wrong, Ellie. That's what you need to focus on. When I came to you before, I had it all wrong. He—" Richard nodded towards the robber where he lay face down on the concrete floor "—isn't the bad guy here. *He* is." He nodded at the dead guy. He might as well have tried to convince her black was white, salt pepper and chalk cheese. She couldn't wrap her head around it.

"We should move," Theo said, not prepared to give her the luxury of time. "We can wring our hands when we're done. Right now, let's just focus on getting this pair into the vault. If we don't get them stashed away we're all royally fucked."

"Here," Richard said, offering her the robber's cellphone.

She took it.

"Open the door," Theo told her as he bent to hook his hands beneath the dead man's limp arms while Richard struggled with his feet.

She did as she was told, standing back as they manhandled the corpse.

As Theo cut across the cellphone's beam the passageway in front of them was plunged into darkness. Ellie raised the phone above her head to shine the way towards the vault.

It was an utterly unremarkable door with an alphanumeric keypad at chest height on the right side. The light was green. The thirty-minute override had run its course. This had obviously been planned in advance. They leaned the body up against the wall while Richard punched in a six-digit code. There was a sharp *snick* as the magnetic bolt disengaged. He reached forward and opened the door. Behind it was a second, older, more traditional steel door with a capstan lock. Ellie aimed the light at his hands as he grasped two of the five handles and began to twist it counter-clockwise. On the sixth revolution his efforts were rewarded with a sigh as the airtight seal broke and the second door swung silently open a couple of inches. Richard heaved it all the way open, then he and Theo dragged the body inside.

The vault was actually divided into two smaller vaults, the first with a bare metal table like something a coroner might use, the second lined with small, medium and large safety-deposit boxes.

She followed them in as they laid the body out on the steel

table, crossing his arms over his chest so they didn't hang down limply at his sides. He was too tall for the table, so his feet still dangled off the end.

Richard crossed himself as he turned his back on the dead man. It was a curious gesture from a man who didn't seem to have a religious bone in his body, but then people did strange things around the dead.

Theo and Richard went back for the other man, who was now stirring, and was able to walk groggily between them. The cellphone's light cast half his face in shadow. She could already see the deep bruising coming to the surface where the balustrade had done its damage. There was blood on his shirt. Richard helped him over to the far corner of the vault, taking his weight as he slumped to the floor. He needed both walls to keep him upright. Ellie noticed that he avoided looking at the body on the steel table.

Ellie began to walk out, but Theo raised a hand to stop her. "You're staying in here with him."

"No," she said. "No, none of us can stay in there. Only the dead guy because he doesn't need to breathe. I disconnected the backup generator. There's no air. You can't lock me in here." She shook her head. She was right, the soft hum of the air ventilation was missing.

"I'll fire it up," Richard promised. "Trust me. There's plenty of breathable air in here. I'll go straight to the generator the moment we close the door. You'll hear the air come on. I promise."

"Seriously? What am I supposed to do? Sit on my hands? Strike up a conversation with a killer while I wait for air to breathe? This is fucked up, you know that, right? Deeply, seriously fucked up."

"I know, I'm sorry. But Theo's right. It's easier for everyone if you just stay in here."

"Not for everyone."

"Look, I know it's asking a lot, I do, but you've trusted me this far, Ellie, please, just trust me a little more, keep an eye on him, make sure he's okay. That was a nasty knock. There's no way of knowing what kind of damage was done. He could have concussion, brain bleed, Christ, he could stroke out. We can't leave him in here by himself."

"In case you haven't noticed, it's a fucking *vault*," Ellie snapped, unable to stop herself from taking a step towards him. Richard flinched, mirroring her step with a backwards one of his own. His hip banged off the corner of the steel table, making the corpse's left hand slide off his chest and flop down to his side. "We're thirty feet underground. The walls are six feet thick, encased in, what, lead? We could survive a nuclear holocaust down here. But if something happens to him the one thing I can't do is call for help. There's no fucking *signal*. This is ridiculous. You can't keep me prisoner in here."

"Please, Ellie. Just sit tight. We won't be long. We'll be back for you in a few hours. I promise."

He backed away from her, without turning his back on her.

"I hate you," Ellie said, and she meant it.

Not that Richard heard her.

He had already closed the door.

She heard the capstan wheel spinning as they locked her in.

47

THE REPLY CAME BACK seconds later.

No.

The Dane had two jobs to do in Chicago. One was to make sure Archer didn't walk out of the bank; the other was almost forty minutes from here, in a warehouse down on the wharf. He wasn't about to leave the bank until he was sure Archer was neutralized. The woman was lying through her teeth, that much was obvious. The weird thing was she didn't seem to be saying much of anything. The officer handling her debrief no doubt assumed it was shock, but the Dane was better at reading people.

A voice from inside the command center called, "We've got the bastard," which threw him for a moment, until a young Hispanic analyst emerged holding a photograph of Samuel

Archer. He passed it to Davenport. The crisis negotiator studied Archer's face without a word. The Dane studied Davenport. Something wasn't sitting well with the man. He handed the photograph to the next man in line, giving him time to fix Archer's face in his mind. They were living breathing HUDS acquiring their targets, locked and loaded. Archer's photograph made it as far as SWAT. It didn't need to go any further.

The Dane took the opportunity the diversion created and approached the freed hostage. She looked up at him as he flashed his credentials just long enough for her to see the letters FBI. "Who are you?"

"Alice," she said. "Alice Fisher."

"I didn't ask you what your name was. I asked you who you were. That's a different thing. I want to know why he let you go. Did he hit you?"

"No."

"You don't work in the bank, so you're a customer, but your bruises and the fact you're first out make you a person of interest, so explain it to me. What's your connection here?"

She looked at him. He could see from her face that she was considering a lie. He didn't say anything. He gave her time enough to hang herself. "We work together at the casino. He runs the floor, I deal the cards on one of the tables. He's a bastard and I hate him. That's why he sent me out first. He didn't want me getting in the way."

It was *almost* believable, which of course was the

foundation of all the best lies. They wrapped themselves up in aspects of the truth.

"And that's it?"

"That's it."

"Tell me what it's like in there. What's his endgame? You know him. What's his mindset?"

"I don't know him," she said. "Not like that." And this time he was sure she was lying.

He resisted the temptation to call her on it. The fact she was lying meant she had something to lie about. The Dane was only interested if that lie had any relevance to his job. If it didn't she could lie away to her heart's content. He looked down at her hands. They weren't moving. They were folded on her lap, resting on a clutch bag. They were perfectly still. Protectively so. The logical conclusion was that there was something in that bag she didn't want the people out here seeing. Maybe she was helping Archer rob the bank, smuggling the real object of the robbery out from the vault right under their noses? That wouldn't be a bad plan. It was like those robberies where the thieves held safety-deposit boxes inside the vault themselves and got away with thousands of dollars simply by moving their ill-gotten gains from one box to another. He didn't care if she was. As long as it wasn't screwing Bonavechio over she could do whatever the hell she liked, including taking down Chicago Liberty.

He tried to think through the possibilities: what else could she be bringing out of there? What would be worth risking it all to get out before the cops stormed the place?

That, he couldn't answer.

"Get us a couple of coffees," he said to a nearby officer. She didn't look best pleased, but with Davenport otherwise occupied she didn't have much choice. The Dane crouched down in front of Alice and took both of her hands in his. At first it looked like a comforting gesture, but then his grip shifted and his thumbs pressed down against the web of veins and arteries inside her wrist. "I'm going to ask you a series of questions and you are going to tell the truth. I'll know if you are lying. Do you understand?"

"Yes."

"Good. I'll start with something simple. What is in that bag you don't want me seeing?"

It wasn't about feeling her pulse trip, of course, what he was really doing was watching her eyes. "Nothing."

Not a flicker.

Maybe he'd got it wrong. Sometimes a bag was just a bag.

"How do you know Samuel Archer?"

"We work together. I already told you. He's my boss."

"So why were you in the bank with him today?" This was one that interested him. They had no reason to be in there together.

"I wasn't with him."

"You just happened to be in the bank when he walked in?"

"No."

"Then what?"

“He was already in there when *I* walked in.” A pause. “I was making a deposit.” He noted again the way her hands protected the bag. It made sense if there was money in there. “He saw me. I think that set him off.”

“How so?”

“He was calm right up until he turned and saw me. Then he changed. It was like he panicked. He hadn’t expected anyone in there to know who he was. When he saw me he knew he was screwed.”

“Because you hate him?”

“I do.”

“Why?”

“Because he’s a bastard.”

“No, really, why?”

“That’s reason enough in my world, *agent*,” the way she said that last word, voice dripping with sarcasm, amused the Dane.

“So you expect me to believe Archer saw you, panicked, and wound up taking everyone hostage?”

“Honestly? I couldn’t give a fuck what you believe.” Her pulse was dead steady. Her gaze didn’t waver. Either she wasn’t lying or was an accomplished liar.

“Why did he send you out first?”

“I told you. Because I’m trouble,” she said, and that he could very well believe.

“In what way?”

“In the I-hate-him way. Everything he said, I contradicted.

I got under his skin. He wanted me out of there."

"And you did this despite the fact he had a gun pointed at you? You're either very brave, Miss Fisher, or very stupid. I am aware that it is wrong to judge someone on looks alone, but I find it hard to believe you are either."

"I've got hidden depths," she said.

"And a smart mouth."

"My momma done raise me good," she said.

"I'm sure she's very proud."

"She has no idea who I am," she said, with an undercurrent of anger that far outstripped any she'd shown towards Samuel Archer. Interesting. "Dementia."

"I'm sorry."

"Why? You don't know her. You don't know me."

"No, you're right. It's just something to say," the Dane said. "Conforming to social norms."

"You are a strange man."

"Indeed."

"You're not FBI, are you?"

"What would make you think that?"

"I've known plenty of cops. You're different. And in this case, like the old *Sesame Street* song, 'One of these is not like the other ones, one of these does not belong.'"

"And yet I'm the one asking the questions."

"You work for Bonavechio? Is that it? Did he send you?"

"I'm here to help you, Alice," he said.

"Did he send you?"

"I don't know what you are talking about." He was a better liar than she was.

"He did, didn't he? You're the cleaner come to mop up Archer's mess."

"I think you should be *very* careful what you say, Alice. We're not exactly alone here. So tell me, how do you fit into all of this? He might be stupid enough to think you're innocent—" he shook his head disparagingly towards Davenport "—but I'm not. So talk to me."

"I'm a criminal mastermind, don't you know?" Alice said, rolling her eyes. "I just robbed the bank, framed Archer for it, and walked out of the front door with a fortune in my clutch. Is that what you want me to say?"

"If it's the truth."

"Is it? You tell me. You're the one playing human lie detector."

"Nothing has changed. I still think you're lying." But before he could press the issue any further, he saw Davenport walking towards them.

"Get away from her. Now."

"I was just—" the Dane started to say. He didn't get to finish. How much had Davenport overheard?

"I don't care what you were *just*. I told you to stay out of the way. That's it, you're done here, Salisbury. I'm not having you interfering. I don't care if Archer's connected to the biggest crime family in Chicago. Right now this is all about getting our hostages out alive. There's nothing for the Bureau to do here. So get yourself behind the barriers with the other Looky-Lous."

The Dane relinquished his grip on Alice Fisher's wrists. "You're making a mistake, Davenport."

"You know, that almost sounds like a threat. But you wouldn't be dumb enough to do that, would you? Because if you are that stupid, that FBI badge of yours won't protect you."

The Dane rose slowly from his crouching position. "Heaven forbid," he said, leaving plenty of room for Davenport to read the silence after the words. "I was only trying to help. I have a particular skill set, as I said. I was merely offering my services."

"We don't need your help, we've got everything covered here. Now, if you don't mind?" Davenport gestured in the direction of the barricade.

The Dane saw Alice's hands go back to her purse protectively.

There was definitely something in there she didn't want the cops knowing about. He thought about snatching it out of her hands and upending the contents onto the road, but with so many guns in close proximity any sudden movement was liable to get him shot by one of the itchier trigger fingers. Bonavechio had claimed he had no link to the woman, but she clearly knew exactly who he was, and that he was likely to send someone like the Dane to fix the mess. He was intrigued. Most people were shallow souls who didn't think beyond what they were having for dinner and when the next episode of their favorite show was on. But he didn't have time to learn her story now. Maybe tomorrow they'd be reacquainted.

"Whatever you say, Davenport. I know when I'm not wanted."

"Good. I'm glad we see things the same way. I hear there's a good coffee shop a couple of blocks away, why don't you go and get yourself a cup?"

"Perhaps I will," the Dane said, with no intention of doing so. He needed to make sure Archer didn't walk out of that bank. Of course, the fact that he was a giant black man didn't hurt. Racial profiling meant his life expectancy could be measured out in minutes now that his photograph was in circulation. The moment he set foot on the sidewalk someone would shoot and call it justified because no matter what they said, black lives mattered just a little less in some of those small minds.

He looked at his watch. He was going to be late for the sit down with Bonavechio's sellers if he didn't go now. He needed to make a judgment call. Gamble that this debacle wouldn't sort itself out before he could get to the warehouse, do what needed to be done and get back, or risk Bonavechio's wrath by standing up the Syrian dealers in the warehouse. That would piss off some unpleasant people, and screw the deal. He could live with that, it was only money and they were only a couple of pissant-no-marks he could visit any evening to make sure they didn't see morning. They were dominoes. It was only one deal, but if Bonavechio was buying their pieces, that meant he already had more buyers in place, and even one hiccup in the chain had ramifications. A guy like Bonavechio, his word was gold. If he said you were getting a shipment of small arms you could take that to the bank. Literally and figuratively, it seemed.

He took a card from his pocket and gave it to the woman. The only thing written on it was the number for a burner phone and the name Kage Salisbury. "Call me if you think of anything I might find interesting."

"Don't," Davenport said. Even so, the woman opened her clutch, slipping the card inside. The movement offered a tantalizing glimpse of the purse's contents, but the shadows hid what was inside beyond basic contours. It wasn't treasure, that was for sure. It was a gun.

Interesting again.

She'd been in there with a gun and hadn't taken a shot at Archer? Yet she claimed she wasn't an accomplice? She wanted him to believe that she hated the man. So, in the time they were in there he was supposed to buy that she'd never had a shot? It didn't work like that. Was that all she was hiding? That she'd had a chance to change the outcome, but hadn't? He would have loved the opportunity to ask her.

"Do you have a number for someone to call?" Davenport asked the woman, gesturing for the Dane to take a walk. "Someone who can come and collect you? Family?"

"I live alone," she said. She dropped her voice, no doubt in the vain hope that the Dane wouldn't hear. "My mother… is in a care home. There's no one."

"We're going to need you to go down to the station for a full debrief, keep you out of the eye of the reporters until everything's blown over. If you just sit tight I'll have an officer collect you."

She inclined her head, as though just remembering something. She had their attention. She was good at this. The Dane knew she was about to say something important; a memory that had just come back to her. She was playing Davenport like a fiddle. "There was a guy at the casino last night… shit, I can't remember the guy's name… He was looking for Archer. Some sort of player come in from out of town. I didn't like the look of him."

"Why?" Davenport said, clearly buying into her story.

"I don't know. There was just something about him."

"Can you remember what he looked like?"

"Tall, fairly nondescript. Well-dressed. Arrogant. It was obvious they had history. You can tell that kind of thing."

"What did he want with Archer?"

"Money," she said. "He wanted money."

Archer's accomplice? Did that explain why he had gone off message and started working for himself? He was going to need to find out what went down between those two last night. There were answers there to questions he hadn't even thought of yet. "They went outside together. Archer was acting really weird after that. You can talk to any of the girls working. Do you think he had something to do with this?"

"Perhaps," Davenport said. "He almost certainly had help."

"Milo," she said suddenly. "That was his name. Milo something. God, what was his surname?" She shook her head. "Sorry. I'll know it when I hear it, but…" She shrugged.

She was good. She was up to her neck in this, the Dane was absolutely certain of that now, doling out little clues to keep them hanging on her every word. Give him twenty-four hours alone with her and she'd give up every secret she'd ever heard, but that wasn't his job. Making sure Samuel Archer didn't get to spill Bonavechio's secrets to Davenport and his crew was. Nothing else mattered.

48

She had lied through her teeth.

It had been rough when the creepy white-haired guy took her hands. She had been sure she was going to screw up, say the wrong thing and land them all in the shit. Then it had hit her: he wasn't with the law, he was Bonavechio's man, come to contain the situation. Instead of scaring her, that put Alice at her ease. She had spent a lifetime dealing with crooks and killers. It was the good guys that messed with her head.

She had made absolutely sure he saw the gun when she slipped his card into her clutch. Let him work that one out. If he was good he'd realize it was far too big a gun for a woman like her to tote around for personal protection. It was an excessive piece. Big gun small dick. It was Samuel Archer all over.

She didn't stick around any longer than she absolutely had to, sneaking away while Davenport was arranging for an officer to escort her back to the station. It hadn't been difficult to slip away with everyone more concerned with what was going on inside the bank rather than outside. She took the L train, buying a new ticket with cash rather than using her card so there was no punch-in punch-out trail for anyone to follow. She changed her look twice on the journey, too, picking up a cheap hoodie from the back of a Goodwill bin, then bunching her hair up inside a baseball cap for the final leg of the journey back to the little boutique hotel, killing time so that she arrived fifteen minutes after the night manager began his shift.

He didn't look pleased to see her as she took the cap off and shook out her hair. Mind you, the broken nose and black eye Archer had given him made it difficult to make out any kind of expression through the bruises. "You," he said. "You are not welcome here. Go. Now. Please." He sounded absolutely terrified, and kept looking over her shoulder. She knew he was looking for Archer.

She looked at his name badge. "He's not coming, Stephen," she said. He didn't look like he believed her.

Alice tried to summon a smile as she leaned up against the reception desk. She toyed with the gold pen that lay on the blotter between them. "I need your help," she said.

He shook his head. "No."

"It's not what you think."

"That's worse, then."

"It isn't. I'm not asking you do to anything more than let me have a room."

"We're fully booked."

"I can make it worth your while," she said with a seductive edge in her voice, hating herself. Archer had turned her into a whore.

"I doubt it," Stephen said.

She picked the pen up. She could see the panic just behind his eyes. He was probably imagining Archer ramming it through the back of his hand to make his point. She put it down again. "Please. I'm not asking you to get involved. It's just a room."

"That's all?"

She nodded.

"And you'll go away and leave me alone after that?"

She nodded again.

"That bastard won't turn up looking to hurt me for helping you?"

This time she shook her head. "No."

"How can you be sure?"

"Turn on the TV." That confused him. "Any local twenty-four-hour news station, check out the stand-off outside Chicago Liberty Bank."

"He's holding up a bank?"

"Hostages and all."

"Fuck me…"

"If that's what it takes," Alice said.

He didn't react to the offer.

"You only want a room? That's it?"

"I can pay for it. Cash."

"But it's just a room? Nothing's going to come back and bite me on the ass? After last night… Horace Greene is a mess. He's out for blood."

"You're not going to be collateral damage, Stephen. I promise. You're doing a good thing here. Can you give me a room next door to Greene's or directly below it?"

He rubbed at his face, his finger and thumb pinching the bridge of his nose. His breathing changed. A sigh. His resistance crumbled. It was that easy.

"I need it for a week, starting last Thursday."

Stephen reached for the wireless keyboard. "Name?"

"Milo…" What was the name Richard had used? Shit. She should have written it down. A painter. Famous. American. Hopper? Warhol? No, that wasn't it. Landscapes. White picket fences. "Rockwell."

"You don't look like a Milo."

"Appearances can be deceptive," Alice said.

"Room 602. Sixth floor. It's yours. Don't tell me what you plan to do with it. I don't want to know. Okay?"

She promised. She put three thousand dollars on the counter and pushed it towards him.

"That's too much."

"Consider it a thank you. Is there another way in and out?"

"Service elevator, round the back. Now I really don't want to know."

"Best you don't," she agreed, taking the key card off him

before he could change his mind. "Does it need the card swipe?" She was thinking about the digital trail. These cards logged each swipe on the system. If the cops saw Milo's room key had opened the staff door at three in the morning that might raise an eyebrow or, thinking about it, maybe, just maybe, it'd be perfect, suggesting Archer's partner had left and, if they wedged the back doors open, never returned. That could work.

She clenched her fist, digging her fingernails deep into her palm as she crossed the foyer to the elevator. This was the last place on earth she wanted to be; last night was still vivid in her mind.

"Suck it up," she muttered under her breath. "You can have a breakdown later."

One night, she promised herself as she rode the elevator up to the sixth floor. *You can do that. Don't think about it yet.* As the doors parted, the sensual voice whispered disconcertingly, "Sixth floor."

She didn't take Archer's phone from her clutch until she had closed the bedroom door behind her.

The room was every bit as luxurious as the room above, but on a smaller scale, the furnishings mercifully different. She could almost pretend it was a different place. The shower was glass. She knew that without even going into the bathroom because part of the bedroom wall was also glass, meaning one could lie on the bed watching water stream down a lover's naked body. She assumed that was all part of the seduction package. Tantalizing glimpses of soapy flesh. Probably not as appealing if your roommate was two hundred and forty pounds of beached whale replete with pale folds of blubber.

She sat on the bed, kicking off her shoes as she thumbed through the cellphone's options until she found Archer's calendar.

All it said for last night was "Player One."

She fixed that, adding a second name beneath, "Milo Rockwell," and saved her changes. The inference was obvious. Now there was a trail that blazed brightly between Archer and the mythical Milo Rockwell. That name was going to keep cropping up: bank records, his visit to the casino, the hotel.

She'd done her part. The rest was down to Theo and the others.

49

THE DANE'S CAR WAS parked in a small lot another block and a half from the police cordon. It was a classic. A 1957 Chevrolet Bel Air, blacker than black, white-rimmed wheels, and fins. The chrome V above the Chevy's radiator grill made the front look like a scowling face. He opened the door, climbed into the red leather seat and threw his laptop bag down onto the passenger seat. The interior still smelled of wax. He fired up the V8 engine and peeled out of the parking bay, not using his blinkers as he rolled out to join the traffic.

It took him forty-five minutes to drive to the warehouse.

That gave him plenty of time to think.

The fact that Archer had chosen today to rob a bank just didn't make sense, but no matter how much he worried at the puzzle the picture wouldn't reveal itself. There was more going on here. Was Archer working with someone else? He had to be, didn't he? He wasn't a prime mover. He was a glorified bagman. He did what he was told.

So who was doing the telling?

The Dane was working in the dark. Bonavechio knew more than he was letting on, the Dane was sure of that. He was equally sure that if challenged, Bonavechio would dismiss his concern with a brusque, "You know what you need to."

Cranes came into view, giant relics of the city's past life towering over the dockside, casting long shadows. He killed the engine outside the corrugated steel doors of the warehouse. He could see the outlines of two vehicles parked inside: a sedan and a huge eighteen-wheeler. The Dane clambered out of his car, but left the door open and the keys in the ignition.

In front of him, two men mirrored the movement, leaving their own vehicles. First impressions: they were slight, not muscle men. They moved with the arrogance of a different kind of strength. They were empty-handed.

The Dane scanned the warehouse. "Where's the merchandise?"

"You're late," the first man said, his Syrian accent thick.

"I'm the back-up plan," the Dane said by way of explanation. "I'm not late at all. The other guy was late."

The seller didn't appreciate the difference.

"I'm authorized to make the transaction, that's really all you need to concern yourself with. You waited long enough to convince me all you care about is the money; let's get this over with. So show me what I'm paying for."

The sellers led him around to the back of the eighteen-wheeler and opened the back to reveal stacks of military-issue crates lined up all the way to the back. Using a crowbar the silent man pried the top off one of them. Fifty handguns packed in straw. The lid came off the second crate, to reveal a host of semi-automatics. "It's all here, as agreed," the man assured him. "Highest quality. Untraceable. A lot of work has gone into this. We've been patient with your boss. We want our money now. Five million. No cash, no toys."

"The laptop's in the car, I'll need it to transfer the money."

"Then go and get it."

The Dane didn't appreciate being talked to like a lapdog. He walked slowly back to the Chevy. It was a power play, letting them know he wasn't frightened of them. It said quite clearly he didn't think they had the balls to shoot him.

He reached into the car for the bag, pulling the laptop out. He put it on the roof of the car.

"I need to get the authorization code," he explained, taking his cellphone from his pocket. He could feel the cold weight of his gun against the base of his spine. He dialed Bonavechio.

"The merchandise is good. They want paying."

"Of course." Bonavechio gave him the details of the "business" account Archer handled for him, including the passwords to assure clearance through the bank's security. It took less than a minute. The arms dealers never looked away from the Dane's fingers as he typed. It couldn't have been that interesting a spectacle, but they had millions of reasons to be fascinated by a few keystrokes.

"Okay gentlemen, I'm going to need somewhere to put all of this money," the Dane said, even as he noticed a problem.

The account was empty. There should have been 5.3 million dollars in there, but it had been cleaned out today. Which explained what Archer was doing in the bank.

He pretended to key in the transaction details as the Syrians dictated their account number. He picked up his phone again. The line was still open.

"I know what Archer was doing in the bank," he said.

"What?"

"Cleaning the Cympac account out. It's empty."

"Impossible."

"And yet it's done."

He registered the surprise followed by hostility on the dealers' faces. He didn't wait for the word from Bonavechio. This was a mess. But it wasn't his mess and he wasn't going to let it bring him down. He was faster than the other men. He drew the Browning before they could pull their weapons and put two bullets into them.

He knew that Bonavechio would have heard the gunshots down the open line.

"Change of plans," the Dane said, walking slowly across the concrete hardstand to the eighteen-wheeler. Through the windshield he saw the panicked face of a third man trying to get the engine started. No doubt the glass was bulletproof. What that meant in reality was bullet-*resistant*, not impenetrable. He put six shots into the exact same square centimeter of glass, first weakening then shattering the glass with the sheer bludgeoning force of repetition. The seventh shot killed the driver.

"What the fuck have you done?" Bonavechio barked at him down the phone.

"Saved your five million bucks that you don't currently have. Don't worry, they won't be looking for a refund."

"I don't understand—"

"You need to look at the numbers. Check every dime Archer was in control of. This one account I'm looking at is empty. And it's not just today. He's been skimming cash one transaction at a time, sending it to some numbered account offshore, always keeping the amount under the declaration threshold. I can only see so far back, but if it follows the same pattern I figure maybe fifteen, eighteen million dollars over the years, depends how long you've trusted him with the keys to the kingdom. You almost have to admire the guy. It takes balls to rob you."

"The cunt. The absolute *cunt*."

"Well, yes. That too."

The Dane could hear Bonavechio's panic and the frantic activity of computer keyboard keys tapping. Then there was silence, which was far eerier.

The Dane was curious. There was something very *off* about all of this.

"I want to check something," he said. "Do you have a friendly cop? Someone I can talk to?"

Bonavechio gave him a name. "Find out what the fuck is going on."

"Trust me. I want to get paid for this."

He put a fresh call through to Bonavechio's bent cop.

"Barnes," the voice on the other end said, utterly uninterested.

"Saul Bonavechio told me you were his man," the Dane said by way of hello. "I need you to run the financials on Samuel Jefferson Archer. Get me everything. Every account he's connected to in any way. Got it?"

"How do I—"

"Don't bother wasting time going on about warrants and rights. Run his financials. Tell me if you see anything out of the ordinary. And do it fast. You can reach me on this number. Do this and Bonavechio will owe you." The Dane was looking for secrets, things not obviously there to be seen.

He killed the call and set about securing the eighteen-wheeler to make sure Bonavechio didn't get ripped off twice in one day. It took much longer than he would have liked, but eventually his phone rang. It was Barnes.

"This guy's neck deep in shit, seriously. He's been moving serious money from accounts he's signatory on, skimming cash. There's enough here to keep White Collar busy for a year trying to figure it all out."

"Anything from today?"

"Maybe. A single payment. There was 5.3 million in there that was moved into an escrow account this morning. It's scheduled to be deposited into an account that didn't exist until today." He'd seen the transaction, but the fact that the destination account was brand new was useful information.

"Give me a name."

"The account's registered to one Milo Rockwell. But when I cross-reference that name I get nothing. No birth certificate, no registration with the IRS, nothing. He's a ghost."

Just like me, the Dane thought. He'd heard that name before.

"You've done good. Very good. Bonavechio will be grateful."

"Well he can do me a favor and fuck off out of my life then. Tell him we're done. This pays off my debt."

"I'll pass the message on," the Dane said, but the cop was gone.

Pulling the dead man out of the driver's seat of the eighteen-wheeler and dumping him unceremoniously on the hardstand, the Dane called Bonavechio.

"What did you say that guy was called?"

"What fucking guy?"

"The one he had a run-in with last night. The one who claimed to be representing a West Coast interest?"

"Why the fuck is that important?"

"Just tell me his name."

"Milo something. I don't fucking remember."

"Rockwell."

"If you say so."

"I say so. You were right to be concerned about your man's

loyalty. Today Samuel Archer paid Milo Rockwell a lot of money. They were working together. Archer sold you out."

Silence can have a lot of different qualities, but only one kind of silence is so fraught with pent-up rage the air around it seems to crackle.

"I want those bastards buried—Rockwell and Archer both. You understand me? Six feet fucking under. No one steals from me."

"You might want to send someone out here to pick up the shipment and dispose of the bodies then."

The last thing he heard before the line died was the impact of Bonavechio's phone being hurled at the wall.

50

THE CLEANUP TOOK AN hour. In that time Richard Rhodes wrestled with the backup generator, finally managing to undo Ellie's effective sabotage while Margot and Beth had scrubbed their hands raw trying to get the blood out of the carpet. Without the bright fluorescents it was impossible to tell just how obvious it was. It wasn't as though they could just rearrange the furniture to cover the mess up.

The phone rang.

Theo answered. "Is it that time again?"

He gestured towards Margot, signaling for her to get her things together. She didn't need telling twice. She wanted to get out of there. Collect Jake and go home. Get into the shower and wash the horrors of the day off her body. She knew she'd never be able to wash them from her mind. And she already had enough demons to last her a lifetime.

She crossed herself reflexively.

She'd been hanging around Beth for too long. The woman looked like she'd aged a decade since the siege began. That, Margot figured, was the cost of losing your soul.

"So what do I get in return?" Theo said into the phone, still looking at her.

She didn't like the security guard. There was just something about him. He seemed to be enjoying this too much.

He made a face, shaking his head. "Man, whatever happened to *quid pro quo*? If I'm sending one of ours out I want something in return… How about you turn the lights back on?" He grunted out a laugh a second later. "Well, I had to ask. I'm guessing a helicopter's still out of the question?" Again with that laugh, though it sounded a little bitter now, like he really was bargaining for his life. She didn't know how he could do it. It was like he was a different person. "Then time. I want time to think. I want a guarantee you won't try to storm this place for at least—" He looked over at the big clock on the wall which had stopped counting down when the power went out "—two hours. Two female hostages are worth that much to you, aren't they? An hour each. That gets us two more people towards a happy ending. Keeps your people happy, gives me a chance to think about how I'm going to stay out of jail." She could hear the negotiator's laughter down the phone line. "Yeah, that's me, ever the optimist," Theo agreed. "Do I have your word?" He nodded. "I'm sending them out. Tell your boys to stand down."

And with those few words she knew she was going home.

But she had things she needed to do before she could enjoy that shower she'd promised herself.

She needed to call Nero and convince him to help them.

The prospect frightened her more than anything else that had happened today. It was one thing for him to be a voice. But to make him complicit in a crime, that was taking their relationship onto a level with John Joseph's second life.

Were they ready for that?

Was she?

It wasn't like she had a choice, though, was it?

"Go," Theo said. "Beth, you too. Remember… drop the name Milo Rockwell into one of your answers. They'll want to know what Archer's state of mind is like. But make it subtle, a throwaway remark about something you overhead. An argument on the phone before they cut off cell reception. Don't get too specific."

Margot nodded. "I've got it. Wish us luck."

No one did.

Theo unlocked the front doors and allowed the two women to slip through, hands above their heads. Margot was genuinely terrified as she walked towards the bank of guns pointing at her. After half a dozen steps the walk became a run.

She sank into the arms of the police officer that ran to meet her halfway. He was all kind words and reassurances; it was over, she was out, she was safe. "It's not," she said. "It's not over. I'll never feel safe again."

The cops hurried them over to a large van where two female officers waited with blankets. One officer led Beth out of earshot—for her own debriefing, Margot presumed—as Margot herself huddled on the steps, shaking.

"We just need to ask you a few questions," the woman said, her hand on Margot's shoulder. "Nothing too difficult, we're not trying to trip you up. But you know where the other hostages are and their condition."

She nodded. "Of course. Yes. Absolutely. But I'm not sure what I can tell you that you don't already know."

"You let us worry about that. Now, what's your name?"

"Margot Moore."

"Okay, Margot. How is everyone? Anyone hurt?"

She shook her head. "No. No. He hasn't hurt anyone."

"That's good. That's really good. So everything's calm in there?"

She nodded again. "Everyone's just sitting around on the chairs in the main lobby."

"What about the robber, Samuel Archer?"

"He's on the counter," she said without thinking. It seemed like the kind of place a bank robber would sit, lording it over them. "Cross-legged. Beside the phones. He's got the gun on his lap." It was going to be the little things that sold the lie.

"Has he said what he wants? What he was trying to achieve by robbing the bank?"

Her gaze darted left, towards the building. She couldn't help herself. "Before the power went out he took a call."

"Did you hear a name?"

"Milo."

That one word brought a flicker of instant recognition with it. Alice had obviously managed to plant the lie. Her repetition of it sold it. "When was this?"

"I don't know. Not long after they locked us in."

"They? There's more than one robber?"

Margot shook her head quickly. "No, no. Theo Monk, the security guard, locked the door. Archer made him."

"Ah, I'm with you. Do you have any idea what Archer talked about to this Milo?"

"Money," she said. Keep it simple. Small lies. They wouldn't have shared any elaborate plans over the phone. It wasn't the movies, villains didn't spill their guts before getting themselves caught.

"How did Archer sound?"

"Frustrated."

"What happened after the call? Did anything change?"

She thought about it, buying herself a few seconds before seeming to recall something. A detail. She looked at the woman and offered an unsure smile. "Sasha, the other teller. He made Sasha do something on the computer."

"A transaction?"

"I couldn't see," she said. She didn't need to say any more. They knew where to start looking for the imaginary Milo Rockwell.

"That's fine. That's more than fine, Margot. A lot more.

Can you think of anything else that might help us? Nothing's insignificant right now."

Margot shook her head slowly, trying to think of another lie, a final piece in the puzzle that would make sure they found their way to the hotel and Archer's body. But she didn't want them getting there before the corpse. "They talked about someone… Archer sounded scared of him."

"Who? Can you remember?" It wasn't the female officer this time. It was a man. He acted like he was in charge. She assumed it was Marcus Davenport, the man Theo had talked to on the phone.

"I… I'm not sure."

"Think," the man pressed.

"Bonamassa…? Bonaducci? Something Italian. Does that mean anything?"

"Could it have been Bonavechio?"

"Maybe. Yes."

"That means something, all right," Davenport said. He grinned fiercely. "You're sure it was Bonavechio? Saul Bonavechio?" She nodded. "Thank you. We'll make sure someone gets you home when you're ready. Is there someone we can call?"

"It's fine."

"Are you sure? It's no problem. We're going to need you to go to the police station now for a proper debrief. It's just procedure, and I'm sorry to add to the hell you've been already been through. I'm sure you just want to go to bed."

"I need to make a call first, let the sitter know I'm running late."

"We can sort that out for you."

"It's fine, it'll just take a second. Is there somewhere I can make a call?"

She was thinking on her feet. She could just call Nero, even if it would have been so much easier to look him in the eye and ask for his help. The real problem was that she had to collect Jake from his sitter. She couldn't palm that off on an officer, it'd be a link back to Adam. She fished her cellphone out of her bag. There was no signal.

"You'll need to walk a couple of blocks for normal service," the officer said apologetically. "Come and find me when you're done and I'll drive you home."

"Will do."

Margot kept the blanket around her shoulders as she walked towards the barrier. She had no intention of returning. She'd flag a cab down and go to Jake as soon as she'd hung up on Nero.

She didn't get an open line until she was six blocks from the bank. She thumbed through her contacts until she found his name.

When he picked up she said, "I need you."

"That's what every boy wants to hear," he said, that laconic sense of humor of his so familiar, so reassuring, after everything that had happened today.

"I need to see you," Margot said.

That was greeted by silence. It stretched out for so long she was sure the signal had dropped. Or he'd hung up on her.

Finally, he said, "I'm not sure that's a good idea."

"Please. It's important. I need your help."

"Whatever you need we can do over the phone. Online. That's where I'm at my best."

"I get that. I really do. But I need to see you. Please. I need to look you in the eye and explain."

"Eyes are overrated," Nero said.

"Don't make fun of me."

"I'm not. But you need to understand… I'm not… well, I told you, I don't see people. It's not who I am."

"I can't do this without you," she said, and it was the truth on so many different levels.

"Then talk to me, Margot. You know I'm here for you. This is how it is."

"I need to see a friendly face."

"That's not good enough."

"I can't do this alone."

"Again, not good enough."

"Please," she said.

"No," he said. "If you care about me at all, please don't make me say no to you again, Margot. Let me help you. You know I'd do anything for you, but—"

"I can't do that," she finished for him.

She didn't ask again.

51

THE MAN WHO CALLED himself Nero lived in a man-made hell.

The projects might have been torn down, but low income and Social Security housing was still a fundamental part of Chicago life. His personal circle was in the heart of high-rise territory. Nero's apartment was at the top of one of the tallest blocks. In the streets below kids milled around, fists buried deep in pockets, hoods pulled up over heads, menacing in their urban camouflage.

The building's interior was drab, decorated with layers of inventive graffiti and gang tags, and the elevator had a sign plastered across the door—OUT OF SERVICE. It promised that the repairman was coming on Wednesday to fix it, though not *which* Wednesday. The only other option was the stairs. All nineteen floors of them, which meant he was locked in.

"One day, I promise, Margot. One day. But not today. I'm not ready for you to see me. So, tell me what you need me to do."

Outside, a door opened and slammed closed a couple of seconds later. Voices rose and fell.

His wheelchair had left scuff marks all the way along the walls and baseboards around the door even though the frames had been widened to accommodate it. Bluish light from a bank of computer screens filled the lounge. There were nine screens in total, supported by a huge steel frame that made the room look like a mission control. One of the screens cycled through black-and-white footage from security cameras around the apartment complex, another showed the familiar façade of Margot's branch of Chicago Liberty, the one beside it focused on the crowd of sightseers gathered behind the police tape to feed whatever vicarious thrill it was they got from being so close to the news cameras.

Nero couldn't take his eyes off the bank, even though he'd watched her walk out a few minutes ago. He waited for her to find the words to tell him what she needed him to do.

"I know you've been watching," she said. It wasn't an accusation. She'd told him often enough she liked having him as her guardian angel. It was just habit now; one of his screens was always tuned to her, either home or work, making sure she was all right. He'd known all day that she wasn't and had felt absolutely useless. He'd called it in as soon as he realized what was going on, but hadn't left a name.

"They killed him," she said.

"Who?"

"The robber," she said. "They killed the robber."

He tried to make sense of what she was saying. "You mean the other hostages?"

"Yes."

"Then why haven't they all just walked out the front door?"

"It was an accident."

"That doesn't make sense, Margot. If the robber is dead, everyone's safe. Why are the others still in there?"

"It's complicated."

"Then make me understand," Nero said. "You said you needed my help. I can't help you if I don't know what's going on."

He listened in silence as she described the events in the bank: the truth about Adam Shaw and how the gun had gone off in his hand; about his disabled son; the crimes of the man who'd died and how he'd used Alice; how they'd decided to help Adam get away with murder; how they'd taken the dead man's money; the false transactions to create a digital paper trail between the dead man and his make-believe co-conspirator; her words leading into what they needed to happen next.

"The security cameras on the street. The ones inside the bank were turned off, but the cops are going to see Adam going inside the bank and not coming out."

"And you want me to make sure they don't see him go in?"

"Can you?"

"Do you have any idea what you're asking?"

"Not really," she admitted.

"It's not like piggybacking the signal to watch," Nero said. "We'd need to find out where they store the servers holding the feed—probably in some classified bunker somewhere—get inside the system, and we're talking top-tier security, where they store the files, work out what kind of filing system they've got, where the data we need is, and then excise it without it being obvious someone's been inside. Otherwise they'll start looking for what's missing, and if we're unlucky, they've got backups they can cross-reference against, meaning we'd have to find those too, or we're shit out of luck."

"Can you do it?"

"I have no idea," Nero admitted. "I'm not even sure *where* I'm supposed to start. But I've got an idea. It's a million-to-one shot, Jim, but it might just work. You're just going to have to trust me."

"Always."

His fingers didn't flutter over the keyboard as he triggered a series of Linux commands, they pecked awkwardly. Even five years old, the damage made sitting awkward. The real pains might have faded, but he'd developed a habit of torturing his body with a series of contortions as he typed to best minimize the phantom ones that had replaced them.

Two of his screens had names on them, and a string of coordinates. Margot's name was among them, halfway down the first. There were others on there. Others he had saved. Brian Anderson, Sarah Matthews, Caleb Carter, Jo-Beth Hart, Annabel Peterson. This was his life now. It had been for almost three years. It had taken two for the self-pity to wear off enough that he could come up with a plan for how he wanted to spend the rest of his life, even if he couldn't go outside.

He started to work, the Linux commands slowly scrolling across the screen, some of them repeating over and over, *sudo, echo, strace*. That last one occurred again and again the deeper he got into the rabbit hole, searching for the files that would help him make Adam Shaw effectively disappear. The images on one of the screens changed.

He had an old vinyl turntable and a couple of thousand records in battered sleeves all neatly slotted away in deep IKEA bookcases. Those black discs were where he chose to escape when he wanted to lose himself; Sammy Davis Jr., Sinatra, Muddy Waters, BB King, Howlin' Wolf, Buddy Guy, Ray Charles, Etta James, Billie Holiday, and Nina Simone. Proper singers. He had all of the songs ripped to MP3 to listen to while he worked without having to navigate the room. He started the player, the volume down low. Janis Joplin's voice conveyed so much sadness. It reminded him of being young.

"You never told me the dead man's name," Nero said.

"Samuel Archer," she said.

"Say that again."

"Samuel Archer."

"What did he look like?"

There was a pause. "He was really big, like a boxer. Black, about thirty years old."

"I know him," Nero said. "I don't want you to think less of

me... but I already told you that I used the Internet to find someone who would be... kind."

"He brought you a girl?"

"Her name was Alice. She was nice. Patient. I didn't know what I was physically capable of. She lay beside me, just letting me feel her skin up against my back. She talked to me." He fell silent.

"I know her story," Margot said. "I don't want to call it coincidence. That doesn't feel meaningful enough. Everything in my life since you came into it feels like it's linked."

"Then call it fate," he said. "He did things to her. She told me she was trying to get away from him, but he owned her. We didn't do anything. Just talked. I didn't want to be another reason for her to hurt, and for a while I felt... normal again."

Her name was on the second screen, near the bottom: Alice Fisher. Nero removed it from his list. Without Archer in her life she didn't need him anymore. "He's connected to some very bad people. They won't let this lie. They'll want to know the truth."

"Which is why we're doing this," Margot said.

"Then I'd better not let you down."

He saw movement on the live feed. Someone else was emerging from the bank—a man in a security guard's uniform. He put his hands behind his head as he walked slowly away from the building, and just as they had with Margot, officers rushed forward to scoop him up and lead him away.

They managed six steps before they all seemed to stumble,

as if some giant invisible hand had reached out from inside Chicago Liberty and shoved them violently.

The center of the screen burned out in bright light, and went blank.

"The feed's dead. Margot? Margot?"

"I'm here. I'm okay," she promised him.

"What just happened?"

"I heard an explosion."

"A bomb?"

"I don't know."

"Get yourself out of there."

"I've got to go and get Jake. Don't let me down. Please. I need you to sort that footage."

"It's done."

52

"WHAT'S HAPPENING OUT THERE?"

Sasha cupped her hands over her eyes and pressed up against the glass like it was some sort of periscope. "They're moving about. A lot. Something's happening. I think they're getting ready to make their move." She could see three men in SWAT gear, each built like a brick shithouse, natural muscles exaggerated by heavily padded body armor. They carried death lightly in their hands. Guns frightened Sasha. Properly frightened her. They served a single purpose, no matter how many arguments the NRA threw up to confuse the issue.

"They're tired of waiting," Theo said. "They're not going to give Archer the time to give us up one at a time."

"But Davenport promised—"

"Either he lied or he's not in control anymore."

"So who is?"

"As usual, the lunatics have taken over the asylum."

"So what's going to happen now?"

"Everything's different. They're going to come in hot. We've got minutes at best."

Richard fidgeted, scratching at his forearm like a junkie. "Are you sure?"

"Positive," Theo said.

"Shit. Shit shit shit shit."

"It doesn't change much," Theo said. "Just accelerates things. I think we should all go out at the same time, but not together. Use different doors."

"Makes sense."

"We can't just walk out there. They'll know we've lied as soon as they come in and can't find Archer," Richard objected.

"Who said anything about just walking out?" said Theo.

"You did."

"No, I said we all go out at the same time. We've got a janitor's cupboards full of chemicals, more than enough to create some diversions."

"What are you thinking?"

"Bombs."

"We're not going to blow the fucking bank up!" Richard said.

"We don't need to." Theo was obviously thinking on his feet. "We just need a distraction. Something small, but with lots of smoke to create confusion."

"I don't see how that helps," Richard said.

"Get the cold packs from the first-aid kits, they're filled

with ammonium nitrate," Sasha said.

"And?"

"Split them open and empty the crystals into a bucket. Dissolve the crystals in a tiny amount of water. Absolutely tiny, we're talking less than half a cup. Then get paper, lots of it, and soak it in the solution. We don't have time to let them dry, so we'll just have to pray we can get them to burn."

"And there will be enough smoke?"

"Trust me, we could sneak a dozen ninjas through it."

"Good job all we need is one oversized black man—or at least the illusion of one they can lose somewhere in the smoke," Theo pointed out.

"It'll work," she assured him. "Science Fair survivor. Trust me."

"How big a bucket?" Richard asked.

"The more paper the more smoke."

"So the bigger the bucket the better?"

She nodded.

"Okay, let's split up, get what we need. First-aid packs, recycling cans, all sorts of paper, newspapers are best as we can roll them tightly. Move. They won't wait for us to get our shit together," Theo said.

Sasha didn't wait to be told twice. She ran through the dark corridors trying to remember where all of the first-aid packs were. She found three along the personal banking wing. There were probably more stashed away somewhere. Margot would have known. Three was good. If the other guys came up with three more from the other side that should be enough to make it look like the whole place was on fire. It wouldn't burn long, but in the short time that it did those ammonium-nitrate-soaked papers would choke the corridors. The problem was that out in the open air it would dissipate too quickly. But, she reasoned, it only had to look like Archer had a plan. He didn't have to actually escape.

Richard came back with two trashcans and the much larger recycling can from the photocopier room, which they could use to flood the main foyer with smoke. Without ventilation it should make things trickier for the cops as they swarmed into the building.

"What about her?" she asked when she returned to the lobby, nodding at Vicky.

Theo said the same thing he had the last time. "I'll get her on side."

"Can we trust her?"

"We have to," Richard said when Theo didn't answer.

They fashioned fifty makeshift smoke bombs out of the rolled-up paper between them, binding them tightly with string and standing them up on their ends inside the containers. The trashcans held a dozen each, the recycling can twenty-five. "It'll work. It has to. Take this to the fire exit," she offered one of the trashcans to Richard. "We need to light them at the same time, and when the corridors are full of smoke, you guys leave through your doors, I go out through mine. Three different exits. The timing's crucial. Five minutes from go. You're going to have move *fast*." They synchronized their watches.

He nodded. "Five minutes. I can work with that."

"Richard?"

He nodded.

"We've got one shot at this. We've got to sell the illusion. They need to be so confused by the smoke that they think there's a chance they missed something. That's all we need. Ready?"

"Now or never," Theo said.

Sasha didn't like the look in his eye. It wasn't just grim determination. There was something else there. Suddenly she didn't trust him. Something had changed in the last quarter of an hour since that last call from Davenport. It was almost as though he saw himself as a real criminal, like he had completely bought into the lie they were trying to sell the cops.

She didn't have time to think about it.

The clock was ticking.

53

SMOKE WAS NEVER GOING to be enough. Smoke was for amateurs.

As far as Theo was concerned, the guys out there would see through it in thirty seconds. They needed a proper distraction.

The answer was in the kitchen.

Richard was an oddball. Most bosses would have made do with a microwave and a couple of vending machines, but not Richard "I want everyone to love me" Rhodes. He had made sure they had a decent range, a fridge with a spacious icebox and a proper sit-down dining table. It was the range Theo was interested in—or more accurately the gas pipe feeding into it. He had to move quickly. Disconnecting the pipe with the gas in full flow wasn't a difficult job if you had the right tools. He didn't. He had his bare hands. He needed some sort of leverage to pull it away from the wall. It didn't need to be much, just enough to break the solder or give him an angle to unscrew one of the couplings so the gas could leak out into the room.

The smoke bomb would take care of the rest.

He still had to work out what the fuck he was going to do with Vicky. She was the fly in the ointment. She only had to open her mouth to ruin them all.

He needed to know that he could trust her.

Theo left the gas slowly leaking into the kitchen and went back to the lobby.

Vicky watched him walk towards her. If looks could kill he'd have been six feet under. He tore the tape off her mouth and pulled the sock out. "Tell me you've changed your mind, Vicky. Tell me you're in this with us."

She struggled against the plastic ties binding her to the chair.

"You've got about twenty seconds to convince me that I should let you walk out of here with me. Please, Vicky. Tell me what I need to hear."

"What are you going to do to me if I don't?"

He sighed. "Do what you think is right, not what you think will hurt the least in the short term."

"You're scaring me, Theo. What do you want me to say?"

"I'm walking out of here in thirty seconds. If I can't trust you to keep your mouth shut then I guess you have to become one of Samuel Archer's victims." He shrugged, as though to say his hands were tied.

"Please."

“Don’t beg. I don’t trust that kind of thing, Vicky. Convince me.”

“You don’t want to do this. You’re not a monster, Theo. You’re a good man. I *know* you.”

“You’re right, but if it’s a choice between you and me, well, sorry to say but I’m a selfish bastard. This is my chance to get my life back. There’s money in the bank, enough to get away, and believe me when I go out that door I am going to run so far so fast no one will have a clue where to find me. Mauritius, Cuba, the Dominican Republic, it doesn’t matter. I’m not going to let you fuck it up for me.”

“I won’t.” She shook her head. “I promise. I won’t say a word.”

“I want to believe you,” he said. In her place it wouldn’t have been a stretch to think he was trying to scare her into silence. He wasn’t that subtle. She didn’t know that though. Even after a decade working together, exchanging pleasantries and little else, no one in here really knew him or what he’d been through before he wound up at the bank. “The problem is I can’t trust you. No matter how much I want to.” Theo walked around behind her. “I’ve always liked you. I want you to know that. Not that it’s any comfort. I wish you’d been with us from the start. I really do.”

He put his hands on either side of her head, his fingers pushing not so gently into her eyes as he tightened his grip. He snapped her neck with one savage twist, feeling the moment the bone stopped supporting the weight of her skull. Killing someone wasn't all that difficult, he realized, stepping away. What happened next wouldn't be half as easy. "I'll just have to learn to live with it," he said to the back of her head.

He checked his watch. He had a minute to get out if he was going to time his exit with the others. Shining the flashlight from his torch across the contours of the lobby he gave the place one last look before pulling the battered old Zippo from his pocket. He could smell the gas now, or rather that cloying smell they put into it. It wasn't thick at the back of his throat yet, but it wouldn't be long before enough of it had leaked into the lobby to make the place a deathtrap.

He leaned forward, lowering his hand into the depths of the recycling can before he flipped the lid on the lighter. He held his breath as he thumbed the wheel. The flint sparked and the naked flame licked at the air.

If he'd misjudged it, he was dead; the truth was as brutally simple as that. But the gas didn't ignite. He touched the flame to the ammonium-nitrate-soaked papers until they started to burn. He counted off five seconds before the smoke started to pour out of the rolled-up sheets. He couldn't hang around with the gas filling every corner of the building. It was only a matter of time before one spark caught the gas and the whole place went up.

He ran across to the front doors, throwing back the bolts.

The smoke was already thick enough to sting his eyes. He coughed as he checked his watch.

He was still thirty seconds early, but he wasn't waiting.

Theo could hear the crackle of the paper burning as he opened the door.

One spark…

"Don't shoot," he called, hands above his head as he emerged. He looked up towards the roof of one of the neighboring buildings, and saw the telltale glint of a sniper's lens. There would be other weapons trained on him, just waiting for him to make a threatening move. It would stay that way until they had visual confirmation he wasn't Samuel Archer and the order to stand down was issued. He walked slowly, eyes front, then officers rushed forward to steer him away from the open doors.

They managed six steps before the sheer force of the explosion punched them off their feet and sent the two of them sprawling across the ground beneath a spray of broken glass.

He craned his head to see smoke and flame pouring out of the building behind him.

The nearest officer struggled to stand, blood streaming down his cheeks. He stared over Theo's head. "Is there anyone in there?"

"Only him. Archer. He sent the others out the back way to confuse everyone."

The cop's radio crackled to life. "*We've got movement back here… lots of smoke… a woman is coming out…*"

54

Officer Andy Jaeger folded Sasha into his arms. The smoke swirled around them.

"That's his none too subtle way of saying he's glad you're okay," his partner said. "Give him a couple of minutes and he'll summon up the courage to ask you out for a drink, won't you, Andy?"

Sasha couldn't help herself; she started to laugh. It wasn't that it was funny, but it was all about the release of tension. She'd set her smoke bomb off early, but that didn't matter now. She wondered if Theo's bomb had failed.

"Just think of me as your own personal Cupid. I'm fat enough, after all," Leigh Parrish said.

"How can I refuse an offer like that?"

"Technically I didn't actually ask," Andy pointed out.

"It's not like you have a choice in the matter," she told him, and now he was smiling too. It was as though she'd been given a fresh lease of life. For a moment she allowed herself to look at him and wonder if he might be number fifty-two. That morning it had felt so important, so wrong to think that there had been fifty-one men, but she was done with shame. She was who she had always been. She liked who she was, even if she wasn't Goldilocks or any of the other names her bad dates had burdened her with. She actually found herself looking forward to finding out who she'd be for Officer Andy. That was part of the fun of falling in love, or lust, or whatever this might end up being.

He still hadn't taken his arm from around her shoulders.

Her laughter died with the sudden shocking blast.

She pulled free of Andy's grip and ran back towards the burning building. Surely that couldn't have been Theo's bomb? He pulled her back. She couldn't hear what he was saying; her ears were ringing. People seemed to be moving in slow motion around her. She saw Parrish shouting something into his radio, his lips moving without any discernible words coming out of his mouth. She thought of her car in the parking lot, the promise of escape. But she couldn't go. "Oh God, oh God," she begged, praying for some sort of divine intervention.

Andy grabbed her shoulders. He was speaking to her, shaking her, but she couldn't focus on his words.

Slowly they began to solidify. "It's over. It's over."

She was crying. She couldn't find the words.

It wasn't until he led her around to the front of the bank that she found out that he'd been wrong. They hadn't all got out.

She saw Richard coming around the other side of the building from the second fire escape and Theo was sat down with a police-issue blanket wrapped around his shoulders. She heard Theo listing the names of everyone who had been in the bank except Ellie, saying she'd been given the day off. She couldn't see Vicky.

"Where is she? Where's Vicky?" she demanded.

Theo just stared at her.

He said nothing.

"You said you'd take care of her. You said—"

"There was nothing I could do," Theo said finally. He couldn't hold her gaze. He looked down at his hands. They were bunching and unbunching in impotent fists. "I… the gas… Archer must have done something with the gas… when I lit the smoke bomb the whole place went up. He won, Sash. He had the last laugh… He killed Vicky. He told me to get out, I thought he was going to follow me, use her as some sort of human shield."

She knew he was lying, but surrounded by half of the Chicago PD she could hardly challenge him without unraveling all of their carefully crafted lies.

She shook her head, the trap she'd help fashion for herself made her sick.

"I'm sorry, Sash. I'm so sorry."

But he wasn't. She could see that in his eyes when he finally looked up again. He was relieved. Vicky wouldn't be around to betray them. All they had to do was cover up two murders for the price of one.

The next couple of hours were awful, worse in many ways than any of the time Sasha had spent as a hostage. They gave their accounts of what had happened against a backdrop of the fire services battling the flames. It took a long time to get the blaze under control. The bank was a mess. She couldn't help but realize the main implication of that: all of the physical evidence of what had happened inside there that day was gone, including the blood on the carpet. It was more than just convenient, it was criminal.

Andy was never far away. He brought her a decent cup of hot coffee, double shot espresso and foamed milk, from the coffee shop down the block. He made sure she was checked out by the paramedics. He kept her company as she gave her statement. And when she was done he offered to take her home.

As he led her over to his car, she saw Brian the compulsive counter, still at his post, still counting. She called, "Hey, Brian! You should be getting yourself home, your mom will be worried."

"Hey Sasha! Ninety-seven today!" She wasn't sure what he was talking about until he held his notepad aloft like a trophy. Whatever color or model he'd been counting today, he'd spotted ninety-seven of them. He was holding out for the hundred before he went home.

"That's fantastic, Brian. Ninety-seven! Wow." She smiled at him.

"Happy you came out today. More going in than coming

out. Like magic. Now it's on fire." He shook his head. "That's sad."

Andy didn't seem to grasp the importance of the compulsive counter's throwaway comment, or if he did, he probably assumed Brian was talking about Archer and Vicky. "It is," she said, as Andy let her lean on him. Walking over to his car she allowed herself to think that maybe, just maybe, she'd get a happy ending after all.

When they arrived at her door there was a moment, her hand on the handle, his eyes on her hand, when she almost invited him up. It was tempting. She craved the contact, the nearness and physicality of it, of not being alone as the shock finally settled and the grief swept in to fill the emptiness inside her, but it would have made things too complicated when her phone went in the middle of the night.

He hid his disappointment well. He didn't even move to kiss her, so she put him out of his misery, stepping in so close the concept of personal space dissolved into her lips on his. It wasn't an earth-shattering kiss. Her world wasn't rocked. But it was nice. And right then nice was exactly what she needed.

"I'll talk to you tomorrow, Andy," she said, stepping back. "I just want to have a bath and sleep like the dead."

He looked like he wanted to skip down the street.

"You do that, Sash," he said, barely able to contain his Cheshire Cat grin.

It didn't matter that it was still early, she managed to fall asleep on the couch within a couple of minutes of sitting down. It was the middle of the night when the vibration of the phone on her chest woke her. She sat up, wiping the sleep groggily from her eyes, and focused on the screen.

> Forty-five minutes. Parking lot behind the bank. Be careful not to be seen.

She called a cab, but gave an address a few blocks over, changed into black jeans, sneakers and a tight-fitting black turtleneck, and tied her hair up before she ran to meet it.

With no traffic on the roads, she was a couple of minutes early. She got the cab to drop her off three blocks away from the bank and walked over, keeping to the shadows.

She saw the police tape around the front, and the two police officers talking in front of a Chicago PD van. Everyone else was gone. She didn't go any closer. She could see enough of the mess from her vantage point. The entire façade was ruined. The glass doors had been torn out of their fixings and the surrounds were buckled and twisted and dripped down from the brick arch like steel stalactites. They were backlit by high-intensity Klieg lights set up inside. No doubt Forensics would arrive in the morning. They had a narrow window of time to get in and out, but with the two-man guard posted to secure the crime scene they wouldn't be walking through the front door.

Richard was waiting for her around the back. One side of

his face was mottled; the bruises from the beating Archer had given him.

Theo emerged from the shadows without a sound. As he stepped into the light the harsh relief stripped away his face so she could see the stark contours of the skull beneath. It looked like a death mask.

"There are two cops around the front," she told them.

"Then we just have to make sure they don't hear us," Theo said. "It's not like we're going to set the alarm off, though, is it?" He held up his keys. "In and out."

"Let's get this over with."

"Two seconds. Wait here."

Before she could object Theo disappeared back into the shadows. It wasn't two seconds. It was closer to two minutes, but then she saw an unfamiliar car roll slowly into the lot, and pull up alongside them.

"It's registered to one Saul Bonavechio," Theo said, clambering out.

"Where did you—? Second thoughts, I don't want to know."

"Ask me no questions, I'll tell you no lies," Theo said.

He left the door open, the keys in the ignition.

They went back into the bank through the same door Sasha had used a few hours earlier. It felt different. It didn't feel like the place she'd spent so many days of her life. As the moved deeper into the building it became more and more apparent that the fire had changed everything. Theo led the way, his Maglite's beam picking out the worst of the water damage where the hoses had finally put out the fire. No one spoke.

She was terrified of what they'd find when they finally opened the vault.

55

NEITHER OF THEM SAID much.

There wasn't a lot for them to say.

They were thrown together by circumstance, and with the robber's meds worn off and the tremors intensifying, he didn't make a good conversationalist.

The vault's reinforced frame dulled the explosion to a soundless shiver. They looked at each other from opposite sides of the small room. The robber—Adam—looked sick, probably from the concussion. He was the one who broke the silence, telling Ellie his story. Midway through she asked, "Why do you think I'd be interested in this?" but he kept on unburdening himself.

When he was done, Ellie got up and started pacing around the cramped space.

"It could be the third world war out there for all we know," she said finally, sinking back down to the floor. She looked at her watch. Time absolutely dragged. “How long do you think we’re going to be trapped down here?”

It was like that for hours, Ellie pacing like a caged animal, Ellie sinking down to the floor, only to rise and repeat the whole process all over again. But at least Richard Rhodes had been good to his word and made sure the generator came online so they weren’t slowly suffocating to death. The break in the pattern came somewhere towards midnight.

“I don’t know why I’m even going to tell you this,” was one of the stranger ways to broach the subject of parental infidelity and identity, “but I’m going to go crazy if I don’t talk to *someone*.” So she told him about the accident that had wiped out her entire family, and then finding the shoebox and those letters with their pretty ribbons and struggling to understand what they meant—especially that last letter dated just a few days before her first birthday—in relation to her life. He listened in silence, his arms wrapped around his knees, knees drawn up to his chest to try to minimize the shakes. She told him about hiring Elias Barker to find her real father, and their conversation just a few hours ago.

“Jesus. So, you mean that Margot’s husband is your father? Will you tell her?”

She shook her head. “I don’t know how to. What am I supposed to say? Hey Margot, guess what, your dead husband was my daddy. Can you imagine?”

“And you’re sure?”

“Yep.”

"I don't envy you that conversation," Adam said.

"It just feels like my whole life has been a lie. I feel so... betrayed. I can't help but wonder: did he know? Did my dad know he wasn't my dad? He must have, mustn't he? She couldn't have kept that from him. And if he knew... then it was all a lie. Everything. I was the cuckoo in their nest."

He clutched tighter at his knees. For a moment she thought he was rocking in place, like someone on the cusp of losing their mind. When he spoke his voice was different. Analytical. "Deception is part of life. The average person tells one and a half lies a day. That's ten and a half lies a week, or almost forty-seven lies a month. Over the course of a year we're talking about over five hundred and forty-seven lies. If you assume a lifespan of seventy-six years, that's over forty-one and a half thousand lies. Most of them are white lies. Others aren't. They're big lies like the one you just uncovered. A quarter of all lies are told to protect someone else, not to make the liar look better. Most people aren't even aware they're lying when they do it."

"That's just depressing."

"Our entire society is founded upon deception. They reckon the average person *hears* two hundred lies a day. That's fourteen hundred lies a week. Six thousand two hundred lies a month, or seventy-three thousand lies a year."

"So what you're saying is get over it?"

"Or get used to it. By the time you're seventy-six you'll count over five and a half million lies floating around you.

And the more people lie the more they come to believe their own lies until they become a sort of truth, which only adds to the deception."

"I don't even want to know how you know this stuff."

"Work. I study people and probabilities. I'm fascinated by all possible outcomes of any given event. I can tell you, to within a reasonable degree of certainty, how long you'll live, your likelihood of divorce, that kind of thing. It's all just math."

"And we all fall into those patterns?"

"Sadly. It would be nice to be surprised once in a while, but any exception really is the one that proves the rule. People think you can tell if someone's lying if they can't look at you when they're talking, but that's wrong. They say we learn to lie as we get older, but that's wrong too. There are even some behavioral scientists who believe babies start lying as early as six months, crying for no reason other than to get food, giggling because they know cuteness will bring a reward."

"That's such a cynical way of looking at the world," Ellie said.

"Maybe it is. Maybe I'm the broken one?"

"Does it have to be one or the other?"

"Did you know you might as well toss a coin to judge if someone is lying to you? Our perception of truth versus lie is so poor. Statistically we can only tell for sure fifty-four percent of the time."

"You've got to be making this stuff up."

"I could be, you'd have a fifty-fifty chance of guessing right.

I could tell you one in six juries get it wrong, or that trained law-enforcement officers have no better lie perception than a layman. We're useless as lie detectors. It's not unreasonable to think that the man who raised you as his daughter had no idea you weren't. But, surely, if he did know, and he still found all that love in his heart for you, that's the important thing. Isn't it?"

She looked at him then, understanding the route his roundabout conversation had taken to get to the heart of the matter—or in this case the matter of the heart.

"He was your father in every single way that mattered," Adam continued. "Being a dad isn't just biological, it's a job description, and I'd say you knew your real father and he knew you. A few letters in an old shoebox don't change that. They might confuse the issue a bit, but eventually you come back to the same truth. Ryan Mason was your father, not John Joseph Moore. He provided the seed, but Ryan nurtured the tree."

"You're the strangest bank robber I've ever met."

He burst out laughing at that. Proper genuine laughter.

"Met a lot of bank robbers, have you?"

"More than my fair share," she said, with a slight smile. She had a good smile. She'd practiced it in the mirror when she was younger, trying different ones on for size, just like she used to practice French kissing into her hand to see what her face would look like when she gave herself to someone that first time, insecurities and all.

"You don't have to tell her, you know. If you don't think

there's a way some good can come out of it, you don't have to increase Margot's pain by revealing her husband had a child by another woman. Sometimes ignorance is bliss. Imagine how your life would have played out if you'd never found that shoebox. You don't have to be *her* shoebox."

"But maybe something good can come of it? You know? I'm alone. She's alone. We've both had our worlds turned upside down."

"Families have been forged in stranger circumstances," Adam agreed.

"So how do I tell her? How do I even broach the subject? I can't exactly sit her down and say 'Hey, you know John Joseph used to play away from home, well guess what?'"

"She's looking after my son. I can tell her she needs to talk to you."

Before she could say yes or no they heard movement on the other side of the door, and the sound of the capstan turning.

56

As Alice approached, Theo was arranging the corpse in the passenger seat, belting him in.

He put a pair of aviator sunglasses on the dead man and stood back to admire his handiwork.

"It'll have to do," he said, and then turned as he heard her step behind him.

"You're late."

"I was asleep."

He tossed a ball cap to her. A second pair of shades fell out of it as she fumbled the catch.

"What are these for?"

"Just put them on." She did as she was told. "You're going to drive back to the hotel. We'll follow you a couple of hundred yards behind. I want you to push the speed limit, break it a couple of times around what would normally be busy intersections, run a set of lights or two."

"Why?"

"Speed cameras. It's the evidence trail."

"You want me to paint a target on my tits while I'm at it?"

"Don't be so melodramatic. If they actually recognize you, you can say he had a gun on you, made you drive him, then cut you loose. With everything else that bastard did to you no jury in the world would convict you."

"Jesus Christ, you're as much of a bastard as he was." Alice shook her head, but even as she did she lowered herself into the driver's seat.

"Keep the brim low and they'll never be able to ID you as his accomplice. We just need them to be able to see Archer in a time-stamped photograph that makes it look like he's alive now, and somehow fooled them all, escaping but only getting as far as the hotel where he was meeting up with his real partner in crime, the mysterious Milo Rockwell. They're in this together, remember, they're stealing from Bonavechio. Something happens, one betrays the other, and that betrayal leaves Archer dead. It works as a narrative. Just make sure you drive erratically. You *need* to get seen."

"But not so erratically you get caught," Adam said. His shakes were much worse now, she noticed. They affected the rhythm of his words as well as the timbre of his voice. He looked like a dying man.

"I won't let the side down," she promised him.

"We'll meet you at the hotel," Theo said, then banged twice on the roof.

"Take a different route," she said. "Don't make it obvious you're following me. The cops aren't stupid, this time of night someone will notice the same cars on the road in every photo and put the pieces together."

"Let us worry about that."

"It's not your neck on the line if this goes wrong," she said, and rolled up the window. The dead man stank. She tried not to think about him in the seat beside her. At least Theo had put a garbage sack on the seat under him so his shit didn't leave a stain. He'd tied Archer's head in place with string so that it didn't flop around as she drove.

She fired up the ignition, feeling the power as the engine came to life beneath her feet. It was stick shift. It had been a long time since she'd driven stick. The gears grated as she peeled away from the fire exit and, lights out, drove out of the lot. She didn't turn the lights on until she was five blocks away.

The roads were deserted.

She looked over at the dead man. The blood on his shirt had dried. It was quite obviously dead blood. Someone had wadded up gauze and stuffed it into the bullet hole like a plug.

She pulled his coat closed, covering the worst of the bloodstain from the cameras, and put her foot down.

The needle moved from thirty to eighty in under ten seconds, the exhaust roaring throatily. The silence was getting to her. She reached down for the dial and found a late-night radio station, which offered up the last few fading bars of Led Zeppelin's "Ramble On" before it blended into Aerosmith's "Dream On." There was comfort in the familiar guitar licks before Steven Tyler's voice promised her she had to lose to win.

She'd lost more than most to Samuel Archer.

She was due a win.

By the time Geddy Lee replaced Tyler telling her they could sail away into destiny she'd already blown through three stoplights and was facing down a fourth.

She pressed her foot down harder, feeling the engine respond.

"I hope you're in Hell," she said to the man beside her. But even that wasn't good enough. Archer was done. Finished. It wasn't like she could wake him up and kill him again.

She was wrong. Of the two of them Alice Fisher was the one living in Hell.

She pulled into the alleyway behind the hotel nine minutes before the others arrived. She'd covered the distance considerably faster than she'd intended, but the benefit of that would be a constant trail of speed camera images triggered in her wake. She parked up beside the chainlink fence. There was a battered blue sign that marked it as the tradesman's entrance. Garbage overflowed from two of the three dumpsters. She could almost smell the desperation lurking behind the fancy façade of the exclusive hotel. She looked up and down the alleyway as she waited, painfully conscious of the corpse in the passenger seat. The last thing she wanted was some curious hooker to come wandering up to her window touting for business.

Finally headlights lit up the rear window as Theo rolled to a stop behind her.

She didn't get out of the car until she saw Theo, Richard and Adam walking towards her.

Theo approached slowly, bending to knock on the side window. He looked wired. She rolled it down.

"Good journey?"

"As good as can be expected."

"And the cameras?"

"I've been here ten minutes, what do you think?"

"Good. Let's get him inside before someone sees us."

She left the keys in the car, but wiped her prints from them. Habit. She had no idea if she'd be returning to the vehicle, but she didn't want to make it too easy for the cops to work out who Archer's mysterious driver was. Theo opened the door, and together with the bank manager manhandled the corpse out of the passenger seat and dragged it to the back door. Adam didn't do anything to help. He held his left elbow with his right hand as if he was trying to hold himself physically together. He should have gone home when they opened the vault. It was obvious he was coming undone. He was becoming a liability.

She'd wedged the door open a crack when she left to go back to the bank. It was still ajar. The night manager had isolated the door so it wasn't on the alarm circuit. It had cost her, but she was happy to pay.

She led the way to the service elevator and pressed the button, holding her breath as the doors opened.

There was no one inside.

Theo propped Archer's body up against the back of the elevator, leaning against him like he was helping out a drunken friend. Richard kept shuffling on the spot, a bundle of pent-up nerves. Adam leaned against the side of the elevator, his head constantly rolling as if he was dancing to some tune only he could hear. A bell chimed and the elevator doors opened on the sixth floor.

Alice hustled down the corridor to the door of Milo Rockwell's suite and swiped it with her keycard. She held it open as the men manhandled Archer into the room and closed it behind them. As Adam hit the lights they saw the mess she'd made. It looked as though a bomb had gone off—or at least a very controlled tornado had passed through on its way back to Kansas. Chairs were overturned, picture frames broken. The TV had been torn off its bracket on the wall, a boot put through the screen. The crystal decanter on the sideboard was reduced to shards of glass, though three of the four tumblers were still whole. It looked as though two very big men had gone at it hard, both of them coming out of the fight as losers.

"Put him down over there," she said, but Theo had other ideas.

He dragged the dead man to where a suggestive

photograph of a lily's sexual organs hung askew, before getting a good firm grip on his lapels and slamming his head back into the middle of the photo. The glass rained down, getting on Archer's clothes and down the back of his shirt. Then Theo reached into the dead man's shirt to unplug the wound. The blood didn't exactly flow so much as ooze out of the corpse. Theo got plenty of it on his hand, then placed his bloody palm on the surface beside the shards of glass and dragged it all the way down to the floor. There were no prints in the streaks.

"There needs to be more blood," Adam said.

"I'm working on it, but there's fuck all left in here," Theo said, shaking the corpse as though trying to drain the dead man of every last fluid ounce of the stuff.

"There should be loads of it, it should be everywhere. There's no splatter. No splash back. It doesn't look like he died here."

"Nothing we can do about that, unless you're volunteering to lend us a couple of pints? No? Okay, then how about you shut up? Maybe they'll think this Milo's one sick fuck who drained Sammy Boy and took his blood off to drink somewhere later in celebration of a job well done?"

"Do you really think—"

"As little as possible," Theo said, cutting him off. "Now, give me his wallet and cellphone and get the fuck out of here, people. We've got one thing missing to paint a proper picture. Shots fired. Alice, give me the gun."

She did as she was told.

As she reached the service elevator she heard six shots ring out clearly, then a moment later saw Theo racing towards her.

It was done.

57

HE'D FOUND THE ROOM registered to Milo Rockwell. There was one glaring problem with the scene: the blood.

The Dane knew death rooms.

He had been in enough of them over the years. They were his stock in trade. This had been staged. It was good, but it wasn't perfect. For all that, Samuel Archer was most certainly dead, and had been for quite a while judging by the lividity of his corpse. Longer than he could have been in this room. Everything had been made to look like there had been a fight. He crouched down beside the body, examining the glitter of broken glass around his collar and the flakes ground into the dead man's cheek. He looked up to the shards of glass still framed on the wall. He could easily visualize the fight that ended with Archer's skull shattering the glass, and the big man desperately trying to stop himself from going down, reaching out with a bloody hand as his legs betrayed him.

The story worked. Whoever had laid the room out knew what they were doing. It would satisfy a cursory inspection. The problem was the blood.

A bullet to the gut ought to have shed more blood. Sure, the dead man's shirt was crusted with the stuff, but the luxurious carpet beneath him wouldn't take much to clean where it ought to have been a case of ripping it up and laying a new one.

And there was no getting around the fact that Archer should have died in the bank. Nothing else made sense. So the question was: who did this and why? It wasn't his dime, he was more than happy to just walk away, it wasn't a matter of professional pride, and no matter what Saul Bonavechio might want, he wasn't the gangster's bitch. Archer was dead, and that was exactly what Bonavechio had wanted. As far as the Dane was concerned it didn't matter how it had happened, he got paid either way. There was nothing to tie him to this, and no reason not just to leave. Apart from curiosity. He didn't like unfinished stories, and that's what this felt like, a big old-style cliffhanger where he'd tune in next week to find out the guy wasn't in the car that went over the cliff at all but had somehow managed to wriggle free before it went careening down the slope. It was a cheat. The Dane didn't like cheats. He liked things to make sense.

There were six bullet holes in the wall, clustered close together, making the outline of a shoulder as though the shooter had missed their mark as Archer came towards them.

Archer's wound was low in the stomach, not high in the shoulder. He filed that observation away.

The Dane went through the room, conscious that the clock was ticking down and no matter how inept Chicago PD were, they'd find their way here eventually. You didn't discharge a gun six times in a hotel room without someone calling the law. It wasn't just the blood that was wrong, he realized. There was no gun. Archer had held the bank up, then come here, winding up in a gunfight. And now there was no gun. That had to mean something.

He called Bonavechio.

"What I said before was wrong."

"What part?"

"That Archer wasn't walking out of the bank."

"That's a pretty big fuck up, my friend. I hope you aren't calling to give me *more* bad news?"

"He is dead now, if that helps?"

"Are you sure this time? Or are you going to call me up in a couple of hours and say the fucker's up and playing Lazarus again?"

"Definitely dead. Gunshot to the stomach. I'm not particularly religious, but I think even Jesus would have trouble bringing him back."

"Make sure. Cut his fucking head off if you have to."

"Won't be necessary. His neck is broken. Someone really wanted him dead."

"Someone *else*?" Bonavechio said.

"He's in a room registered to Milo Rockwell."

"That motherfucker again? I'm really beginning to hate that name. You know what you have to do."

"It might be prudent to draw a line under yesterday, end things here."

"No one fucks with me and lives to walk away. It's bad business. Kill the fucker," Bonavechio said, ending the call.

The Dane frisked the dead man for his wallet and phone, then set his laptop up on the coffee table, a few feet away from Archer's head. The SSD had the operating system booted up in seconds, the built-in 4G card had it online a couple of seconds later. He went through Archer's wallet looking for anything that would lead him to the money. People are simple. Even complicated people are far more straightforward than they'd like to think. Archer was no exception. His address was there, along with credit cards and driver's license, social security number, everything he needed. The Dane photographed each one front and back before slipping them back into the wallet, then pocketed the dead man's keys and was on his way.

He stopped as he crossed the exaggeratedly seductive foyer and pointed a finger at the man behind the desk. "You can help me," the Dane said.

It was obvious from the frightened way the man's head came up—and the way his knuckles whitened—that he'd been expecting this moment.

Dreading it.

"Of course, sir. How can I be of assistance?"

"You've got a dead body upstairs, but I'm sure you know that." He gave the night manager the room number. "The guy's name was Samuel Jefferson Archer—ah, I see you know the name—well, Samuel's been ventilated. The room has been trashed. There was obviously a confrontation between Archer and your guest." The night manager closed his eyes. "I want you to describe him to me. Everything you can remember. If you try to pretend you have no idea what I'm talking about they'll be carrying two body bags out of the hotel in the morning. Do we have an understanding?"

"It wasn't a him," the man said. "It was a her. Milo Rockwell was a woman."

By the time the night manager had finished spilling his guts he'd vividly described the first hostage Archer had released from the bank. The Dane had known Alice Fisher was holding something back; he'd assumed it was her shame that she hadn't pulled her gun on Archer to influence the chain of events, but he'd assumed wrong. She was a much better liar than he'd given her credit for. He thought about it. She'd been the first one to mention Milo Rockwell's name, placing him at the casino the night before, leading the cops by the nose. She was smart. Maybe she was even the brains behind Archer's betrayal? Men would do funny things for a sniff of pussy. It even fit with the timeline. She'd come straight here from the bank to book the hotel room, convincing the night manager to make it look like the mythical Milo had been in town for a week.

"Am I going to have to kill you?"

"No," the man said, barely squeezing the word out.

"I knew you were going to say that. I can see the future sometimes, but only when it's important, like now. Do you want me to tell you what I see?"

"No."

"That's unfortunate," the Dane said. He reached around to the grip of the gun nestling in the holster at the base of his spine, drew and fired in one smooth motion, putting a single bullet between the man's eyes.

He walked out the front door. It was a race between him and the Chicago PD; first one to the girl would win it all. He had a head start; he knew who he was looking for. That didn't mean much in this city.

58

ALICE KNEW SHE'D NEVER be able to stop running, and as long as her mother was an emotional millstone she'd never get far enough away to ever feel safe.

She knocked softly on the door and went in without waiting for an answer.

The room was deep in shadow, the contours of the old woman tucked up in bed picked out by the silver of moonlight.

She'd come to say goodbye, even though her mother would never know she'd been there. The one small mercy was that the rapid progression of her dementia promised a kind of peace she would have been denied if she'd been aware enough to know she'd never see her daughter again.

Alice sat down on the edge of the bed, taking her mother's hand in hers. "Hey Mom," she said, as the woman stirred. She wanted to believe she saw her mom's lips twitch into a smile at that. All she really wanted was for her mother to know that everything was going to be okay, that she needn't worry about her little girl anymore. Of course, none of this was for the woman in the bed. She had no idea who Alice was. This whole conversation was for Alice.

She couldn't risk staying in one place for very long. For the last week Alice had moved from seedy motel room to sleazy hotel room, crisscrossing the city. Thanks to the news segment she'd seen, she didn't dare stay in one place for more than twenty-four hours. The report had been focused on the hotel at the center of not one but three scandals inside twenty-four hours: the brutal assault that had ended Horace Greene's fledgling career; the shooting of the night manager Stephen Lewis; and the discovery of Samuel Archer's body in room 602. Alice Fisher knew she could never go home again.

Reading between the lines, Bonavechio's fake FBI agent had found the staged scene with Archer's corpse before the cops and from there it didn't take a genius to figure out he'd got what he needed out of the night manager—a physical description of Milo Rockwell—and put a bullet in the man's head to ensure he couldn't tell the cops the one crucial detail they were missing: Room 602 had been booked and paid for by a woman.

The cash she'd paid the night manager had bought a surveillance camera blackout for one night only, ensuring there was no footage to betray them, but she had to believe Stephen had talked before he was killed. She was marked.

Alice looked at her watch, willing the hands to stop for a

little while, freezing this moment until she was ready to go.

She heard the door open, and assumed it was the night nurse come to check in on her mother. She turned to offer a smile that died on her lips when she saw the white-haired man in the doorway.

"Milo Rockwell, I presume?"

She didn't reply as he closed the door softly and leant back against it.

"You should have run, Alice. Sentimentality is a killer."

Alice didn't let go of her mother's hand.

"I've got one question for you. Be truthful and I'll make it easy." Even as he said it, the assassin took a gun from its holster and fixed a suppressor in place, making sure she was in no doubt what the easy option was. "I know you're Milo. There's no point lying. I've had time to piece together what Archer did to you, and saw for myself what you did to him. I have no problem with that. You saved me a job. I'd have been inclined to let you live. I mean it's not as though you got away with any of that cash in escrow. That bounced back the minute Milo Rockwell was implicated. The only damage is to Bonavechio's pride. The problem is Saul Bonavechio isn't a forgiving man. He wanted you to know why you were dying tonight—because you were in it with Archer, because Archer screwed him and Archer's dead it falls to you. You understand how it is."

"I get it." She didn't bother pleading. It wouldn't have made any difference. "I knew someone like you'd come eventually.

So what do *you* want to know?" she asked, sounding braver than she felt. Her grip tightened on her mother's hand.

"Does it end with you?"

She looked him in the eye, grateful for the shadows as she lied. "Yes." He didn't know about the Victor LaSalle account, about Adam, or the involvement of the others. But if he kept digging he would find out. By dying she could give Adam the same gift he'd given her. She could save his life, at least for a little while longer.

"I believe you," the white-haired assassin said, walking around the bed to stand behind her.

Alice felt the suppressor against the back of her head as she said what she'd come here to say.

"Goodbye, Mom."

59

Adam watched as the two women pushed Jake on the swings.

His son was having the time of his life, laughing and urging Ellie Mason to push him higher while Margot Moore made funny faces to amuse him.

It was done. Victor LaSalle's bank card and transaction book—containing sixteen deposit slips, sixteen withdrawal slips—had arrived six months ago and with it the security of Jake's future was assured. The numbers more than added up. He'd returned to the lawyer's office, torn up the letter and thrown away the locker key. He had no interest in opening that particular box.

Margot and Ellie had had the conversation about John Joseph, and the tears, Margot had promised, were ones of joy when she realized Ellie had a reason to be in her life forever—not for pain at the remembered betrayal. She even confided in him that she was thinking of asking Nero to help her find the daughter she'd given up for adoption years ago. He'd offered before but she'd been unsure. Now she was coming around to the idea. They weren't exactly an ordinary family, but that just meant they'd make an extraordinary one for his son.

He'd seen Sasha half a dozen times since the robbery. She'd come by to check in on him and meet Jake. He'd started out by thinking of them all as living on parallel lines, but the problem with that was parallel lines never met. That caused him to revise his thinking; they were more like lifelines on a palm, only crossing at a major intersection of life. They weren't friends. They wouldn't have the time to become friends, either, but for a single day their lifelines had crossed. The second time she'd visited, Sasha had been on her way to meet Officer Andy for their first proper date. They'd been together for five months now.

Richard Rhodes had got his way; the first newspaper headline had called him the Robin Hood Bank Manager. Adam had read the story with something approaching dread; the hostage situation at the branch had triggered a full forensic audit by the fraud department which had turned up a number of anomalies around interest payments to multiple corporate accounts. For weeks Adam had been sure that they were coming for him next, that Richard will spill everything to save his own skin, but it never happened. The article didn't go into details, and Sasha didn't know much more than what was in the papers, but she seemed to think that because he hadn't profited from the crime the DA would be keen to plea bargain the charges down. It wasn't exactly the win Richard had hoped for, but in light of the publicity the bank had decided to swallow the losses, replacing the interest he had diverted without penalizing the people he'd helped.

None of them talked about the fate of Victoria Mann or Theo Monk. Adam knew what Theo had done to her colleague, and as sickening as it was, he and the others had no choice but to keep silent. To do anything else would unravel the lies they'd told. He'd scanned the papers for news of his arrest, but when it didn't come realized the ex-cop had used all of his training to run far and as fast as he could. Maybe he hadn't stopped running. Chances are he never would. The money wouldn't last forever, eighty-five grand wasn't that much in the grand scheme of things.

He'd read about Alice's murder, not putting the name and the woman he knew together at first. It just seemed so utterly tragic that she should claw her way out of the hell Samuel Archer had put her through, only to die at her mother's bedside. There was nothing in the article linking her murder to what had happened at the bank, but it couldn't have been some random act of violence. It had to be about what they had done.

The only other person he hadn't heard from since the robbery was Beth. Margot had told him that she'd handed in her resignation the morning after, and booked a vacation to Rome. He assumed she'd gone to beg forgiveness.

Adam saw a white-haired man watching him from across the playground. Little kids ran around between them as they raced from the jungle gym to the slide. Adam's gaze shifted towards Jake, Ellie and Margot. It was a gift beyond words knowing he could die safe in the knowledge that his son was looked after.

Adam wrestled with the blanket covering his lap, his fingers struggling to close around the fabric with any sort of strength. He hated the helplessness of the wheelchair and the constant pressure on his lungs that signaled that his chest muscles were finally failing him. Each breath was labored. The left side of his face had drooped, making him look like a stroke victim. He couldn't talk very clearly anymore. The "dies" had claimed him for their own. Dyskinesia, dysphagia, dysarthria, and dyspnea. His hand trembled as he lifted the oxygen mask to cover his mouth and nose. The breath wouldn't come. He'd done so much dying in the last six months, but the truth was he could last another six months or six years, his body slowly betraying him one muscle at a time. It was so hard to look at every new dawn as the gift it was.

Jake's giggles carried to him across the playground. Pure unadulterated joy. There was no better sound in the world.

When he looked back he saw the white-haired man walking towards him.

He was ready to go now.

ABOUT THE AUTHOR

STEVEN SAVILE HAS WRITTEN for *Doctor Who*, *Torchwood*, *Stargate*, *Warhammer*, *Battlefield 3* and other popular game and comic worlds. He won the inaugural Lifeboat to the Stars Award for *Tau Ceti* (co-authored with International Bestselling novelist Kevin J. Anderson), and his thriller *Silver* was one of the Top 30 bestselling ebooks of 2011. He is the author of the Titan Books novels *Sherlock Holmes: Murder at Sorrow's Crown* (co-authored with Robert Greenberger) and *Primeval: Shadow of the Jaguar*, which won the International Media Association of Tie-In Writers Award. He lives in Sweden.

ALSO AVAILABLE FROM TITAN BOOKS

THE BLOOD STRAND

A FAROES NOVEL

CHRIS OULD

Having left the Faroes as a child, Jan Reyna is now a British police detective, and the islands are foreign to him. But he is drawn back when his estranged father is found unconscious with a shotgun by his side and someone else's blood at the scene. Then a man's body is washed up on an isolated beach. Is Reyna's father responsible? Looking for answers, Reyna falls in with Detective Hjalti Hentze, but as the stakes get higher and Reyna learns more about his family and the truth behind his mother's flight from the Faroes, he must decide whether to stay, or to forsake the strange, windswept islands for good.

"A winner… for fans of Henning Mankell and Elizabeth George"
Booklist (starred review)

"An absorbing new mystery"
Library Journal

"A convincing atmosphere of the isolated isles"
The Times

ALSO AVAILABLE FROM TITAN BOOKS

THE FIRE PIT

A FAROES NOVEL

CHRIS OULD

When long-buried skeletal remains are unearthed at an isolated farm on the island of Borðoy, Hjalti Hentze is charged with investigating the death. But as Hentze's investigation turns to the commune that occupied the farm in the 1970s, Jan Reyna discovers a connection to the death of his mother and to long-repressed memories from his childhood.

Increasingly driven to exorcise his personal demons, Reyna pursues an ever-darker conspiracy of murder and abuse spanning four decades, from the Faroes to Denmark and back.

However, as Hentze puts the same pieces together, he has a growing realisation that Reyna may be about to follow a course of action from which there can be no return.

PRAISE FOR THE AUTHOR

"Unmissable and thrilling fiction"
Lancashire Evening Post

"Grittily realistic crime"
Independent

AVAILABLE FEBRUARY 2018

ALSO AVAILABLE FROM TITAN BOOKS

IMPURE BLOOD

A CAPTAIN DARAC NOVEL

PETER MORFOOT

In the heat of a French summer, Captain Paul Darac of the Nice Brigade Criminelle is called to a highly sensitive crime scene. A man has been found murdered in the midst of a Muslim prayer group, but no one saw how it was done. Then the organisers of the Nice leg of the Tour de France receive an unlikely terrorist threat. In what becomes a frantic race against time, Darac must try and unpick a complex knot in which racial hatred, sex and revenge are tightly intertwined.

"Engrossing… an auspicious debut for Darac"
Publishers Weekly

"A vibrant, satisfying read"
The Crime Review

"Glorious setting and taut writing – a real winner"
Martin Walker, bestselling author of *Bruno, Chief of Police*

ALSO AVAILABLE FROM TITAN BOOKS

WRITTEN IN DEAD WAX

A VINYL DETECTIVE NOVEL

ANDREW CARTMEL

He is a record collector—a connoisseur of vinyl, hunting out rare and elusive LPs. His business card describes him as the 'Vinyl Detective' and some people take this more literally than others. Like the beautiful, mysterious woman who wants to pay him a large sum of money to find a priceless lost recording—on behalf of an extremely wealthy (and rather sinister) shadowy client. Given that he's just about to run out of cat food, this gets our hero's full attention. So begins a painful and dangerous odyssey in search of the rarest jazz record of them all…

"Marvelously inventive and endlessly fascinating"
Publishers Weekly

"This charming mystery feels as companionable as a leisurely afternoon trawling the vintage shops"
Kirkus

"An irresistible blend of murder, mystery and music"
Ben Aaronovitch, bestselling author of *Rivers of London*

ALSO AVAILABLE FROM TITAN BOOKS

THE BURSAR'S WIFE

A GEORGE KOCHARYAN MYSTERY

E.G. RODFORD

Meet George Kocharyan, Cambridge Confidential Services' one and only private investigator. Amidst the usual jobs following unfaithful spouses, he is approached by the glamorous Sylvia Booker. The wife of the bursar of Morley College, Booker is worried that her daughter Lucy has fallen in with the wrong crowd. Aided by his assistant Sandra and her teenage son, George soon realises that Lucy is sneaking off to the apartment of an older man, but perhaps not for the reasons one might suspect. Then an unfaithful wife he had been following is found dead. As his investigation continues – enlivened by a mild stabbing and the unwanted intervention and attention of Detective Inspector Vicky Stubbing – George begins to wonder if all the threads are connected...

"An auspicious start by Rodford"
Booklist

"As pleasing as any popular primetime TV cop drama"
Killer Nashville

"Rodford's sense of delight in transposing American noir to modern, multicultural Cambridge is palpable"
Reviewing the Evidence

ALSO AVAILABLE FROM TITAN BOOKS

DUST AND DESIRE

A JOEL SORRELL NOVEL

CONRAD WILLIAMS

Joel Sorrell, a bruised, bad-mouthed PI, is a sucker for missing person cases. And not just because he's searching for his daughter, who vanished five years after his wife was murdered. Joel feels a kinship with the desperate and the damned. He feels, somehow, responsible. So when the mysterious Kara Geenan begs him to find her missing brother, Joel agrees. Then an attempt is made on his life, and Kara vanishes... A vicious serial killer is on the hunt, and as those close to Joel are sucked into his nightmare, he suspects that answers may lie in his own hellish past.

"An exciting new voice in crime fiction."
Mark Billingham, No. 1 bestselling author of *Rush of Blood*

"Top quality crime writing from one of the best."
Paul Finch, No. 1 bestselling author of *Stalkers*

"Take the walk with PI Joel Sorrell."
James Sallis, bestselling author of *Drive*